The Stillness Protocol
by
Jon-Michael Billingslea

Copyright © 2026 Jon-Michael Billingslea

All rights reserved.

No part of this publication may be reproduced, distributed, or transmitted in any form or by any means without prior written permission of the author, except in the case of brief quotations embodied in critical reviews and certain other noncommercial uses permitted by copyright law.

This is a work of fiction. Names, characters, organizations, places, events, and incidents are either the product of the author's imagination or used fictitiously.

ISBN: 9798249636371

First Edition

Printed in the United States of America

Chapter 1
Scale

Toronto ARC Clinical Network — 2047
Snow dragged sideways across University Avenue, thin and relentless, catching in the seams of the hospital's glass façade. The streetcars moved through it without slowing, red bodies humming past banks and research towers, wires sparking faintly against the gray.
Inside, the intake board refreshed.
148.
173.
219.
Dr. Nadia Serrano stood at the upper railing overlooking the waiting floor. The glass was cool beneath her palm. Below, winter coats lay folded over laps. Meltwater pooled in dark crescents beneath boots. A woman in a navy parka pressed a tissue to her nose and held it there, not crying, just holding.
The board refreshed again.
    241.
Director Alan Mercer's voice came from behind her.
"We lifted the caps."
Nadia didn't turn immediately. "All of them?"
"All of them," he said.
She turned then. He looked energized, jacket unbuttoned, tie loosened just enough to signal momentum.
"Phase II authorization cleared at 05:10," he said. "Full expansion."
"That wasn't the projection," she said.
"It is now."
The board ticked upward.
    312.
On the lower level, intake nurses moved in clean diagonals between stations—triage, consent, biometrics. The choreography had tightened since Phase I. No wasted steps. No raised voices. Just a steady current of people being guided forward.
A man in work boots leaned forward in his chair, elbows on knees, staring at the floor between them as if something were moving there.
"Primary complaints?" Nadia asked.

"Grief clusters. Insomnia. Panic spikes," Mercer said. "Layoffs in Scarborough accelerated demand."

"That doesn't explain this curve," she said.

"It explains enough."

417.

The number pulsed red for a half-second before stabilizing.

Nadia crossed to a workstation and pulled up the queue.

Complicated grief.

Chronic stress response.

Night terrors.

Persistent distress unresponsive to first-line interventions.

The banner across the top read:

ARC Phase II — Distress Regulation Pathway Active

"Overtime's approved," Mercer said. "We're adding two intake blocks tonight."

"Compliance review?" she asked.

"Cleared."

"Long-term variance?"

"Within threshold," he said.

"Relative to what baseline?" she asked.

He gave her a look. "Emotional volatility."

Below, man in work boots was guided into Screening Room 4.

The board hit 463.

A junior researcher approached with a tablet. "We're scheduling first-dose blocks into next week."

"Already?" Nadia asked.

"Yes."

"How many confirmed?" she asked.

"Five hundred twelve."

The snow outside thickened. Wind pushed it against the glass in sheets that flattened and slid.

Nadia descended to the screening corridor.

Screening Room 4 opened twenty-four minutes later. The man stepped out. His shoulders were still bent, but his breathing had steadied. A nurse touched his elbow lightly.

"Qualifies," the nurse said.
"Any contraindications?" Nadia asked.
"None flagged."
The man looked at her.
"Is it going to stop the night?" he asked.
"It reduces physiological distress intensity," she said. "It does not remove memory."
He nodded quickly.
"I don't want it removed. I just need to sleep."
She studied his face. Stubble grown without intention. Eyes rimmed raw. The kind of exhaustion that rearranges posture.
"You'll complete baseline imaging," she said. "Then dosing."
His exhale came out like he'd already been given something.
"Thank you."
Upstairs, the intake board crossed 500.
Mercer leaned against the railing.
"This is what scale looks like," he said.
On Nadia's terminal, updated modeling projections populated automatically. The adoption curve had been adjusted upward—steeper than the last revision. She zoomed in.
Original forecast: moderate urban uptake.
Revised forecast: dense network adoption.
"Who authorized the revision?" she asked.
"Regulatory and Senate liaison," Mercer said. "Duarte pushed it."
She didn't answer.

The consent script for Phase II had shifted subtly:
ARC assists in distress regulation and improves functional stability. Long-term tracking ongoing.
Ongoing.

Her phone vibrated in her coat pocket.
Adrian.
She stepped into the stairwell to answer.

"You see the morning feed?" he asked.
"No."

3

"They said ARC expanded. Said it's helping."
"It expanded," she said.
"You sound tired," he said.
"It's a surge day."
For a moment, there was silence.

"Do you think it would help someone like me?" he asked.
The stairwell light hummed above her.
"They'd have to screen you," she said.
More Silence came.

"I didn't sleep last night," he said. "Not even an hour."
The intake board downstairs ticked again.
"Let's talk tonight," she said.
"Okay."
He didn't hang up immediately.
"I just need the edges dulled," he said quietly.
The call ended.

When she stepped back onto the intake floor, the first-dose schedule had populated.
37 TODAY
The man from Screening Room 4 was being escorted toward the dosing wing.

The doors opened.
Cold air followed another wave of arrivals through the lobby entrance.
The intake board refreshed.
    538.
Mercer exhaled, satisfied.
"Tomorrow will be higher."
Nadia opened a blank document on her private drive.
Cursor blinking.
She typed:
Personal Log — Intake Variance
And saved it.

Chapter 2
Acceleration

Toronto ARC Clinical Network — 2047

The snow had stopped by morning. Salt crusted the sidewalks in a thin white film that cracked under shoes.

Inside Conference Room C, the blinds were half-lowered against the glare off neighboring towers. A long table. Twelve chairs. Stainless carafes sweating onto paper coasters.

Nadia arrived last.

Mercer stood at the head of the table, jacket off, sleeves rolled once at the wrist. A projection glowed behind him—uptake curves, heat maps, intake velocity.

"Phase II is now full-scale," he said as she took her seat. "Enrollment caps are removed across all Toronto sites effective immediately."

A murmur moved around the table.

Dr. Patel from outcomes monitoring leaned forward. "Across all sites?"

"Yes."

"Even Scarborough East?"

"Yes."

"Staffing isn't aligned for that," said Patel.

"It will be," Mercer said.

The slide changed.

Throughput Targets — Updated

Baseline: 60 daily screens per site.
Revised: 140.

"Those numbers assume three additional intake nurses," Patel said.

"They're approved," said Mercer.

"Approved doesn't mean hired."

"They'll be hired."

Nadia folded her hands on the table.

"What changed between last week and this morning?" she asked.

Mercer met her eyes. "Demand," he said.

"That curve is predictive," she said.

"It's real-time now." He clicked again. A live feed of the intake board appeared. Numbers rolling.

"We're averaging five hundred submissions every twelve hours," he said. "We cannot artificially restrict access."

Dr. Huang cleared her throat. "What about longitudinal tracking windows?"

"Condensed," said Mercer.

"To what?" asked Huang.

"Six-week initial review instead of twelve," said Mercer.

"That eliminates comparative variance," said Huang.

"It accelerates relief."

Nadia leaned back slightly. "Acceleration reduces clarity."

"It reduces suffering," Mercer said.

And then there was silence.

He moved to the next slide.

Operational Adjustments
— Consent briefings standardized
— Imaging compressed into parallel tracks
— Dosing blocks extended to 20:00

"Twenty hundred?" someone asked.

"Yes," Mercer said.

"That's fourteen-hour days."

"Rotational."

Nadia looked down the table. Several of the younger clinicians avoided eye contact.

"What about clinical discretion?" she asked.

"It remains."

"With revised quotas?"

"Targets," Mercer corrected.

Patel tapped her pen against her notebook. "Targets create pressure."

"Pressure exists already," Mercer said. "That's why they're here."

The door opened briefly. An assistant slipped in a folder and placed it beside Mercer.

He opened it without comment.

"Senator Duarte's office called at 06:30," he said. "Regulatory confidence is strong. We have political cover."

Nadia felt the room shift slightly at that.

"Cover for what?" she asked.

"For scale," Mercer said.

He closed the folder.

"Every hour we slow this down," he said, "someone goes home without relief."

Nadia watched condensation slide down the carafe beside her.

"What's the threshold for pausing expansion?" she asked.

Mercer smiled faintly. "Adverse events."

"Defined how?"

"Medically."

"And psychologically?" asked Nadia.

"Subjective dissatisfaction isn't an adverse event."

"That's not what I asked."

He held her gaze.

"Clinical destabilization," he said evenly. "Hospitalization. Harm."

"And if that doesn't appear?" Nadine asked.

"Then we continue."

The slide shifted again.

Projected Six-Month Uptake — Revised

The curve climbed steeply and held.

Nadia studied it.

"Who revised the modeling assumptions?" she asked.

"Regulatory analytics," said Mercer.

"Under whose authority?"

"Mine."

The room quieted.

"You adjusted predictive inputs?" she asked.

"I approved them," he said.

"Based on?"

"Observed demand elasticity."

"That's a short window."

"It's a… strong signal," he said.

Nadia opened her tablet and pulled up the original Phase II model.

Adoption was meant to plateau gradually.

The new projection didn't plateau. It steepened, then stabilized higher.

"This assumes retention beyond initial relief," she said.
Mercer didn't answer immediately.
"It assumes people continue treatment if it works," he said.
A few heads lifted.
Patel shifted in her seat. "We're compressing the twelve-week psychological follow-up. That data will thin."
"We'll expand sampling later," Mercer said.
"After expansion?"
"Yes."

The assistant reentered quietly and whispered something into Mercer's ear.
He nodded once.
"First-dose block filled through Friday," he said to the room. "We're adding Saturday."
"That wasn't cleared," Huang said.
"It is now," said Mercer.

Nadia stood.
Chairs scraped slightly.
"If we expand intake without proportional monitoring," she said, "we lose resolution."
"We gain access," Mercer said.
She met his eyes. "Access without resolution isn't neutral."
"It's relief."
The silence stretched.

Finally, Mercer clicked off the projection.
"Phase II is active at scale," he said. "If you have operational concerns, submit them in writing. We reconvene in seventy-two hours."
Chairs shifted. Folders closed. The meeting dissolved in quiet clusters.

Nadia remained seated.
Mercer approached the table's end.
"You're worried," he said.
"Yes."
"About what, specifically?" he asked.

"Velocity," she said.

He nodded once, as if acknowledging a weather report. "Velocity means it's working."
"It means it's moving faster than we modeled."
He leaned closer, voice lower.
"We modeled conservatively," he said. "People are asking for this."

"And if we mis-modeled?" Nadia asked.
"Then we adjust."
"After expansion?"
"Yes," said Mercer.

She watched him for a moment.
"You're committing the system to scale before variance stabilizes," she said.
"I'm committing the system to relief," he replied.
Across the hall, a nurse hurried past with a stack of consent tablets.
The intake board on the corridor monitor ticked upward again.
Mercer straightened his sleeves.
"Send me your concerns," he said. "In writing."
He walked out.

Nadia remained in the empty conference room.
Through the blinds, the city looked scrubbed and bright after the storm.
Salt dust lifted in the wind and settled again.
She opened her tablet.
The draft she had titled the night before blinked on the screen.

Personal Log — Intake Variance
She added a new line beneath it.
Phase II caps removed systemwide. Monitoring window compressed. Throughput targets doubled.
She hesitated.
Then typed:
Model revision approved before stabilization.
She hit save.

Outside the conference room, the dosing corridor doors opened again. And did not close for several minutes.

Chapter 3
Booked

Toronto — 2047
The apartment windows faced west. Late light slid across the hardwood in a thin amber band and caught on the edge of the kitchen counter. Nadia unlocked the door and stepped inside.
The sink was empty. The kettle sat cold on the stove. Adrian's shoes were lined neatly against the wall—closer together than usual.
"Adrian?" she called.
"In here."
He was on the couch. Lights off. Curtains half-drawn. The television screen reflected the room without showing anything.
He didn't look up immediately.
"You're home early," he said.
"It's past seven," she replied.
He nodded once, as if recalibrating.
She hung her coat carefully. "Did you eat?"
"Toast."
She crossed the room and sat in the armchair opposite him.
The air felt still. The radiator clicked once and stopped.
"How was today?" he asked.
"Busy."
"That's what the feed said."
"You watched it?"
He nodded. "They ran a segment. Said the expansion was successful."
"It was announced," she said.
He studied his hands.
"They said it's helping."
"It is," she said.
He let out a short breath through his nose.
"I signed up."
The words sat between them.
Nadia didn't move.
"For screening," he added. "Initial assessment."
She folded her hands in her lap.
"When?" she asked.

"Tomorrow."
"You didn't tell me."
"I'm telling you now."
She held his gaze.
"Why tomorrow?"
"Because I don't want to wait."
The amber light shifted lower on the floor.
"You said we'd talk," she said.
"We are."
"You booked it before we talked."
"Yes."
Silence.

He leaned forward, elbows on his knees.
"I can't keep doing this," he said.
"Doing what?"
"Waking up at three every night. Counting the hours until morning. Walking into the kitchen and feeling like the air is heavier than it should be."
"You're grieving," she said.
"I know what grieving is."
"And?"
"And this isn't easing."
She watched him carefully.
"ARC therapy reduces distress intensity," she said. "It doesn't fix what happened."
"I don't want it fixed," he said. "I want it livable."
She didn't answer.
He stood and walked to the window, pulled the curtain back an inch, then let it fall.
"I tried therapy," he said. "I tried running. I tried not talking about it. I tried talking about it."
"And?"
"And I'm still not sleeping."
The radiator clicked again.
She kept her voice even.
"Screening doesn't obligate you to dose."

"I know."
"You can decline."
"I know."
"Then why does it feel decided?" she asked.
He turned toward her.
"Because if they say I qualify... then it is."
Her jaw tightened slightly.
"Why?"
"Because I don't want to feel like I'm choosing this," he said.
"This?" she asked.
He gestured vaguely around the room.
"This version of me."

She leaned back in the chair. Then, she stood slowly.
"You could have told me before booking it," she said.
"I didn't want you to talk me out of it."
"That's not how this works."
"It is for me," he said.
The room tightened.
"You're asking me to support something I'm professionally evaluating," she said.
"I'm asking you to support me."
"That's not the same."
"No," he said. "It isn't."
They stood facing each other now, the coffee table between them.

"It's work," she said.
She exhaled slowly.
"If you enroll, I can't oversee your case."
"I wouldn't want you to," he said.
"You'd be assigned another clinician."
"Good."
"You're comfortable with that?"
"Yes."
"Why?"
"Because you won't be trying to measure me," he said laughing.
She held still.

"I don't measure you," she said.
"You do," he replied, not unkindly. "You notice everything."
The light had fully left the floor now. The room was gray.
She reached for the lamp and turned it on. Warm light filled the space between them.

"Screening is tomorrow?" she asked again.
"Yes."
"Which site?"
"University."
Her hospital.
She nodded once.

"I can flag a conflict-of-interest request," she said. "Preemptively."
"I'd prefer that."
"So, this is settled?" she asked.
"Yes," he said.
The word came clean.

She looked at him for a long moment.
"If you qualify," she said, "and you proceed, you understand there's no immediate reversal."
"I understand."
"You understand follow-up is structured."
"Yes."
"You understand—"
"I understand," he said again.
Silence pressed in.
"All right," she said.
He blinked.
"All right?" he repeated.
"I won't try to stop you."
His shoulders lowered slightly, as if he'd been braced.
"Thank you," he said.
She walked to the kitchen and filled the kettle, set it on the stove.
Behind her, he remained standing.

The kettle began to hum softly as it heated.

He crossed the room, quiet steps on the hardwood, and came up behind her at the stove.
His arms went around her middle—firm, not tentative. His forearm settled across her waist like a bar, his hand finding the far edge of her hip. Nadia let out a small sound that wasn't a protest.
"Am I in trouble, mister?" she asked, half a laugh.
"No, You *are* trouble," he said.
She tipped her head back to look at him. His face was close enough that she could see the thin red line at the corner of one eye, the lack of sleep sitting there.
He looked at her like he used to—like she was a fact.
Nadia laughed again, softer, and their eyes met. For a second, the tension in her shoulders loosened on its own.
She turned back to the stove, fingers finding the kettle handle, but he leaned in and pressed his mouth to the back of her head—hairline first—then the curve behind her ear. Kisses traveled to her neck. Then, another lower, until along her shoulder through the fabric of her shirt, then the line of her back where her spine rose.
She turned, caught between the stove and him, and offered her hands in protest.
"I don't think you've considered tha—"
She was cut off before completing the sounds.
One kiss, long enough that her hands tightened in his shirt. When he pulled back he didn't give her room to speak, just kissed her again—two more, steady, but less assertive kisses—then a scatter of small ones, quick and precise, like he was counting her into a calmer place. Her breath came out uneven. The room felt smaller, warmer.
When he stopped, he rested his forehead against hers.
"Considered what?" he asked.
Nadia blinked once.

"I—" She tried to catch the sentence by its tail. It wasn't there.
Her mouth opened, then closed.
"Forget it," she said, laughing lightly, as if that solved it.

Adrian rolled his eyes with a fondness that almost looked rehearsed. "You always do that," he said, and released her.

His hand slid off her hip last, a final, quiet squeeze, and then he turned away from the kitchen.

In the living room, Adrian picked up his phone and opened the confirmation email again.

Screening Appointment — 09:40

He pressed confirm.

The notification sound was small but distinct.

Nadia heard it.

The kettle clicked off.

Chapter 4
Restricted

Morning came bright and hard. The sidewalks were wet from overnight melt, the salt on the curb edges turning to gray paste. Nadia walked faster than usual, scarf tight at her throat, badge tapping lightly against her coat zipper.
Inside the University site lobby, the air smelled like disinfectants and coffee.
Adrian was already there.
He stood near the wall-mounted clinic map, hands in his pockets, shoulders set as if he'd practiced standing still. His hair was damp at the temples. When he saw her, his face softened for a second, then reset.
"You came!" he said.
"I work here…" Nadia replied, rolling her eyes at him.
He looked past her, down the corridor.
"Are you okay?" she asked.
"I'm fine."
"You didn't sleep," she said.
His mouth tightened. "No."
They didn't touch. There was too much motion. There were too many people. A young woman with red eyes stared at her phone. An older man held a clipboard with both hands as if it could drift away.
Adrian shifted his weight.
"Screening's at 09:40," he said.
"I know."
He glanced at her badge. "Do you know who's screening me?"
Nadia didn't answer immediately.
"Not me," she said.
A nurse called a name at the intake desk. Someone stood. A chair squeaked. The waiting room sound was low and continuous—breath, fabric, distant printers.
Adrian's phone buzzed. He checked it and held the screen up toward her without handing it over.

ARC PHASE II — SCREENING CHECK-IN
Please confirm arrival at Intake A

He pressed the on-screen button.
A moment later, Nadia's own device vibrated.

AUTOMATED NOTICE — CLINICAL ACCESS RESTRICTION
Conflict-of-interest flag detected.
User: Serrano, Nadia.
Patient: Hale, Adrian.
Access to chart restricted pending review.

She stopped walking.
Adrian watched her face. "That was you?"
"No," Nadia said.
He blinked. "You said you could flag it."
"I said I could," she replied. "I didn't."
He looked at her phone again, at the way her thumb hovered over the notification as if she could will it away.
"So it's already in," he said.
"It's automatic," she said.
"Triggered by what?"
Nadia's eyes flicked to the screen.
Detected proximity / shared address / emergency contact match.
Her jaw tightened.
"It's triggered by system criteria," she said.

Another notification arrived.
RESTRICTION UPDATED — EFFECTIVE IMMEDIATELY
Chart access removed. Clinical interaction prohibited.
Direct communication with assigned clinician regarding patient status prohibited.
Violations subject to review.

Nadia stared at the line that mattered.
Clinical interaction prohibited.

She looked up.
Adrian was watching her carefully, as if checking whether she'd flinch.

"You're barred," he said.
"Yes."
His eyes moved around the lobby again, taking in the other couples, the lone bodies, the intake desk, the security camera in the corner.
"That's... clean," he said.
Nadia swallowed. "It's policy."
He leaned closer, just enough that his voice dropped.
"So you can't even ask how it went?" he asked.
"I can't open your chart," she said. "I can't communicate with the clinician assigned to you."

A voice called from the desk.
"Adrian Hale?"
He straightened.
A clinician stood in the opening behind the intake counter—mid-thirties, hair clipped short, face neutral in the practiced way of people trained to hold distress without absorbing it. Her badge read:
DR. L. MORENO

Adrian glanced at Nadia. A question in his eyes. Permission, maybe. Or a test.
Nadia said, evenly, "They'll take care of you."
Dr. Moreno waited.
Adrian nodded once, more to himself than to either of them.
He stepped forward.
Nadia followed, then stopped when she reached the line on the floor that marked staff-only access. A strip of yellow tape. A sign on the glass door:
AUTHORIZED PERSONNEL.

Dr. Moreno held the door open for Adrian.
He looked back at Nadia one last time.
"You're really not coming?" he said.
Nadia's voice stayed calm. "I can't."
Something in his face tightened, then smoothed again.
"Okay," he said.
Dr. Moreno's hand rested lightly at Adrian's elbow—guiding, not comforting.

The door closed.

Nadia was left on the public side of the line, the glass reflecting her coat, her badge, her face.
Her device vibrated again.
COMPLIANCE NOTICE — ACKNOWLEDGEMENT REQUIRED
You have been restricted from patient Hale, Adrian's record.
Please confirm you understand and will comply.
Two buttons.
ACKNOWLEDGE
REQUEST REVIEW
Her thumb hovered.
She pressed **REQUEST REVIEW**.
A new field opened.
Reason for review request:
Nadia typed:
Spouse/partner. High risk of harm if communication blocked. Will comply with chart restrictions. Request permission for non-clinical status updates only.
She hit send.
The system responded immediately.
REQUEST RECEIVED — PENDING
Estimated response: 5–7 business days.
Nadia stared at the line.
Five to seven days.
From the corridor beyond the glass, she could see Adrian's back as he followed Dr. Moreno down the hall. He didn't look back again.

A nurse pushed a cart past the door. Wheels clicked over tile seams. The fluorescent light made everything look slightly damp.
Nadia's phone vibrated one last time.
APPOINTMENT STATUS — IN PROGRESS
She stood very still, listening to the faint hum of the building.
Then she turned off her screen.
And walked toward the staff elevators, alone.

Chapter 5
Consent

Toronto ARC Clinical Network — 2047

The consent room was smaller than Nadia remembered.
Frost clung to the lower corners of the window where the seal met glass. A single overhead panel light hummed faintly. Two chairs on one side of the table. One on the other.
Nadia stood outside the door.
She wasn't supposed to be here.
Through the narrow glass strip, she could see Adrian seated across from Dr. L. Moreno. His coat folded over the back of the chair. His hands flat on the tabletop, fingers spread as if steadying something.
Dr. Moreno's tablet projected a soft blue glow onto the surface between them.
"ARC Phase II treatment is indicated for persistent distress unresponsive to first-line interventions," Dr. Moreno said evenly. "You've reviewed the pre-screen materials?"
"Yes," Adrian said.
"Any current medications?"
"No."
"Substance use?"
"No."
"Recent hospitalization?"
"No."
Dr. Moreno nodded once and advanced the screen.
Nadia leaned slightly closer to the glass.
She could hear only fragments through the door.
"Primary goal?" Dr. Moreno asked.
"To sleep," Adrian said. "And to not feel like I'm bracing all the time."
Dr. Moreno's tone did not change.
"The compound reduces physiological distress markers and intrusive activation patterns," she said.
"I understand," Adrian said.
Dr. Moreno rotated the tablet toward him.

"Common transient effects include fatigue, mild dissociation, altered affect intensity, appetite fluctuation. Rare events include destabilization requiring intervention."

Adrian nodded.

"Questions?" Dr. Moreno asked.

There was a pause.

Nadia felt it in her chest.

"Is there a duration limit?" Adrian asked.

"Treatment length varies," Dr. Moreno said. "Some patients discontinue after relief stabilization. Others continue under monitored dosing."

"And if I stop?"

"You may discontinue at any time," Dr. Moreno said. "Follow-up is structured to assess residual symptoms."

Nadia closed her eyes briefly.

The language was clean. Accurate. Contained.

Dr. Moreno advanced again.

"ARC therapy is voluntary," she said. "By signing, you acknowledge informed consent and agree to monitoring protocol."

She tapped the section header.

Long-Term Data Use Authorization

Adrian scanned the text.

"What does this mean?" he asked.

"It permits de-identified use of your treatment data for safety and efficacy monitoring," Dr. Moreno said.

"De-identified," Adrian repeated.

"Yes."

He kept reading.

Nadia watched his eyes move left to right.

The paragraph below was smaller.

Continuation Clause

Participation in ARC Phase II may involve adaptive protocol modifications based on aggregate response modeling.

Adrian looked up.

"What's adaptive protocol modification?" he asked.

Dr. Moreno did not hesitate.

"Adjustments to dosing intervals or assessment structure based on cohort-level outcomes."

"So you can change it?" Adrian asked.
"Within approved parameters."
"Without asking me?" he asked.
"You would be notified of any material changes," Dr. Moreno said.
"Notified," Adrian repeated.
"Yes."
Silence.
Nadia's hand tightened on the doorframe.
Adrian leaned back slightly.
"And there's no long-term neurological risk?" he asked.
"None identified within current monitoring windows," Dr. Moreno said.
"Monitoring windows," he said.
"Yes."
"How long are they?"
"Six weeks initial. Ongoing follow-up at structured intervals."
Adrian nodded.
He looked at the tablet again.
His thumb hovered near the signature line.
Through the glass, Nadia saw the exact moment his shoulders shifted forward—decision settling into posture.
"Do you have additional questions?" Dr. Moreno asked.
Adrian shook his head.
"No."
Dr. Moreno held the tablet steady.
"Please sign to indicate informed consent."
Adrian hesitated for half a breath.
Then signed.
The signature glowed briefly before locking into the system.
Nadia felt the click in her own body.
Dr. Moreno tapped confirm.
"First-dose block is available today," she said. "We have an opening at 14:20."
Adrian blinked.
"Today?" he asked.
"Yes."
He exhaled once, through his nose.
"Okay," he said.

Nadia stepped back from the door.

The hallway felt narrower now.

Inside the room, Dr. Moreno extended her hand.

"Thank you, Mr. Hale," she said. "We'll begin baseline imaging shortly."

Adrian stood and shook her hand.

"Thank you," he said.

The door opened.

Dr. Moreno exited first, eyes briefly meeting Nadia's before sliding past her without acknowledgment.

Adrian followed.

He stopped when he saw Nadia standing there.

"You heard?" he asked.

"I heard enough," she said.

He studied her face.

"They had a slot today," he said. "I took it."

"You didn't have to," she replied.

"I did," he said.

There it was again—that clean certainty.

A nurse approached with a clipboard.

"Mr. Hale?" she asked.

"Yes."

"Imaging suite is ready."

Adrian glanced at Nadia.

"I'll see you after?" he said.

She nodded.

He followed the nurse down the corridor.

The door to Imaging closed behind him.

Nadia remained in the hallway, staring at the consent room door.

Her phone vibrated.

PATIENT STATUS — CONSENT COMPLETE
FIRST DOSE SCHEDULED — 14:20

She turned off the screen.

Chapter 6
Administration

Toronto ARC Clinical Network — 2047

The imaging corridor smelled faintly metallic.

Nadia stood at the far end, outside the restricted threshold. Through the glass partition she could see the preparation bay: three reclining chairs separated by frosted dividers, a rolling vitals cart, a nurse adjusting tubing with precise, economical movements.

Adrian sat in Chair Two.

His coat was gone. A paper band circled his wrist. The fluorescent light caught the edge of his cheekbone, sharpening it.

A nurse clipped a monitor to his finger.

"Heart rate's elevated," she said.

"I'm fine," Adrian replied.

"Baseline only," she said.

On the wall monitor above him, his vitals populated in green.

Nadia shifted her weight but did not step forward. Her badge would not open that door.

Dr. Moreno entered the bay, gloves already on.

"Mr. Hale," she said, checking the tablet in her hand, "baseline imaging complete. No contraindications."

Adrian nodded.

"Any new questions before administration?" she asked.

He shook his head.

"No."

Dr. Moreno glanced at the nurse. The nurse nodded once.

A small vial was removed from a sealed container. Clear liquid. No color shift.

The nurse drew it into a syringe.

Nadia's throat tightened, but her face did not change.

Dr. Moreno held the syringe up briefly— just for confirmation.

"ARC Phase II compound," she said. "Single-dose initiation."

Adrian looked at it.

"Okay," he said.

The nurse swabbed the inside of his arm.

Cold alcohol. A small circle of shine on his skin.

"You may feel warmth or mild pressure," Dr. Moreno said.
Adrian gave a short nod.

The needle entered cleanly.
Nadia watched the angle, the steady push of the plunger, the way Adrian's jaw flexed once and then settled.
The syringe emptied.
The nurse withdrew it and placed a square of gauze over the puncture.
"All set," she said.
Dr. Moreno checked the monitor again.
"Observation window: thirty minutes," she said. "We'll monitor for acute response."
Adrian leaned back into the chair.
For a moment, nothing happened.
Then his shoulders lowered slightly.
Not dramatically. Just enough.
"You feeling anything?" the nurse asked.
"Warm," he said.
"Where?"
"Chest."
"Any dizziness?"
"No."
Nadia's hand curled into her coat pocket.
On the wall monitor, his heart rate began to descend, one beat at a time.
Eighty-eight.
Eighty-three.
Seventy-nine.
He closed his eyes.
Dr. Moreno made a note on her tablet.
"Respiration normal," she said.
Adrian inhaled slowly.
Exhaled.
The tension that had lived in his neck for weeks eased by degrees, like a fist loosening without instruction.
Nadia saw it before he did.
He opened his eyes again and looked toward the glass.
He found her immediately.

There was surprise in his expression.

"It's quieter," he said.

Dr. Moreno followed his gaze but did not comment.

"Define quieter," she said.

Adrian frowned slightly, searching for precision.

"My chest isn't... bracing," he said.

Dr. Moreno nodded once.

"Continue to observe," she said.

The nurse adjusted the monitor lead.

Across the bay, another patient shifted in their chair, eyes closed, lips parted.

The room was calm.

Controlled.

Nadia stepped closer to the glass.

Adrian held her gaze for several seconds.

His breathing remained steady.

"Heart rate stable," the nurse said.

Dr. Moreno tapped her screen again.

"Initial response within expected range," she said.

Adrian's eyelids lowered briefly, then lifted.

He gave Nadia a small, almost embarrassed smile.

"I'm okay," he said.

She nodded.

The words did not reach him through the glass, but the gesture did.

He leaned his head back against the chair and closed his eyes again.

The monitor continued its steady rhythm.

Seventy-six.

Seventy-four.

Seventy-two.

The nurse checked the injection site.

"No adverse reaction," she said.

Dr. Moreno removed her gloves.

"Observation continues," she said. "If stable at thirty, discharge with follow-up schedule."

Nadia's phone vibrated in her pocket.

She didn't look at it.

Through the glass, Adrian's face had changed.

Not empty.

Not altered beyond recognition.

Just unguarded.

The crease between his brows had smoothed.

The set of his mouth had softened.

He exhaled again.

Longer this time.

On Nadia's screen, without her touching it, a notification appeared.

DOSE ADMINISTERED — 14:23
STATUS: STABLE

She looked from the message back to him.

There was no visible mark except the small square of gauze taped inside his arm.

Thirty minutes passed.

Dr. Moreno approached him again.

"How would you rate your current distress intensity?" she asked.

Adrian opened his eyes.

He considered.

"Lower," he said.

"Numerical?"

"Four," he said. "Maybe three."

"Baseline was eight," Dr. Moreno said.

He nodded.

"Okay," she said. "We'll discharge with instructions."

The nurse removed the monitor clip from his finger.

Adrian sat up slowly.

He looked steady.

Dr. Moreno handed him a small printed sheet.

"Hydrate. Avoid major decisions for twenty-four hours," she said. "We'll see you in one week."

Adrian nodded again.

He stood.

For a moment he swayed—not dramatically, just recalibrating.

Then he was upright.

The door opened.

He stepped into the hallway.

Nadia faced him.

"Well?" she asked.

He searched her face as if comparing something.

"It worked," he said.

Not triumph.

Not relief exactly.

Just fact.

Behind him, the dosing bay doors closed.

And did not reopen.

Chapter 7
Sleep

Toronto — 2047

The street outside the clinic looked the same as it had that morning—salt-streaked curb, wet asphalt, slush packed into the gutter. The difference was only in Adrian's pace.

He walked without stopping to brace.

Nadia kept beside him, matching his stride. The cold air pinched at the inside of her nose. He didn't tug his scarf higher. He didn't rub his hands together. He moved like the temperature was information instead of threat.

At the corner, he paused for the light.

"You're quiet," Nadia said.

He blinked once, as if checking himself. "I'm… calm," he said.

The word came out flat, not defensive.

A cyclist hissed past, tires cutting through meltwater. Adrian didn't flinch. They crossed on green. The crosswalk signal chirped as they reached the far side.

In the apartment building lobby, the heat hit them in a soft wave. Adrian exhaled as if he hadn't noticed he'd been holding air all day.

The elevator smelled faintly like someone's laundry detergent.

He watched the floor numbers rise.

"You're okay?" Nadia asked again.

He looked at her, then looked away.

"Yea, really. Feels like… I can stand inside myself a little easier," he said.

Nadia didn't answer.

The elevator chimed.

Inside the apartment, late daylight had shifted into the blue edge of evening. The kitchen counter held the mug from the night before, still unwashed. The kettle sat where Nadia had left it, cord looped neatly. Adrian took off his shoes and lined them against the wall.

He did it slowly, as if the motion mattered.

"You want tea?" Nadia asked.

"Later," he said.

He went to the couch and sat. Not collapsing. Just sitting.

Nadia moved around him—coat off, bag set down, kettle filled. She listened for the sounds she knew from him: the restless foot, the shallow breath, the sharp swallow that came when his thoughts spiked.

None of them came.

He watched her hands.

"You look tired," he said.

"I am," she replied.

"Eat something," he said.

It was ordinary advice, the kind that used to come from him only when he was trying to prove he was still present.

Nadia turned the stove on low and set the kettle down.

The click of the burner sounded too loud in the quiet.

Adrian leaned back and closed his eyes.

For a moment she thought he might fall asleep right there.

He didn't.

He opened his eyes again and watched her, almost carefully.

"What are you thinking?" he asked.

"That I can't see your chart," Nadia said.

He nodded and laughed. "Good."

"That's not what I meant."

He let that sit.

The kettle began to warm. A small hum rose from the metal.

Adrian's phone buzzed on the coffee table. He looked at it but didn't pick it up.

Nadia watched the screen light fade.

"Do you feel—" she started.

He looked up. "Different?"

She stopped.

He finished for her, like he'd been waiting for the question.

"Yes," she said.

He considered.

"I feel lighter," he said. "But not happy."

Nadia's fingers tightened around the kettle handle without lifting it.

"Do you feel sad?" she asked.

He frowned slightly, as if trying to locate it precisely.

"I can reach it," he said. "It's just not… grabbing me."
Nadia turned her eyes back to the stove.
"Okay," she said.
She poured two mugs once the water boiled, set one in front of him.
Steam fogged the surface of the coffee table, then dissipated.
Adrian picked the mug up with both hands and drank.
His shoulders remained loose.
He set it down again with care.
"I want to go to bed," he said.
Nadia's head lifted.
"Now?" she asked.
He nodded.
It was still early. The sky outside the window had only just turned fully dark. Streetlight glow climbed the glass.
Adrian stood and walked toward the bedroom.
Nadia followed.
The bedroom was cool. The sheets were rumpled from the last night he'd left them and returned again and left again.
Adrian pulled the covers back and sat on the mattress.
He looked at Nadia.
She sat beside him, close enough that their shoulders touched.

He lay down.
He didn't scroll his phone.
He didn't stare at the ceiling.
He didn't do the thing he always did—counting silently, eyes open, waiting for the first wave of panic to arrive.
He just lay there.
Nadia watched his face in the dim light.
His eyelids lowered.
His breathing slowed.
One minute.
Two.
His mouth parted slightly on an exhale.
Nadia waited for the correction—for the sudden inhale, the jerk of his leg, the restless turn.
It didn't come.

His breathing deepened.

His body let go in stages, each one visible: jaw unclenching, brow smoothing, hands opening where they'd curled into fists without him noticing.

Nadia lay back beside him, still on top of the covers.

She watched the ceiling.

She listened.

The radiator clicked.

A car passed below, tires whispering on wet street.

Adrian slept.

She turned her head toward him and saw it—his face slack with actual rest, not the half-sleep he used to get in exhausted bursts.

Relief, made physical.

In the darkness, her phone lit once on the nightstand.

A silent notification.

She didn't touch it.

Adrian's breathing stayed steady.

She lay there until her eyes were heavy.

Then, quietly, she reached for her phone and turned the screen face down.

Chapter 8
Manageable

Toronto — 2047

Morning light came in clean and colorless.

Adrian was already awake.

He sat at the kitchen table with a bowl of cereal, milk barely disturbed, spoon resting against the rim. The window above the sink was edged with frost. Traffic moved below in steady lines.

Nadia stood in the doorway for a moment before speaking.

"You slept," she said.

Adrian looked up. His eyes were clear.

"Yeah," he said. "All the way through."

"How long?"

"Since ten."

No hesitation. No recalculation.

Nadia crossed to the counter and poured coffee.

"Dreams?" she asked.

"Don't remember any."

She handed him a mug.

He took it with both hands and drank immediately, as if the temperature didn't need testing.

"You look better," she said.

"I feel better."

The words came simply. No triumph. No edge.

He picked up his spoon and ate.

"Do you remember," he said, "the night at the lake?"

Nadia's hand paused on the counter.

"The storm," he said. "When the dock lights went out."

She sat down across from him.

"Yes," she said.

He nodded once, almost thoughtfully.

"I kept replaying that before," he said. "Over and over."

Nadia waited.

"The sound of the sirens coming across the water," he added.

The kitchen felt smaller.

"And?" she asked.

He looked down at his cereal.

"I can still see it," he said. "It's just… not sharp."

Nadia didn't blink.

"What's not sharp?" she asked.

"The part where I—" He stopped, corrected himself. "The part where it happened."

She kept her voice steady. "Describe it."

He frowned slightly, not distressed—concentrating.

"There was rain," he said. "And the dock boards were slick."

"Yes," she said.

"And I remember holding her," he said.

His voice stayed even.

"I remember the weight," he added.

Nadia watched his hands.

They didn't tighten.

"And what do you feel when you think about that?" she asked.

He considered the question like it was technical.

"Sad," he said.

"How sad?"

He lifted one shoulder faintly.

"Manageable."

She leaned back slightly.

He took another bite of cereal.

"It's not gone," he said, noticing her face. "It's just not crushing."

Nadia nodded once.

He finished the bowl and stood.

"I'm going to shower," he said.

She stayed at the table.

The bathroom door closed. Water started a moment later.

Nadia stood and walked to the hallway mirror.

She studied her own face.

The water ran steadily.

From the bathroom, Adrian's voice came faintly through the door.

"You know what's strange?" he called.

"What?" she asked.

"I don't feel guilty for sleeping."

She closed her eyes briefly.
"That's not strange," she said.
"It is," he replied. "I thought it would feel wrong."
The water shut off.
Steam drifted out when the door opened.
Adrian stepped into the hallway.
He walked back into the bedroom to dress.
Nadia stood alone in the hallway.

On the kitchen table, his empty bowl sat with milk pooled at the bottom, the spoon resting neatly inside.
Her phone buzzed.
She didn't look at it immediately.
From the bedroom, Adrian's voice again:
"Do you want to go back to the lake this summer?"
The question landed softly.
Nadia turned toward the doorway.
"What?" she asked.
He stepped out fully dressed.
"It might be good," he said. "To stand on the dock again."
His tone was level.
"Why?" she asked.
"To see it without it wrecking me."
He smiled slightly.
"We could try."
Nadia stared at him.
Try.
The word settled wrong.
He checked his watch.
"I should head in," he said. "Follow-up instructions said normal activity."
He picked up his coat.
At the door, he paused.
"I'm glad I did it," he said.
No hesitation.
No flicker.
He kissed her forehead—gentle, present.
Then he left.

The apartment door closed.
Nadia stood still for several seconds.
Then she walked back to the kitchen table.
She sat in his chair.
She closed her eyes and forced herself to replay the lake.
The storm.
The dock.
The weight.
Her chest constricted immediately.
Breath shallow.
Tears rising without permission.
She opened her eyes again.
Across the table, his mug sat half-full.
Steam gone.
On her phone screen, the clinic notification waited.

FOLLOW-UP CHECK — PATIENT REPORT: POSITIVE RESPONSE

Nadia unlocked the device.
There was a small optional field at the bottom.
Additional observations (clinician only):
She stared at it.
Then locked the screen again without typing.

Outside, traffic moved.
Inside, the apartment felt steady.
Nadia looked at the chair where Adrian had been sitting.
She reached for her laptop.
And opened a new entry.

Chapter 9
Protected

Toronto ARC Clinical Network — 2047

The hearing room wasn't in Queen's Park. It was worse.

A conference center off University, leased for the day, with portable metal detectors and temporary signage taped to glass doors.

ARC PHASE II — SAFETY UPDATE
AUTHORIZED ATTENDEES ONLY

Outside, February light reflected off old snowbanks that had turned gray at the edges. Inside, the air was dry and warm, the kind that made your eyes feel slightly sanded.

Nadia arrived early anyway.

A security guard checked her badge and waved her through. Beyond the checkpoint, a hallway had been turned into a staging lane: staff in lanyards, media assistants with earpieces, a row of bottled water laid out with the same care as surgical instruments.

She walked past a cluster of clinicians she recognized from outcomes and monitoring. No one was speaking at full volume. Everyone held the quiet posture of people who knew their words could be used against them later.

At the end of the hall, double doors opened into the room.

Rows of chairs. A raised dais. A screen already lit with a waiting slide—white background, the ARC logo in the corner, a simple title centered.

PHASE II: EARLY SAFETY FINDINGS
TORONTO NETWORK

Mercer stood near the front, jacket immaculate, hands loose at his sides as if he'd slept eight hours.

When he saw her, he tilted his head in greeting like they were arriving at the same dinner.

"Nadia," he said.

"Alan."

"You look like you're heading to court," he said.

She didn't answer that.

He glanced at the screen. "Good turnout."

"Because it's being framed as reassurance," she said.

"It is reassurance," he replied, and looked almost pleased that she'd said it out loud.

People began to file in—senior staff, administrative directors, a few policymakers Nadia didn't know by name but recognized by the way others subtly moved aside for them. A small knot of media sat behind a velvet rope with notebooks open, microphones resting on their thighs. The doors closed with a soft hydraulic click.
A woman in a dark blazer stepped to the podium and introduced herself as moderator, though her tone said compliance officer.
"Thank you for attending," she said. "Today's purpose is to review early monitoring results for Phase II and confirm continued operational clearance."

Operational clearance.

Nadia felt the words settle in her body like weight.
The moderator looked down at her notes. "We will begin with Director Mercer, followed by Dr. Patel from outcomes monitoring, then a brief statement from Senator Duarte's office."
So he'd brought her into the room to be watched.
Mercer took the podium.
He didn't tap the microphone. He didn't need to. The room leaned toward him on its own.
"Three weeks ago," he began, "we removed enrollment caps across Toronto sites. Since that change, we've screened over eight thousand residents and initiated treatment for a first cohort of twenty-seven hundred."
The slide behind him changed to a clean bar graph—treatment numbers climbing in neat blocks, each block labeled with a site name.
"We did this," he continued, "because need was measurable. Distress demand was measurable. Relief outcomes are measurable."
He paused, as if letting the word relief act like a hand pressed to the forehead of the room.
"Monitoring has been active since Day One. We are not guessing. We are not improvising. We are tracking safety, stability, functional improvement, and adverse events in real time."

He clicked again.
EARLY SAFETY SUMMARY
— No significant increase in acute destabilization
— No increase in hospitalization rates relative to baseline
— High reported functional stabilization

The bullets were smooth.
Confident.
Nadia watched the room respond anyway—the subtle exhale of people who wanted permission to stop being scared.
Mercer let them have it.
"The question that matters most," he said, "is whether scale introduces risk. The answer, based on current data, is no."
He let the word no land like a gavel.
Another slide.
ADVERSE EVENTS
Rate: 0.6%
Most common: transient fatigue, mild dissociation.
Severe: rare, manageable with protocol support.

Manageable.

Nadia felt her jaw tighten and forced it to loosen again.
Mercer continued. "When we started Phase II, we promised the public we would not widen access without accountability. This is accountability."
He moved his gaze deliberately, as if making eye contact with each section.
"Today, we confirm Phase II remains within safety thresholds. We confirm monitoring supports ongoing expansion. We confirm that this is a stable intervention at scale."

Stable intervention at scale.

She wrote the phrase down in her head without moving her hand.
Mercer stepped back from the podium and made room for Dr. Patel.
Patel looked less sure. She carried a folder, not a tablet.

When she began speaking, her voice was careful in a way that made Nadia feel grateful and anxious at the same time.

"Our monitoring team assessed early post-dose stability," Patel said. "We're tracking emergent adverse events and comparing them against baseline clinical presentation."
She clicked to a slide that looked more like work.

COHORT MONITORING WINDOW
Initial: 6 weeks
Current analyzed segment: 10–21 days post-initiation
So early.
Patel showed charts—distress ratings dropping, sleep reports increasing, self-reported functioning rising. The lines were clean and upward, like a sales pitch.
Then she paused, turned slightly toward the screen, and said, "A note on interpretation."
The room sharpened.
"Most metrics we have right now are self-report," she continued. "And self-report is still valuable, but it is not the only form of stability. Our longer-term monitoring is still in progress."

Mercer's face didn't change, but Nadia saw the shift at the edge of his eyes—the small tightening that said: don't.
Patel kept going anyway.
"In addition," she said, "we are monitoring for variance. Not only mean response. We want to know if there are subgroups responding differently."
There it was. The word Nadia had been looking for all morning.
Variance.

Patel clicked to another slide.
VARIANCE ANALYSIS
— No significant cohort divergence detected in early window
— Outliers under review

Outliers under review.

Nadia waited for the definition. It didn't come.
Patel looked down at her folder as if her next sentence mattered.
"We have flagged a small subset of participants reporting affect intensity changes," she said, "but current evidence does not indicate clinical impairment."

Affect intensity changes.
Not distress. Not sleep. Not functioning.
The room absorbed the phrase without panic because it was shaped like a footnote.

Mercer stepped forward and reached the podium again before Patel fully cleared it. The motion was subtle, but it shifted ownership back to him.
"Thank you, Dr. Patel," he said warmly. "That's exactly why we monitor."
He turned to the moderator with a practiced look: we're done here.
The moderator nodded, then introduced the next speaker.
A man from Duarte's office approached the podium. Not Duarte himself—an aide with a clipped tie and a face that held no usable emotion.
"Senator Duarte sends her regards," he said. "She asked me to convey her support for the ARC Clinical Network and to reaffirm the Senate's commitment to continued access."

Continued access.

He glanced down briefly, as if reading from something that had been approved by three lawyers.
"We have reviewed the early safety findings. We consider the program in good standing. We consider the monitoring process sufficient. We consider the expansion justified."

Justified.

Nadia felt the room exhale again, harder this time.

The aide continued. "In addition, the Senator will be introducing a motion next week to formalize Phase II as a protected health response under emergency relief authority."

Protected.

She looked up sharply.
Mercer's expression didn't shift, but Nadia saw satisfaction in the way he held his shoulders—like a door had clicked into place behind him.
The aide added, "This will ensure stability of funding and operations, and prevent disruption due to administrative fluctuations."

Prevent disruption.
Prevent pause.

The moderator thanked him, then opened the floor for questions.
A clinician asked about staffing. Mercer answered smoothly.
A journalist asked about eligibility criteria. Mercer answered smoothly.
A policymaker asked about throughput. Mercer answered smoothly.
Everything had an answer.

Nadia waited until there was a lull and then stood.
Her chair scraped. A few heads turned. Patel looked at her quickly, then away.
The moderator nodded toward her. "Dr. Serrano."
Nadia hadn't introduced herself. But they knew who she was. Her badge had been checked twice to get into the room.
"My question is about the variance analysis," she said, keeping her voice level. "You're reporting no significant cohort divergence in an early window. What are you treating as divergence? What's the threshold?"
There was a small stillness, the kind that happens when a room senses the wrong kind of clarity arriving.
Patel's eyes flicked up again, almost pleading.
Mercer smiled slightly.
"Good question," he said. "We're using standard deviation shifts against baseline distress markers and functional metrics."

"Functional metrics defined as what?" Nadia asked, "in the early window? Sleep and self-report?"
Mercer's smile held.
"Sleep is a functional metric," he said. "So is return to work. So is reduced crisis utilization."
"And affect intensity changes?" Nadia asked. "Where do those sit in your model?"
The word model made Mercer's eyes narrow by a fraction.
"They sit under quality-of-life tracking," he said. "Which remains positive."

Nadia kept going because she could feel the room wanting her to stop.
"How are you distinguishing between reduced distress and reduced affect salience?" she asked. "Those aren't interchangeable."
A few people shifted in their seats.
Mercer didn't look angry. He looked patient.
"We're distinguishing by impairment," he said. "If someone reports changes but remains stable and functional, we treat it as non-pathological."

Non-pathological.

Nadia felt something in her chest flare and forced it down.
"So you're defining safety as the absence of visible collapse," she said.
That line made the room tighten.
Mercer's voice softened. "Safety is the absence of harm."
"And harm is defined as what?" Nadia asked, "in a monitoring window that hasn't reached the long-term endpoints?"
The moderator's mouth tightened slightly.
Mercer's smile thinned.
"We are not ignoring long-term endpoints," he said. "We are proceeding with the information we have. That's how medicine works."

Nadia looked at the slide behind him—clean lines, confident words, the feeling of inevitability.
Behind her eyes, she saw Adrian's face across the breakfast table. Clear. Calm. Saying manageable.

She sat back down.

The moderator thanked her and moved to the next question quickly, like wiping a spill before anyone had to name it.

The rest of the Q&A continued in a controlled rhythm. Mercer answered. The room agreed. The graphs stayed clean.

When the session ended, people stood and began to talk in clusters. Conversations had the relieved buzz of a storm warning that had been lifted.

Nadia stayed seated for a moment, watching the way Mercer was surrounded. Administrators. Policymakers. The aide from Duarte's office. People smiling as if they'd been handed a future.

Patel approached Nadia's row cautiously.

"Don't," Patel said quietly, before Nadia could speak.

Nadia looked up at her.

Patel's face held exhaustion. "They're going to call it settled now."

"Is it settled?" Nadia asked.

Patel didn't answer directly. She glanced toward Mercer, then lowered her voice.

"We don't have enough time in the window," she said. "We don't have enough resolution."

She paused.

Patel added, "And we can't write concerns the way we used to. Everything routes through compliance now."

Nadia stared at her. "Since when?"

Patel's mouth tightened. "Since this morning."

She handed Nadia a printed sheet, folded once, like contraband.

At the top:

PHASE II — COMMUNICATION GUIDELINES (EFFECTIVE IMMEDIATELY)

Below, a list of rules. Language constraints. Reporting pathways. Escalation procedures.

One line caught Nadia's eye.

All variance concerns must be submitted through centralized review. Individual clinicians may not distribute internal analyses without authorization.

Nadia felt her palms go slightly damp.

Patel's voice was barely audible. "They're calling it protection."
Nadia looked up again. Mercer was laughing with someone from the Senate liaison team. His hand rested lightly on the person's shoulder as if they were already aligned.
"Thanks," Nadia said, and folded the paper into her pocket.

Patel hesitated, then said, "How's Adrian?"
Nadia's throat tightened.
"I don't know," she said.
Patel blinked. The answer hit her late, then settled with a grim understanding.
"Right," Patel said. "The restriction."
She stepped back as if proximity itself could be audited.

Nadia left the room through the side corridor to avoid the main exit, where the media were now gathering around Mercer.
In the hallway, her phone buzzed.
A clinic notification.
She looked at it despite herself.

PHASE II — STATUS UPDATE
Monitoring milestone: PASSED
Operational clearance: CONTINUED
Communication guidelines: ACKNOWLEDGEMENT REQUIRED

Two buttons.
ACKNOWLEDGE
REQUEST REVIEW

Her thumb hovered.
She pictured Adrian this morning—finished bowl, steady voice, asking about the lake like it was a weekend plan.
She pressed ACKNOWLEDGE.
The phone vibrated once, confirming compliance.
Then a second notification arrived immediately, as if it had been waiting for her permission to exist.

SENATE NOTICE — EMERGENCY RELIEF AUTHORITY
ARC Phase II designated protected intervention pending vote.

Protected intervention.

Nadia stood still in the hallway while people moved around her—heels on tile, badge lanyards swinging, the soft rush of institutional momentum. Outside, through the glass doors, the winter sun hit the snowbanks and made them briefly look clean.
Nadia put the phone back in her coat pocket without turning off the screen and kept walking.

Chapter 10
Variance

Toronto — 2047

The hospital parking structure was almost empty when Nadia reached her car.

Salt crusted along the concrete ramps. Meltwater gathered in shallow gray pools under fluorescent strips that hummed faintly overhead.

She sat in the driver's seat without starting the engine.

Her phone screen was still open to the clinic notification:

FOLLOW-UP CHECK — PATIENT REPORT: POSITIVE RESPONSE

Distress Rating: 4

Sleep Duration: 7h 52m

Adverse Events: None Reported

She locked the screen.

Then unlocked it again.

The numbers did not change.

Inside the hospital, two floors up, Director Mercer stood in front of a live dashboard.

"Green across sites," Patel said from the side console. "No destabilizations. No acute escalations."

"Retention?" Mercer asked.

"Seventy-three percent requesting continuation consult."

Mercer nodded.

"Push the release," he said.

Patel hesitated. "Already?"

"Yes."

She turned to her keyboard.

Across internal messaging channels, a summary began to populate:

ARC Phase II — Initial Stability Confirmed

Early cohort shows reduced distress intensity without destabilization.

Mercer adjusted his cufflinks.

"Schedule the Senate briefing," he said. "If the first cohort stays clean through week two, we move to regional replication."

Patel glanced at him.

"That's faster than—"
"Than what?" Mercer asked.
She didn't finish.
He watched the retention graph climb in clean arcs.
"Momentum matters," he said.

In her car, Nadia opened her laptop.
She connected to her private network.
A blank document appeared.
Cursor blinking.
She titled it:
Private Line — Variance Tracking
She hesitated.
Then typed:
Case Reference: Hale, A.
Dose: Single initiation.
Immediate relief response within expected physiological band.
Observed effect: Distress memory intact, affect intensity reduced.
She stopped.
Deleted the last line.
Rewrote it.
Observed effect: Distress memory intact. Affective engagement altered.

She stared at the wording.
Altered how?
She left it.
Her phone vibrated.
Adrian.
She answered.

"You're still at work?" he asked.
"In the garage," she said.
"I'm making dinner," he said.
There was a clatter in the background. A cabinet closing.
"You don't have to," she said.
"I want to," he replied.
His tone was steady. Even.

"How are you feeling?" she asked.
"Fine," he said.
No pause.
"Anything unusual?" she asked.
He laughed lightly. "Like what?"
"I don't know," she said.
Silence.
"No," he said. "It just feels… quiet."

There it was again.
Quiet.
She closed her eyes.
"Okay," she said.
"You sound like you're interviewing me," he said.
"I'm not."
"You are," he said.
Another silence.
"Come home," he said.
"I will."
The line clicked off.

Upstairs, Mercer's assistant stepped into the control room.
"Media wants a statement," she said.
"Approved copy only," Mercer replied.
"And the retention forecast?"
"Include it."
Patel looked up from her screen.
"That's speculative," she said.
"It's trending," Mercer corrected.
He turned back to the dashboard.
"Highlight reduced emergency admissions," he added. "And workplace productivity indicators."
Patel hesitated. "We don't have validated productivity data yet."
"We have employer surveys."
"That's not clinical," she said.
"It's persuasive," Mercer said.
He folded his arms and watched the green bars stabilize.

"Get ahead of the story," he said.

In the parking structure, Nadia typed again.
Comparison note — Day 1 post-dose:
Sleep restoration immediate.
Guilt response absent.
Trauma recall intact.
Somatic constriction absent.
She stared at the words.
Somatic constriction absent.
She replayed the lake in her own mind.
The dock.
The rain.
The weight.
Her chest tightened instantly.
She forced herself to breathe through it.
She added:
Self-test: Recall produces full physiological activation.
She sat back.
The garage light flickered once overhead.
On her dashboard screen, a small notification appeared from the internal system—visible through her secondary login.
Phase II — Public Summary Released.
She opened it.
ARC Phase II demonstrates strong early relief outcomes without destabilization. Cohort stability exceeds projections.

Exceeds projections.

Her jaw tightened.
She opened a second tab and accessed archived modeling files.
Original projected uptake curve: gradual climb, plateau at 0.32 adoption density in high-distress regions.
She opened the revised file from two days ago.
Projected plateau: 0.44.
She zoomed in.
Retention adjustment coefficient had changed.

She scrolled.
Authorization signature: Mercer, A.
Timestamp: 05:08.

Before the caps were lifted.
Before stabilization.

She returned to her private document.
New header:
Model Variance — Adoption Curve Revision
She copied both projections into the file.
Original.
Revised.
The difference was visible even without numbers.
She added:
Revision authorized prior to longitudinal stabilization window.
She paused.
This was no longer observation.
It was comparison.

Her phone buzzed again.
Unknown number.
She declined it.
A moment later, a text arrived.
Dr. Min-Jae Kwan.
You seeing the release?
She stared at the message.
Typed:
Yes.
Three dots appeared immediately.
Retention curve's aggressive, he wrote.
She looked back at the revised model.
You approved it? she typed.
No.
She waited.
Five seconds.
Ten.

Then:
Be careful what you document.
Her pulse ticked once harder.
Why? she typed.
Three dots again.
Because revisions usually follow data, he wrote.
This one preceded it.
Nadia stared at the line.

Preceded it.

She looked at her own document.
Private Line — Variance Tracking.
She highlighted the entire file.
For a moment, she considered deleting it.
Instead, she created a duplicate.
Encrypted the copy.
Saved it to an external drive.
Then returned to the original and added one final line:
Private monitoring initiated. Not for institutional review.
She closed the laptop and started the car.

As she pulled out of the garage, snow began again—thin and sideways, catching in the streetlights.
Upstairs, Mercer approved the Senate briefing deck.
At home, Adrian stirred a pan and hummed quietly under his breath.
Nadia drove through the city without turning on the radio.
She did not delete the file.

Chapter 11
Contagion

Toronto — 2047

The café on Bloor was louder than Nadia remembered.
Steam hissed from behind the counter. Milk pitchers struck metal with small, bright sounds. A row of laptops glowed along the window where snow had begun collecting in thin seams against the glass.
Adrian was already seated when she arrived.
Not alone.
Across from him sat Daniel Hale—older by a few years, shoulders rounded forward the way men sit when they expect impact. Nadia recognized him from the lake.
Daniel stood when she approached.
"Hey," he said, voice thin from lack of sleep.
"Hi," Nadia replied.
She took the empty chair beside Adrian.
Daniel's coffee sat untouched.
"You look better," Daniel said to Adrian.
Adrian shrugged slightly. "I am."
Daniel studied him openly, as if looking for something missing.
"You're not—" Daniel started, then stopped. "You don't look wrecked."
"I'm not," Adrian said.
Nadia watched Daniel's fingers tighten around his cup.
Adrian nodded once.
Nadia's eyes moved to him.

Daniel leaned forward.
"I heard you started ARC," he said.
Adrian didn't look at Nadia before answering.
"Yeah."
Daniel waited.
"And?" he asked.
Adrian took a sip of his coffee.
"It works," he said.
The words landed with weight.
Nadia kept her face neutral.

Daniel blinked. "How so?" he asked.
Adrian searched for precision.
"It just... kind of, does."
Daniel stared at him.
"It doesn't make it gone. It just makes it survivable," Adrian replied.

Survivable.

Daniel looked down at his hands.
"They screened you?" he asked.
"Yeah," said Adrian.
"Hard?"
"No."

Nadia inhaled slowly.
Daniel's eyes flicked to her.
"You work there?" he asked.
"Yes," Nadia replied.
"And?" he asked.
She chose her words carefully.
"It's indicated for persistent distress unresponsive to first-line treatment," she said.
Daniel gave a short laugh.
"That's me," he said.
Adrian leaned forward slightly.
"You don't have to keep doing it," he said.
Nadia felt the shift.
Daniel looked at Adrian with something close to hope.

Daniel nodded once.
"I saw the hearing," he said. "They said it's safe."
Nadia's jaw tightened.
"It's monitored," she said.
Daniel didn't look at her.
He was watching Adrian.
"How does it take?" he asked.
"Same day," Adrian said.

Daniel exhaled.

"Same day," he repeated.

Nadia set her coffee down carefully.

"Daniel," she said, "screening doesn't obligate you to dose."

He looked at her, confused.

"I know," he said. "But if they say I qualify..."

He didn't finish.

Adrian did.

"Then it makes sense," Adrian said.

Nadia turned to him.

"Adrian," she said quietly.

He met her eyes.

"What?" he asked.

There was no defensiveness in it.

Daniel glanced between them.

"I just don't want to keep feeling like this," he said. "I want to feel better."

The word hung there.

Adrian nodded again. "You will," he said.

Nadia felt the moment tipping.

Daniel pulled out his phone.

"What's the site?" he asked.

Adrian answered without hesitation.

"University's fast," he said. "Scarborough's backed up."

Nadia's hand tightened on her cup.

Daniel typed.

The intake page loaded.

He looked up once more. Then he pressed the scheduling button.

Appointment options populated on the screen.

Tomorrow.

Thursday.

Friday.

He chose tomorrow.

The confirmation page flashed.

ARC Phase II — Screening Confirmed

09:10 — University Site

Daniel set the phone down on the table.

"There," he said.

He looked at Adrian like something had already shifted.

"Thank you," he added.

Adrian didn't look triumphant.

He looked certain.

After Daniel left, Nadia and Adrian stayed seated.

The café noise returned around them.

"You didn't have to do that," Nadia said.

"Do what?" Adrian asked.

"Recommend it."

He frowned slightly.

"I didn't recommend it," he said. "I told the truth."

Nadia held his gaze.

"You're part of the data now," she said.

He blinked.

"So?"

"So when you say it works, people believe you."

"It does work," he replied.

She leaned back in her chair.

"That's not the only variable," she said.

He looked at her carefully.

"You think I shouldn't have told him?" he asked.

She didn't answer immediately.

"Daniel makes his own decisions," she said.

"So do I," Adrian replied.

The line landed clean.

He stood.

"We're allowed to feel better," he said.

Nadia stood too.

Outside, the snow had thickened again, drifting against the window.

As they stepped onto the sidewalk, Daniel's confirmation notification echoed in Nadia's mind.

Tomorrow.

09:10.

University.

Another intake.

Another dose.

Nadia reached into her coat pocket and felt her phone there, solid and warm.
She did not open it.
But she knew what she would add to the private log tonight.
Adrian walked beside her, shoulders loose, breath steady.
Behind them, inside the café, two students at the window were talking.
"Did you hear?" one said. "It helps."
The other nodded.
"I'm thinking about it."
The door closed.
And the street absorbed the sound.

Chapter 12
Velocity

Toronto ARC Clinical Network — 2047
The administrative floor was warmer than the clinical wing.
Carpet instead of tile. Frosted glass instead of clear partitions. The noise of the intake lobby reduced to a distant, indistinct hum.
Nadia didn't knock.
Mercer's office door was already half-open.
He stood near the window, phone pressed to his ear, city towers reflected faintly in the glass behind him.
"Yes," he said. "Retention is exceeding projection. No destabilizations reported."
Pause.
"Yes. We're prepared to extend blocks through Q2."
He turned slightly when he saw her but didn't stop speaking.
"No, Senator, I understand the visibility. We'll keep messaging aligned."
He ended the call and set the phone down.
"You're early for the briefing," he said.
"I'm not here for the briefing," Nadia replied.
He studied her face.
"Close the door," he said.
She did.
The latch clicked softly.
Mercer moved behind his desk but didn't sit.
"What's the concern?" he asked.
"Velocity," she said.
He gave the faintest smile.
"Again?" he asked.
"Yes," she said.
He sat this time.
She remained standing.
"We're compressing monitoring windows," she said. "Doubling throughput targets. Revising adoption modeling before stabilization."
"We're responding to demand," Mercer said.
"We're shaping it," Nadia replied.
He folded his hands. "Clarify."

"You lifted caps before the first cohort cleared longitudinal review."
"They cleared acute review," he said.
"That's not the same."
"It's sufficient."
"For whom?" she asked.
"For the people sleeping for the first time in months," he said evenly.
Nadia held his gaze.
"There are qualitative shifts emerging," she said.
"Such as?" he asked.
"Affect compression."
He waited.
"Define that," he said.
"Participants reporting intact memory but reduced physiological engagement."
"That's the mechanism," he said.
"Yes," she said. "But we don't know the downstream impact."
"We monitor."
"At six weeks," she said. "Reduced from twelve."
"Six weeks captures destabilization risk," he said.
"It doesn't capture behavioral adaptation," she said.

He leaned back slightly. "Behavioral adaptation to what?"
"To relief," she said.
He exhaled once. "You're implying dependency."
"I'm implying retention variance."

He reached for his tablet and turned it toward her.
The retention graph rose in clean lines.
Seventy-four percent continuation consult request.
"Variance in which direction?" he asked.
She didn't touch the screen.
"We don't know yet," she said.
"Exactly," he replied.
Silence.

He tapped the graph.

"No adverse events," he said. "No hospitalizations. No reported destabilizations. Emergency admissions trending downward."

"That's acute," she said.

"That's measurable," he replied.

Nadia stepped closer to the desk.

"The consent language includes adaptive protocol modifications," she said. "Aggregate-based adjustments."

"Approved by ethics," he said.

"Before longitudinal clarity," she insisted.

"Before political pressure," he corrected.

She paused.

"What political pressure?" she asked.

He held her eyes for a beat.

"You watched the hearing," he said.

"That's not what I asked."

He leaned forward.

"Insurance providers are watching this. Employers are watching this. Provincial health is watching this. If we demonstrate stability, funding expands. If we hesitate, access narrows."

"This isn't about funding," she said.

"It's always about funding," he replied.

The words were not sharp. Just factual.

Nadia crossed her arms.

"You revised the uptake model," she said.

"Yes," he said.

"Upward."

"Yes."

"Before six-week stabilization?" she asked.

"Yes," he said.

"Why?"

He didn't answer immediately.

"Because the original model underestimated demand elasticity," he said.

"Based on how many days of data?" she asked.

"Enough."

"That's not a number."

"It's enough," he repeated.

Nadia studied him.

"You're assuming continuation if relief holds," she said.

"I'm observing it," he replied.

"We don't know what continuation does over time."

"We know what untreated distress does," he said.

The intake board notification pinged faintly from the wall screen outside his office.

She heard it through the door.

He glanced toward the sound.

"You want me to slow enrollment?" he asked.

"Yes," she said.

"How?"

"Reinstate partial caps until twelve-week review."

He shook his head.

"That's not happening," he said.

"Why?" she asked.

"Because people are lining up," he said. "Because legislators are endorsing it. Because we have no destabilization signal to justify a slowdown."

"We don't have resolution either," she said.

"Resolution isn't the metric," he replied.

She took a breath.

"What is?"

"Relief," he said.

The word sat between them.

Nadia's jaw tightened.

"I want raw cohort-level affect reporting," she said. "Unfiltered."

"You have access to summary data," he said.

"I want uncleaned feeds."

His eyes narrowed slightly.

"Cleaned," he repeated.

"Normalized," she said.

"Data is standardized," he replied.

"I want the pre-standardization set."

He leaned back again. "That's not your scope."

"I'm outcomes research," she said.

"You're outcomes within assigned parameters," he corrected.
"Then expand them," she said.
"No."
The word was calm.
Final.
Silence filled the office.

Outside, someone laughed too loudly in the corridor, then stopped abruptly.
"You're worried about something you can't name," Mercer said.
"I'm watching something I can't measure," Nadia replied.
He held her gaze.
"Well, until you can measure it," he said, "it doesn't justify restricting access."
She stepped back.
"Who approved the revised retention coefficient?" she asked.
"I did," he said.
"Based on what consultation?" she asked.
"My authority," he said. The answer landed much heavier than the others.
Nadia nodded once.
"So this is institutional," she said.
"It's operational," he replied.
She reached for the door.
"Send your concerns in writing," he added.
She paused.
"Will you act on them?" she asked.
"If they meet threshold."
"And who sets threshold?" she asked.
He didn't answer.
She opened the door.
The intake board down the corridor flashed:
612 ACTIVE
41 DOSES TODAY
The number pulsed green.
Behind her, Mercer's voice came one last time.
"Nadia."
She turned slightly.

"It's working," he said.
She looked at the board.
Then back at him.
She exhaled.

She walked down the corridor.
Her badge tapped lightly against her coat.
In her pocket, her phone vibrated.
AUTOMATED NOTICE — DATA ACCESS PARAMETERS UPDATED
User: Serrano, Nadia
Scope: Outcomes Summary Tier Only
Raw cohort access removed pending review.
She stopped walking.
Read it again.
Raw cohort access removed.
She locked the screen.
Then continued toward the elevator.
The intake board refreshed.
And did not slow.

Chapter 13
Stable

Toronto ARC Clinical Network — 2047
The complaint did not arrive through the formal channel.
It came as a message routed through internal clinician chat, flagged with a yellow triangle instead of red.
Dr. Nadia Serrano opened it at 06:42 while standing in her kitchen, coat half on, coffee untouched.
Subject: Post-Dose Affect Question
From: Dr. L. Moreno
Marked: Informal Clinical Consult
Nadia read it once. Then again.
Patient reports persistent reduction in emotional intensity beyond expected stabilization window.
No distress reported. Functional metrics improved.
Spouse reports "flattening."
Requesting perspective before logging variance.
Nadia stared at the word.

Flattening.

Not in the official lexicon.
She typed back:
Duration since first dose?
The reply came thirty seconds later.
Six weeks.
Continued dosing at recommended interval.
Nadia grabbed her bag and left the apartment without finishing her coffee.

The clinic smelled faintly of antiseptic and wet wool. Early arrivals sat in orderly rows, intake tablets glowing in their hands.
Dr. Moreno was already in her office.
Door closed.
Nadia knocked once and entered.
Moreno didn't look defensive. She looked procedural.

"You saw it," Moreno said.
"Yes," Nadia replied.
Moreno turned her screen so Nadia could see.
Patient ID anonymized.
Male. 34.
Initial complaint: acute grief + insomnia.
Baseline distress: 8/10.
Six-week distress: 3/10.
Sleep normalized.
Return-to-work achieved.
All green indicators.
"Spouse reports affect reduction," Moreno said. "Uses word 'flat.' Patient denies impairment."
"Specific examples?" Nadia asked.
Moreno scrolled.
Spouse reports patient did not cry at funeral of close friend.
Patient states: "I was sad. It just didn't overwhelm me."
Nadia read the line twice.
"Was the friend recent?" she asked.
"Yes."
"Prior baseline comparison?"
"Before dosing, patient cried during intake when discussing deceased child," Moreno said.
Nadia's eyes lifted.

Child.

"Current presentation?" Nadia asked.
Moreno folded her hands. "Calm. Cooperative. Engaged. No anhedonia. No apathy. Goal-directed behavior intact."
"Spouse dissatisfied?" Nadia asked.
Moreno hesitated half a second.
"She asked whether this was reversible."
"And?" Nadia asked.
"I told her emotional range varies during stabilization."
"Did you log it?" Nadia asked.
Moreno's jaw tightened.

"Not yet."

"Why?" Nadia asked.

Moreno held her gaze.

"Because it isn't distress," she said.

Silence.

Outside the office door, a cart rolled past. Wheels ticking over tile seams.

Nadia looked back at the screen.

Six weeks.

Continued dosing.

"Has he requested dose increase?" Nadia asked.

"No."

"Dose decrease?"

"No."

"He's satisfied?" Nadia asked.

"Yes."

"And she isn't?" Nadia asked.

Moreno didn't answer.

The patient arrived at 08:10 for follow-up.

Nadia stood in the observation room behind the one-way glass. She wasn't assigned to the case. She wasn't supposed to be there. But Moreno had left the access feed open.

The man sat in the chair calmly.

Hands folded.

Posture straight.

Moreno spoke first.

"How have you felt since your last dose?" she asked.

"Stable," the man replied.

"Any resurgence of intrusive thoughts?" Moreno asked.

"No."

"Sleep?" she asked.

"Seven hours."

"Any loss of interest in daily activities?" she asked.

"No."

"Energy level?" she asked.

"Good."

Moreno nodded once.

From the hallway outside, a woman's voice could be heard faintly arguing with a nurse.

"That's my husband," she was saying.

Nadia turned her head toward the sound.

Moreno continued.

"Your spouse has expressed concern," she said evenly.

The man blinked once.

"She misses who I was," he said.

"Do you feel different?" Moreno asked.

"Yes," he said.

"How?" she asked.

"I don't break," he said.

No hesitation.

"Do you want to break?" Moreno asked.

"No."

The hallway voice grew louder.

"You can't tell me I can't sit in on this."

Security murmured something low.

Moreno kept her tone flat.

"Are you experiencing sadness?" she asked.

"Yes."

"How intensely?" she asked.

"Low," he said.

"Do you feel detached from people you love?" she asked.

He thought about it.

"No," he said.

Outside the room, the woman's voice cracked.

"He didn't cry."

Moreno did not react.

"Do you feel love for your spouse?" she asked.

"Yes," he said immediately.

"Describe it," she said.

He paused.

"I mean… I lover her," he said.

Nadia's stomach tightened.

68

Moreno nodded.

"Do you wish to continue treatment?" she asked.

"Yes," he said.

"Understood," Moreno replied.

She entered something into the tablet.

Nadia leaned closer to the glass.

On the screen:

FOLLOW-UP STATUS: STABLE

CONTINUE DOSING: YES

ADVERSE EVENT: NO

Her hand pressed flat against the glass before she realized she'd done it.

Outside, the spouse's voice finally broke into full sobbing.

Security escorted her away gently.

The man inside the room did not turn his head.

After the appointment ended, Moreno exited first.

She saw Nadia standing in the hall.

"You watched?" Moreno asked.

"Yes," Nadia replied.

Moreno handed her the tablet.

"Tell me where to log it," she said.

Nadia looked at the screen.

There was no category for flattening.

There was:

☐ Sleep disruption

☐ Panic recurrence

☐ Dissociation

☐ Mood destabilization

☐ Other (Specify)

Nadia selected:

☐ Other

A blank field opened.

She typed:

Spousal report of affect reduction inconsistent with baseline presentation.

She stared at the sentence.

Then added:

Patient denies distress.
She hit save.
The system paused.
Then a small banner appeared:
ENTRY RECEIVED — REVIEW NOT REQUIRED
WITHIN EXPECTED RESPONSE RANGE
Nadia's eyes lifted slowly.
Moreno saw it too.

"That's new," Moreno said.
"Yes," Nadia replied.
They stood there, both looking at the tablet.
Within expected response range.
Moreno took the tablet back.
"I'll continue dosing," she said.
It wasn't a question.
Nadia didn't answer.
Moreno walked away down the corridor.
Nadia remained standing under the fluorescent lights.
Down the hall, intake doors opened again.
Another wave entered.
On the corridor monitor, the intake board ticked upward.

That evening, Nadia opened her private log.
Personal Log — Intake Variance
She added a new line.
First spouse-reported affect reduction. Logged as "within expected response range." No escalation triggered.
She stared at the phrase.

Expected.

She closed the laptop.
And did not delete the entry.

Chapter 14
Infastructure

Toronto ARC Clinical Network — 2047
The message arrived through an old channel.
Not the hospital network. Not the outcomes portal.
A direct text.
MJ: Coffee. Offsite.
Nadia stared at the name for a long second before replying.
When?
MJ: Now.

The café was three blocks east of the clinic, across from a pharmacy and a law office with frosted windows.
Late morning light slid through the glass, reflecting off salt-streaked sidewalks. The air inside smelled of espresso and citrus cleaner. No hospital badges. No intake screens.
Dr. Min-Jae Kwan sat in the corner booth with his back to the wall.
He hadn't changed much. Same narrow shoulders. Same careful posture. The only difference was the way he watched the door before she entered.
"Nadia," he said.
"Min."
They did not hug.
She slid into the seat across from him.
"You shouldn't text me on personal channels," she said.
"You shouldn't log spouse-reported flattening as 'other,'" he replied.
Her jaw tightened.
"You saw that?" she asked.
He stirred his coffee once and set the spoon down.
"I see a lot of things," he said.
"That wasn't escalated," she said.
"No," he agreed.
"Because it wasn't destabilization."
"Because it was recoded," he said.
She held still.
"Recoded how?" she asked.
He looked at her over the rim of his cup.

71

"There's a normalization filter applied before outcomes review," he said.
She didn't blink.
"Applied by whom?" she asked.
"Analytics," he said.
"That's not a person."
"It doesn't have to be."
The espresso machine hissed behind the counter.
Nadia leaned back slightly.
"What does the filter do?" she asked.
"It collapses variance into expected bands," he said.
"That's standard smoothing," she said.
"This isn't smoothing," he said.
Silence.

He took out his phone, turned the screen toward her briefly.
Two columns.
RAW RESPONSE SET
STANDARDIZED REPORT SET
The entries were similar. Not identical.
She leaned forward.
"What am I looking at?" she asked.
"Pre-aggregation affect reporting," he said. "Before normalization."
She scanned the rows.
Subjective intensity — spouse observation
Affect latency
Response delay
Expressive variance
Some values highlighted in yellow.
"These don't appear in the summary," she said.
"No," he agreed.
"Why?" she asked.
"Because they're categorized as relational impact, not clinical instability," he said.
"And relational impact doesn't trigger review?" she said.
"No."
She sat back.

"That's categorization, not manipulation," she said.
He didn't argue.
He just watched her.
"Look at the timestamp," he said.
She did.
Raw entries logged at 09:14.
Standardized export generated at 09:16.
Two minutes.

"That's automatic," she said.
"Yes."
"Based on threshold modeling."
"Yes."
"Approved modeling."
"Yes."
She folded her hands on the table.
"Then what's your concern?" she asked.
Kwan held her gaze.
"The thresholds moved," he said.
She didn't respond immediately.

"When?" she asked.
"Three weeks ago."
Caps lifted overnight.
"Moved how?" she asked.
He took his phone back and scrolled.
"Range for 'expected affect compression' expanded."
"By how much?" she asked.
"Fourteen percent."
She did the math in her head without meaning to.
"That's within tolerance," she said.
"It used to be six," he said.
The café door opened. Cold air rushed in, then faded.

Nadia's fingers pressed lightly into the tabletop.
"Who approved the change?" she asked.
"Administrative analytics," he said.

"Under Mercer?" she asked.
"Yes."
She looked away for the first time.

"So you're telling me flattening is being reclassified as expected response?" she asked.
"I'm telling you the band widened."
"That's not the same thing."
"It functionally is," he said.
Silence stretched between them.

A barista called out a name at the counter.
Nadia lowered her voice.
"Why are you telling me this?" she asked.
Kwan leaned back.
"Because you're still looking at raw signal," he said.
She didn't like the phrasing.
"And?" she asked.
"And you won't have access much longer."
Her eyes sharpened.
"What do you mean?"
"There's a tier restructuring memo circulating," he said.
She felt something drop in her stomach.
"I already lost raw cohort access," she said.
"Yes."
"This is further?" she asked.
He nodded once.
"Outcomes will receive summary-tier only. No variance flags unless destabilization threshold breached."
"That removes comparative analysis," she said.
"It reduces noise," he replied.
She stared at him.
"That's what they're calling it?" she asked.
"Yes."
A long pause.

"Are you saying the data's being falsified?" she asked.

"No," he said immediately.
"Then what are you saying?"
He met her eyes.
"I'm saying the definition of concern changed."
The words hung there.
Nadia's mind ran backward through the last four weeks.
The spouse in the hallway.
The banner: within expected response range.
The expanded retention curve.

She looked at him again.
"Is this about optics?" she asked.
"It's about clearance," he said.
"For what?" she asked.
He hesitated. Then said it. "National adoption."
The café noise receded in her ears.

"National?" she repeated.
"Phase II is Toronto," he said. "Phase III is provincial. After that…"
He didn't finish.
Nadia sat very still.
"You're still inside the system," she said.
"Yes."
"And you're telling me this offsite."
"Yes," he said.
"Why?" she asked again.
He took a breath. "Because I don't think anyone's recalibrating for long-term relational variance," he said.
"That's not a clinical category."
"No."
"Then what is it?" she asked.
He held her gaze. "A human one."
The barista dropped a metal scoop into a bin. The sound rang sharply.

Nadia looked down at the table. "Show me the memo," she said.
"I can't send it," he said.
"Then show me."

He hesitated. "That would log," he said.
"Everything logs," she said.
"Yes."
They sat there, the tension between risk and caution visible but unspoken.
Finally, he nodded once.

"I'll show you a screenshot," he said. "Nothing exportable."
"When?" she asked.
"Tonight," he said. "Different location."
She nodded.
Kwan stood first.
"Delete this thread," he said quietly.
She met his eyes. "I don't keep threads," she said.
He gave a faint, humorless smile.
"That's why I texted you."
He left the café without looking back.

Nadia remained seated.
Outside, a bus passed, brakes hissing against wet pavement.
She took out her phone and opened her personal log.

Personal Log — Intake Variance
She added:
Affect compression band expanded from 6% to 14%. Reclassified as expected response. Tier restructuring pending.
She stared at the words.
Then added one more line.
National adoption referenced.
She locked the phone, stood, and walked back toward the clinic.

Chapter 15
Retention

Toronto ARC Clinical Network — 2047
The notification arrived at 06:12.
Nadia was awake. She had been for twenty minutes already, lying still while the radiator clicked and the sky outside the bedroom window shifted from charcoal to thin blue.
Her phone vibrated once against the nightstand.
SYSTEM NOTICE — INTERNAL REVIEW INITIATED
User: Serrano, Nadia
Access Tier: Conditional
Reason: Data Irregularity — Phase II Monitoring
She didn't open it immediately.
Beside her, Adrian slept on his back, one arm folded loosely over his chest. His face was smooth in sleep now. No crease between the brows. No clenched jaw.
She slid out of bed without waking him.

In the kitchen, frost feathered the lower corner of the window. The city below moved in pale early lines—delivery trucks, bundled pedestrians, a streetcar gliding past the hospital corridor she knew by heart.
She opened the notification.
An internal link populated beneath it.
FLAG SOURCE: Outcomes Monitoring — Raw Query Access
Trigger: Unscheduled Extraction Attempt
Status: Under Administrative Review
Her thumb hovered over the screen.

Unscheduled extraction attempt.

She had requested access to raw variance tables the night before. Not altered anything. Not exported anything. Just opened a secondary analytics pane and compared flattened affect reports against dosing frequency.
She had closed it before midnight.
The kettle clicked on.

Another notification layered over the first.
MEETING REQUEST — 08:30
Director Mercer
Location: Office 14B
She locked the screen.

Behind her, the bedroom door opened softly.
Adrian stepped into the hallway, barefoot, hair still flattened on one side.
He leaned against the doorframe and watched her.
"You're up early," he said.
"So are you," she replied.
He shrugged lightly. "Couldn't get back to sleep."
She turned. "You slept."
"Yeah." He smiled faintly. "Just didn't need more."
He came into the kitchen and reached for a glass, filling it at the sink.
"You going in today?" he asked.
"Yes."
He nodded.

She studied him as he drank.

"You okay?" he asked.
"I have a meeting," she said.
"With?"
"Mercer."
He set the glass down.
"About what?" he asked.
"Monitoring," she said.
He held her gaze a second longer than usual.
"Is that bad?"
"It depends."
On what, she didn't say.
He crossed the small space between them and kissed her forehead—brief, habitual. Then he stepped back.
"I'm going to go for a run," he said. "Clear my head."
She watched him tie his shoes.

The apartment felt larger after the door closed.

At the clinic, security checked badges twice.
Not visibly different. Just slower.
Office 14B sat at the end of the administrative corridor, walls lined with framed press releases and photographs of ribbon cuttings.
Mercer stood behind his desk when she entered.
He didn't gesture for her to sit immediately.
"Morning," he said.
"Alan," she said.
He closed the door.
The click was deliberate.
He walked around the desk and leaned against its edge instead of taking his chair.
"Outcomes flagged your account," he said.
"I saw."
"Do you want to tell me why you were pulling raw Phase II variance tables at 23:14?"
"I couldn't sleep," she said.
He watched her.
"That's not an answer," he said.
She met his eyes.

"I wanted to compare subjective flattening reports against dosing continuation rates," she said.
Mercer's expression didn't change, but his shoulders shifted slightly.
"That's not part of your current assignment," he said.
"It used to be."
"We reorganized."
"I noticed," she said.
He exhaled slowly.
"You're pulling at threads," he said.
"I'm reading data."
"Outside your lane."
"My lane involves long-term safety," she said.
"Your lane," he corrected gently, "involves clinical stabilization."
Silence.

He crossed to his desk and tapped a key. A screen on the wall lit up.
A dashboard.
Green bars.
Retention curves trending upward.
Adverse event reports flat and minimal.
"This," he said, gesturing toward the screen, "is what oversight sees."
She didn't look away from it.
"What do you see?" he asked.
"I see six-week windows," she said.
"And?"
"And nothing beyond them."
He smiled faintly. "That's because nothing beyond them is required yet."
"Yet," she repeated.
He let the word pass.

"You requested access to longitudinal raw tables that are still being normalized," he said. "That triggers compliance review."
"I didn't export anything," she said.
"You accessed."
"That's not a violation."
"It's a deviation," he said.
He let the distinction sit.

She stepped closer to the screen.
"Show me the subjective flattening category," she said.
Mercer didn't move.
"It's under non-critical affect variance," he said.
"Show it."
He hesitated, then clicked.

A smaller graph appeared in the corner.
A thin line. Almost flat.
Reported Affective Blunting — 1.8%
"Self-reported," he said. "Within tolerance."
"What's tolerance?" she asked.
"Below five."

"Who set five?"
"Consensus," he said.
She turned to him. "On what evidence?"
"On the absence of functional impairment."
She held his gaze.
"Absence of reported functional impairment?" she said.
He didn't answer.

She stepped back from the screen.
"You compressed follow-up windows," she said. "You adjusted modeling inputs. You increased throughput. Now you're smoothing categories."
"We're standardizing language," he said.
"You're diluting signals."
He straightened.
"You are not the only clinician in this building," he said. "And you are not the sole guardian of emotional nuance."
"I didn't say I was," she said.
"Well, you're acting like it."
Silence.
The radiator in the corner ticked.

Outside his window, snow slid from a ledge and broke apart against the glass below.
"You're too close to this," Mercer said finally.
She didn't ask which this.

He continued. "You have a personal conflict on record. Your partner is enrolled. That alone puts you under observation."
She didn't blink.
"Are you questioning my objectivity?" she asked.
"I'm protecting the program," he said.
"From what?"
"From doubt that isn't evidence-based."
She folded her arms.
"What happens if flattening increases?" she asked.
"Then we review," he said.
"When?"

"When it crosses threshold."
"And if it doesn't cross threshold but accumulates quietly?" she asked.
He stepped closer.
"Quiet accumulation," he said evenly, "is not the same as harm."
She felt the word land in her body.

Harm.

"People are sleeping," he continued. "They're functioning. They're returning to work. Domestic incidents have declined. ER psychiatric admissions are down twelve percent in three weeks."
"I've seen the numbers," said.
"Then what are you afraid of?"
She thought of Adrian at the kitchen table, describing the lake like a case file.

Manageable.

"I'm not afraid," she said.
Mercer watched her for a long moment.
"Compliance will clear this," he said. "You'll retain your access. But stay within assignment scope."
He turned the screen off.
The room dimmed slightly without its glow.
"Understood?" he asked.
She nodded once. "Understood."
He opened the door for her.

As she stepped into the corridor, her phone vibrated again.
ACCESS STATUS — CONDITIONAL
Monitoring Active
No Further Action Required

She stood still for a second, then walked toward the clinical wing.
Across the hall, a television mounted near the waiting area played a morning segment on mute.
A lower-third banner scrolled beneath a smiling anchor:

ARC PHASE II — MONITORING SHOWS SAFE EARLY RESULTS
Patients in winter coats sat beneath it, staring at their hands or their phones.
A nurse called a name.
A man stood.
He walked toward the screening corridor.
Nadia watched him go.
Her phone vibrated once more.
A text from Adrian.

Ran 5K. Felt good.
Coffee later?
She typed back:
Yes.

She slipped the phone into her pocket and walked toward Outcomes Monitoring.

Chapter 16
Eirenex

Toronto ARC Clinical Network — 2048
The denial notice came through at 21:14.
Nadia had requested archived modeling inputs from the week caps were lifted. Not live dashboards. Not summaries. Raw forecast revisions.
ACCESS REQUEST — DECLINED
Reason: Tier Realignment

Tier realignment.

No additional explanation.
She stared at the message for several seconds, then forwarded it.
To: Min-Jae Kwan
Tier realignment?

His reply came nine minutes later.

From: Min-Jae Kwan
Check the archived build versions. Not the live dashboards. Metadata only.

That was all.

At 22:03 she was in the sub-basement records room.
Older terminals. Slower systems. No polished interface.
She logged in under outcomes review clearance — still valid for archive queries.
Search: PHASE II MODEL REVISION
Three files appeared.
PH2_FORECAST_V1
PH2_FORECAST_V2
PH2_FORECAST_V2_FINAL
She opened V2.
The curve rose sharply, then leveled. Conservative retention assumptions.
Six-week stabilization window.

She opened V2_FINAL.
The curve rose sharper.
Retention assumptions extended.
Language tightened.
She opened file properties.
Created: 05:02
Modified: 05:08
Published: 05:10
Six minutes between revision and publication.

She scrolled further down to internal tag fields.
Internal Program Code: EIRNX_ADAPTIVE_TRACK
Her hand stopped.
EIRNX.
She highlighted it.
Copied.
Searched.
Two archived folders surfaced.
EIRNX_COMMUNICATION
EIRNX_TRANSITION_PLAN
She opened the first.
A slide deck loaded.
White background.
Minimalist design.
Title:
EIRENEX
Phase Transition Strategy
She did not move.
Slide 2:
Lexical Alignment Plan
— "ARC therapy" maintained for clinical settings
— "Eirenex" introduced in parallel stakeholder communications
— Gradual public migration recommended post-stability validation

Post-stability validation.

She scrolled.

Brand Rationale:
Short-form name improves recall
Removes clinical barrier language
Positions treatment as ongoing support rather than intervention

Ongoing support.

She opened the second folder.
EIRNX_TRANSITION_PLAN.
Timeline graphic.
Internal adoption: Q2
Stakeholder briefings: Q3
Public-facing brand shift: Q4
She checked the file date.
Three weeks before caps were lifted.
Her jaw tightened slightly.
Caps were lifted under ARC.
The rebrand planning had already been built.

She searched the document for "Phase II."
Result:
Toronto Phase II functions as stability validation cohort.
Stability validation.
Not distress relief.
She leaned back in the chair.

Her phone vibrated.
Kwan.
You see it.
She typed:
It's already branded.
He replied:
Internally.

She looked at the green logo again.
ARC's branding had been clinical. Blue. Institutional.
Eirenex was clean. Commercial.

She typed:
Why shift?
A pause.
Then:
Because Phase II isn't meant to stay Phase II.
She stared at the words.
Is this regulatory? she typed.
No immediate answer.
When it came, it was shorter.
'It's positioning'.

Positioning.

Not expansion.
Not safety.
Not outcomes.
Positioning.

She tried exporting the slide deck.
FILE EXPORT REQUIRES EXECUTIVE AUTHORIZATION.
She canceled.
Then pulled out her phone.
Took three photos:
The green logo.
The lexical alignment slide.
The timeline graphic.
The fluorescent lights flickered once above her.
She logged out of the archive system.

When she stepped back into the corridor, nothing looked different.
A nurse pushed a cart past her.
An overhead speaker paged respiratory therapy.
On the wall-mounted monitor near intake, the banner still read:
ARC Phase II — Distress Regulation Pathway Active
She stood beneath it.

ARC on the wall.

Eirenex in the basement.
She pulled out her phone and opened her private log.

Personal Log — Intake Variance
She added one line.
Internal brand name: Eirenex. Transition plan predates cap removal.

She closed the entry, then turned off her screen and walked toward the elevators.

Chapter 17
Normalization

Toronto — 2047

The kitchen window was open a crack.
Cold air slipped in along the frame and moved the edge of the curtain in slow, steady pulses.
Adrian stood at the counter with both palms flat against the surface.
Nadia watched him from the doorway.
"You're early," she said.
"I left work," he replied.
He didn't turn around.
The kettle was on but not boiling. He hadn't turned the burner high enough.
"What happened?" she asked.
He exhaled through his nose.
"Nothing," he said.
Silence.
She stepped closer.
His shoulders weren't tense. That was the problem.
"What do you mean nothing?" she asked.
"I mean I didn't panic," he said. "I didn't freeze. I didn't feel like I was going to break."
He turned then.
"But I also didn't feel anything."
The refrigerator motor hummed behind them.
Nadia held still.
"About what?" she asked.
"My team got cut," he said. "Three people. Walked out with boxes."
"And?" she asked.
"And I watched," he said.
His voice stayed even.
"I knew I should feel something," he added. "Anger. Fear. Something."
"What did you feel?" she asked.
He thought about it.
"Clear," he said.
The word landed wrong.

Nadia crossed her arms.

"That's not pathology," she said carefully. "It's stability."

"It didn't feel like stability," he replied.

"It felt like I was observing myself."

She didn't answer.

He pushed off the counter and moved toward the table.

"I keep waiting for it to settle into something normal," he said. "It hasn't."

"You're in early window," she said.

"It's been weeks," he said.

"Yes."

"That's not early."

She sat across from him.

"Are you sleeping?" she asked.

"Yes," he said.

"Nightmares?"

"No."

"Intrusive replay?" she asked.

"Less," he said.

She nodded.

"So the primary symptoms are reduced," she said.

"That's not the question," he said.

"What is the question?" she asked.

He leaned forward.

"Is this the level?" he said. "Or does it go further?"

Her stomach tightened.

"What do you mean further?" she asked.

"I mean—" He stopped. Recalibrated. "Can it be adjusted?"

She held his gaze. "Adjusted how?"

"Dose," he said.

The room went quiet.

"You want to increase?" she asked.

"I want to feel like myself again," he said.

"You are yourself."

"No," he said.

He stood abruptly and paced once across the narrow kitchen.
"I'm functional," he said. "I'm productive. I'm not drowning."
"Yes," she said.
"But when you look at me—" he stopped walking "—you're measuring something."
She didn't blink.
"You think I don't see it?" he asked.
"I'm not measuring you."
"You are."
He leaned both hands on the table.
"I don't want to be manageable," he said. "I want to be okay."
Nadia's voice stayed level.
"Okay isn't a dosage category," she said.
He stared at her.
"That's not what I meant."
"I know what you meant."
Silence stretched.

Outside, a streetcar screeched lightly along its track.
He lowered himself back into the chair.
"If this is partial," he said quietly, "I don't want partial."
She felt the words like impact.
"More compound doesn't mean more you," she said.
"How do you know?"
"Because flattening increases with intensity."
He didn't look surprised.
"So there is more," he said.
She didn't answer quickly enough.
He saw it.
"You've seen it," he said.
"I've seen variability," she replied.
He leaned back.
"Then I want variability," he said.
"No," she said.
The word came out sharper than intended.
He stared at her.
"You can't tell me no," he said.

"I can tell you I think it's a mistake."
"It's my body."
"Yes," she said.
"And I'm not assigned to you," he said.
"No."
The air between them shifted.
"You think I don't know what distress feels like?" she asked quietly.
"That's not what I said."
He rubbed his face once.

"I'm not trying to fight," he said.
"You are," she replied.
Silence again.
Then:
"I have a follow-up next week," he said.
"I know."
"I'm going to request a dosage review."
Her pulse kicked once in her throat.
"You're already stable," she said.
"That's your word."
"It's clinical."
"I'm not a chart," he said.
He stood.
"If this thing can be tuned," he continued, "I want it tuned."
"To what?" she asked.
He paused.
"To quiet."
The word felt colder than the open window.
"We don't know what that costs," she said. "I'm not convinced that they do either."
Neither of them moved.

After a long moment, he picked up his phone.
He opened the clinic portal.
REQUEST FOLLOW-UP MODIFICATION
He tapped it.
"Adrian," she said.

He didn't look up.

"Additional notes?" the screen prompted.
He typed:
Experiencing emotional dampening. Request evaluation for dose optimization.
Her breath felt shallow.
"Adrian."
He hit submit.
The confirmation appeared instantly.
REQUEST RECEIVED — SCHEDULING IN PROCESS
He locked the phone and set it face down.
"There," he said.
Nadia sat very still.

The kettle, forgotten on the stove, began to click as the water inside finally reached heat.
Neither of them moved to turn it off.
Outside, the curtain shifted again with the cold air.

Chapter 18
Protocol

Toronto ARC Clinical Network — 2047

The server room was colder than the hallway.

Not dramatically. Just enough that breath felt thinner.

Nadia stood in front of Terminal 3B, badge clipped to her coat, hands steady on the keyboard. The glass wall reflected her face back at her—composed, almost bored.

Behind her, two junior analysts argued quietly over a data export.

"…cohort B needs to be separated by intake week."

"It already is."

"Then why—"

Their voices blurred into background noise.

On her screen:
PATIENT FOLLOW-UP SCHEDULE — HALE, ADRIAN
Next assessment: Day 7
Dose status: Initiation complete
Continuation flag: Pending clinician review

Pending.

Dr. Moreno's name sat beside the continuation field.

Nadia's access banner glowed amber at the top of the screen.

LIMITED VIEW — FAMILY RELATIONSHIP IDENTIFIED

She wasn't supposed to be here.

Technically, she wasn't.

She had routed her login through aggregate monitoring, not individual chart view. It wasn't the same as opening his file. It was structural. Structural meant defensible.

Her phone buzzed in her pocket.

She didn't check it.

On the adjacent monitor, intake velocity numbers climbed in quiet increments.

She shifted back to Adrian's schedule panel.

There it was.
Recommended dosing interval: Maintain weekly continuation pending symptom score ≥ 4.
Symptom score ≥ 4.
He'd reported three.

She stared at the number.
Three meant relief.
Four meant continuation justified without question.
Three meant discretion.
Her fingers hovered over the field.
This was small.
Not altering compound.
Not altering chart notes.
Just adjusting the follow-up structure.

She opened the scheduling backend.
AUTHORIZATION REQUIRED
Enter supervisor override code.
She paused.
Her heart rate was steady. She checked her own wrist unconsciously.
Override codes were issued to senior research leads for system balancing—moving patients between blocks when capacity shifted.
It was meant for flow correction.
She entered her code.
The field opened.
Recommended dosing interval → Biweekly review.
She did not change his symptom score.
She did not delete Moreno's notes.
She adjusted the interval only.
The system flagged the modification.

CONFIRM CHANGE?
This adjustment affects automated continuation modeling.
Yes / No

She stared at the warning.

Automated continuation modeling.
Her jaw tightened slightly.
She pressed YES.
The field shifted.
Next assessment: Day 14.
The amber banner at the top flickered, then stabilized.
CHANGE LOG CREATED
User: Serrano, Nadia
Modification: Schedule interval update
Reason field required.
A small text box appeared.
She typed:
Patient-reported stabilization below continuation threshold. Review cadence adjusted to match subjective distress.

It was accurate.
Technically.
She hit save.
The system processed for two seconds.
Then returned to neutral.

On the other side of the glass, one of the junior analysts laughed at something small and harmless.
Nadia stepped back from the terminal.
Her reflection in the glass looked exactly the same.
Her phone buzzed again.
This time she checked it.

Adrian:
"Still feel steady."
She stared at the message.

Steady.

She typed back:
"Hydrate. Let me know if anything shifts."
Three dots appeared immediately.

"Nothing shifting…"
She slipped the phone back into her pocket.

Behind her, a new notification populated on the main intake board.
CONTINUATION RATE — WEEK 1 COHORT
Projected Retention: 87%
Eighty-seven percent.
She looked at the number.
If his review was pushed to Day 14, he would fall outside the Week 1 continuation spike.
It might not matter.
It might.

Dr. Patel's voice drifted in from the hallway.
"…retention velocity is stronger than predicted. We'll have to adjust cohort modeling again."

Adjust.
Everything was adjusting.

Nadia walked out of the server room and into the corridor.
Her shoes made no sound on the polished floor.

At the end of the hall, Mercer stood speaking with a policy liaison. He didn't see her at first.
"Retention is stabilizing," Mercer was saying. "Which means relief is sustaining."
Relief is sustaining.
Nadia slowed.
The liaison nodded. "And continuation?"
"High," Mercer said. "Very high."
His eyes flicked up and caught Nadia's for half a second.
She didn't look away.
He finished his sentence without breaking rhythm.
"…which confirms demand elasticity."
The liaison moved on.
Mercer approached her almost immediately.

"*You're* quiet lately," he said.
"Busy," she replied.
"Monitoring board meets Friday," he said. "We'll present continuation metrics."
She nodded.
"Any anomalies?" he asked casually.
She held his gaze.
"No destabilizations," she said.
It wasn't what he'd asked.
He studied her a moment longer than necessary.
"Good," he said finally.
He walked past her.
Nadia continued down the hall toward the elevators.
Her pulse was still steady.

Inside the elevator, alone, she let her shoulders drop a fraction of an inch.
It was a small adjustment.
Small enough to rationalize.
Small enough to undo if needed.
Small enough that no one would call it interference.
The elevator doors opened to the lobby.

Outside, snow had begun again—fine and dry, lifting in thin spirals across the pavement.
Nadia stepped into the cold.
Her phone buzzed once more.

Adrian:
"Thinking about going back to work next week."
She stared at the message.
Work next week.
She typed:
"We'll see how you feel."
She did not add anything else.

Across the street, a digital billboard rotated through public service announcements.

One frame lingered as she waited for the light.
ARC
Relief Is Possible.
The light changed.
She crossed.

Chapter 19
Drift

Toronto ARC Clinical Network — 2047
The email arrived at 06:12.
Nadia saw it before she was fully awake.

Subject: Compliance Review — Immediate Meeting Required

She read it twice.
No greeting. No explanation. Conference Room B. 08:00.
She set the phone down and stared at the ceiling.
Adrian slept beside her.
His breathing was even.
She did not wake him.

The hospital corridors were quieter than usual at that hour.
Fluorescent lights hummed faintly above polished floors. A custodian pushed a mop bucket past her without looking up.
Conference Room B was already occupied.
Mercer sat at the far end of the table.
Beside him: a woman Nadia recognized from legal oversight. Short hair. No visible jewelry. Tablet open.
And Dr. Moreno.
Nadia stopped just inside the doorway.
"Good morning," Mercer said.
No one else echoed it.
She took the chair opposite them.
Her badge tapped lightly against the table edge.
The oversight officer spoke first.
"Dr. Serrano, this is a procedural review," she said. "We need clarification regarding a recent scheduling adjustment."
Nadia's hands remained folded.
"What adjustment?" she asked.
Moreno slid a tablet across the table.
Adrian's record header was visible.
A single entry highlighted.

User: Serrano, Nadia
Action: Review cadence modification
Interval change: 7 days → 14 days
Nadia did not touch the tablet.
"I adjusted monitoring cadence," she said.
"Without being the assigned clinician," the oversight officer replied.
"I have senior system privileges."
"You have research privileges," the officer corrected.
Mercer watched silently.
Nadia shifted her gaze to Moreno.
"Was the patient destabilized?" Nadia asked.
Moreno answered evenly. "No."
"Was the adjustment clinically unsafe?" Nadia asked.
"That is not the question," the oversight officer said.
Nadia looked back at her.
"What is the question?" she asked.
The officer tapped her tablet once. "Why did you intervene in a restricted case?"
Nadia held her breath for half a second.
"I did not alter dosage," she said. "I adjusted review timing based on symptom report."
"Which was below continuation threshold," Moreno said.
"Yes," said Nadia.
"Continuation threshold does not prohibit weekly review," the officer replied.
"It implies flexibility," Nadia said.
Mercer leaned forward slightly.
"Not unilateral flexibility," he said.
And ther there was silence.
The air in the room felt colder than the hallway.

The oversight officer swiped to another screen.
"Your badge permissions were limited two weeks ago," she said. "You requested review of that limitation."
"Yes," Nadia said.
"That request is still pending."
"Yes."

"And during that pending period, you accessed backend scheduling," said the officer.

"I have system-level clearance," Nadia repeated.

"For research modeling," the officer said. "Not personal proximity."

The word proximity landed deliberately.

Moreno's voice remained flat. "The patient has since requested dosage evaluation," she said.

Nadia's eyes moved to her. "When?" she asked.

"Yesterday," Moreno said.

Nadia's stomach tightened.

Mercer watched her carefully.

"Your adjustment delayed the evaluation window," he said.

"By one week," Nadia replied.

"Which interfered with cohort modeling," Mercer said.

"There is no confirmed destabilization," she said.

"There is confirmed interference," the oversight officer replied.

The word interference hung in the air like something formal.

Nadia did not lower her gaze.

"What is the outcome of this review?" she asked.

The oversight officer folded her hands.

"Effective immediately," she said, "your backend scheduling privileges are revoked."

Nadia didn't react outwardly.

"You will retain research analytics access," the officer continued, "but no patient-level structural modification capability."

Mercer added, softly, "This is precautionary."

Nadia looked at him. "Is it?" she asked.

"Yes," he said.

Moreno closed her tablet.

"The patient's evaluation has been rescheduled," she said.

"For when?" Nadia asked.

"Day 7," Moreno replied.

Back to original.

Nadia nodded once.

The oversight officer slid a document across the table.
"Please sign acknowledgment of corrective action."

Nadia read the header.
Formal Warning — Boundary Violation

Her name was spelled correctly.
She did not ask for a pen. She used her own.
Signed.
The officer collected the document.
"This will not be escalated further at this time," she said.

At this time.

Mercer stood.
"Let's keep our focus on stability," he said.
Nadia remained seated.
"Is the system unstable?" she asked.
Mercer met her eyes. "No," he said.
"Then why does it need protection from one scheduling change?"
Moreno looked at Mercer.

Mercer did not answer immediately.
Instead, he said:
"Because the system depends on trust."
Silence.
Nadia stood.
Her badge felt heavier against her chest.
She walked to the door.
Before leaving, she turned back once.
"Did the patient report destabilization?" she asked Moreno.
"No," Moreno said.
"Then the change did no harm."
The oversight officer responded evenly. "It did harm."
Nadia paused. "How?" she asked.
"It introduced variance," the officer said.
The word landed like accusation.

Nadia held her gaze, and then she left the room.

Her badge failed at Terminal 3B.
ACCESS DENIED.
She stared at the message.
She tried again.
ACCESS DENIED.
A junior analyst nearby glanced at her, then quickly looked back at his screen.
Nadia stepped away from the terminal.
Her phone buzzed.
Adrian.

She stepped into an empty hallway before answering.
"Hey," he said.
His voice sounded clear.
"They moved my evaluation up," he added.
"When?" she asked.
"Tomorrow."
Her pulse ticked once.
"Did you request that?" she asked.
"I think so," he said. "I filled something out."
She closed her eyes briefly.
"How are you feeling?" she asked.
"Steady," he said.
The word felt thinner than before.
"Okay," she replied.
There was a pause.
"You sound far away," he said.
"I'm at work," she answered.
"Right," he said.
Another silence.
"I want to see if it can go further," he said.
Nadia leaned against the wall.
"I know," she said.
The line was quiet for a moment longer.
"Love you," Adrian said.

She didn't hesitate.
"Love you," she replied.
The call ended.

Across the corridor, a large display screen showed updated intake metrics.
CONTINUATION RATE — WEEK 1 COHORT
89%
Higher than before.

Nadia stood there, watching the number.
Her badge no longer opened backend systems.
Her modification had been reversed.
Her warning was logged.
The model had absorbed the disruption.
And adjusted.

She reached into her bag and pulled out her personal laptop.
Not the hospital-issued one.
She opened it.
A blank document.
She typed:
Personal Log — Variance Event
And began writing.

Chapter 20
Aggregate

Toronto — 2047
The clinic confirmation arrived at 07:02.
Nadia saw it before Adrian did.
APPOINTMENT REMINDER — CONTINUATION EVALUATION
Today — 09:10

Adrian was at the kitchen sink, sleeves pushed up, rinsing a plate he hadn't needed to wash twice.
"You have a reminder," she said.
"I know," he replied.
The water ran too long before he shut it off.
He dried his hands carefully. Folded the towel once. Hung it straight.
Nadia watched the small rituals.
He walked to the table and sat down.

He looked at her.
"You don't like it," he said. "You don't like how I am."
Nadia's mouth tightened.
"I didn't say that," she said.
He leaned back.
Nadia sat across from him.

"Do you feel flat?" she asked.
He shook his head once.
"No?" he said.
The radiator clicked.
He looked down at his hands.
Nadia waited.
Silence stretched.
He looked at more her, trying to understand what she needed from him.
She looked at him wondering what she needed as well.

He stood.

"I don't want to be measured today," he said.
"I'm not measuring you," she said.
He studied her face.
"You want me to stop," he said.
Nadia inhaled slowly.
"I want you to decide without pressure," she said.
He let out a small, humorless breath.
"Nadia, I had already done that."
He picked up his phone from the table.
The screen was already open to the appointment.

CONTINUE TREATMENT
RESCHEDULE
DISCONTINUE

His thumb hovered.
Nadia did not speak.
He looked at her one last time.
Then pressed **DISCONTINUE**.
The screen shifted.
ARE YOU SURE?
Discontinuation may result in return of symptoms.
He swallowed.
"Yes," he said quietly, and pressed confirm.
The phone vibrated once.

STATUS UPDATED — TREATMENT PAUSED
Paused.

He set the phone face down.
Neither of them moved for several seconds.
"Alright, it's done," he said. "Are you happy?"
Nadia nodded. "Yes, Adrian. I am. Ok? I'm happy."
He stood there as if waiting for something to happen immediately.
It didn't.
The apartment was quiet.
Outside, traffic moved.

He rubbed his hands together once, then stopped himself.
"I'm going to regret this," he said.
"You might," she said. "You might not."
He looked at her, searching.
"You're relieved," he said.
She held his gaze.
"Yes, I am. But, I'm more scared, Adrian" she said.
"Of what?" He frowned slightly.
He walked to the window and pulled the curtain back an inch.

Light cut across his face.
"I just don't want to struggle every day," he said.
Nadia felt the sentence in her chest.
"You won't," she said.
He turned toward her and they embraced.
"What if the pain is part of her?" she asked.
Adrian didn't have an answer that.

He let the curtain fall.
"I'll call work," he said.
He stepped into the bedroom and closed the door.
Nadia remained at the table.

Her phone buzzed.
CLINIC NOTICE — PATIENT HALE, ADRIAN
Continuation status: Withdrawn
Monitoring window adjusted.

Adjusted.

She stared at the word.
From the bedroom, she heard him speaking on the phone—steady, polite, saying he wouldn't be in today.

She opened her laptop.
Personal Log — Variance Event.
She added a new line:

Adrian discontinued voluntarily.
In the bedroom, his voice rose slightly—laughing at something the person on the other end had said.
It sounded real.
Not forced.
But thinner than it used to be.
Nadia closed the laptop before she could finish the entry.
The bedroom door opened.
He stepped back into the kitchen.
"Coffee?" he asked.
She looked at him.
"Yes," she said.

He filled the kettle and set it on the stove.
The click of ignition sounded sharper than usual.
They stood side by side, not touching.
The kettle began to hum.
Neither of them spoke.

Outside, snow started again—light, almost invisible against the gray.
Inside, the protocol had one fewer participant.
Adrian's name remained in the system.

Chapter 21
Recommitment

Toronto — 2050
Spring came late that year.
The snow did not melt all at once. It collapsed inward. Sidewalk edges shrank in uneven ridges, exposing old salt and grit beneath.
Nadia stood at the kitchen sink, hands submerged in warm water, watching the last shelf of ice slip from the building across the street.
Behind her, Adrian set two plates on the table.
Not carefully.
Not recklessly.
Just placed.
He had not returned to ARC.
He had not asked.

Nadia left six weeks later.
Her clearance had expired the week she resigned.
Her access was terminated within the hour.
Clinical privileges revoked.
System login archived.
She consulted privately now.

Three years had passed.
The system had scaled without them.
The word Eirenex now appeared on transit ads.
RELIEF, REFINED.

Nadia did not comment on the branding.
She dried her hands.
"You're quiet," Adrian said.
"I'm thinking," she replied.
"About work?"
"No."
He waited.
She turned to face him.
"I had coffee with Tina today," she said.

Adrian's jaw tightened slightly.
Tina had dosed. Continued. Continued again.
"And?" he asked.
"She's pregnant."
Adrian nodded once.
"Okay," he said.
Nadia studied him.
"You don't have anything else to say?" she asked.
"What would you like me to say?"
She held his gaze.
"That you want that," she said.
He didn't look away.
"Well, I do," he said.
No hesitation.
Clear.
She felt something move in her chest.
"I know we haven't talked about it," she said.
"I mean, yea. We've straight up prevented it," he replied.
"Yes."
Silence.

Traffic moved below the window. A bus hissed at the curb.
"That was then, though. This is now," Nadia said.
"I know." He sat down. "So what are we doing?" he asked.
The question was not abstract.
She felt it.
"We decide," she said.
"Decide what?"
He leaned back in the chair and looked at his hands.
She crossed the room and sat across from him.
She leaned forward.
"Do you want to have a child with me, Adrian?" she asked.
"Yes," he said.
"You're sure?"
"Yes."
"Not because I brought up Tina?"
"No."

"Do you promise?" she asked.
"Yes," he said laughing.
"Because you want one?"
"Yes."
Each answer landed without wobble.
She watched his face for any sign of uncertainty.
There was none.

"I'm thirty-eight," she said.
"I know, sweetheart," he said.
"I left the program," she said.
"I know."
"And you still want to do this?"
"Yes," he said.
He stood abruptly.
Not in anger.
In decision.
He moved to the window and looked down at the street.
A stroller passed below.
He watched it.
Nadia stood slowly and joined him.
He turned toward her.
She held his gaze.

"You dosed," she said.
"Briefly," he said.
"Yes."
"And?"
"And we don't know anything beyond what they published," she said.
"They published safety clearance," he replied.
She did not respond.

He stepped closer.
"Are you worried about it?" he said.
"I don't know," she replied.
"Well, that helps no one."
"I know."

He studied her face. "You're still running models in your head," he said.

"Yes," she said.

He exhaled once.

"Then let's stop modeling," he said.

He stepped closer again.

"I'm not a dataset," he said.

She swallowed.

"I know."

He reached for her hands.

She let him.

"I want to try," he said.

"Even if we don't know everything?" she asked.

"Yes."

"Even if it scares you?"

"Yes," he said.

"Even if it scares me?" she asked.

"Yes."

Silence held them there.

Outside, wind lifted the last strips of snow from the curb.

She looked at him.

Not as a clinician.

Not as an analyst.

As the man who could take hold of her in the kitchen at any time and cut her sentences off with a kiss.

"Okay," she said.

The word felt different this time.

He blinked once.

"Okay?" he repeated.

"Yes."

His shoulders lowered slightly.

The echo was not lost on either of them.

He pulled her into him.

Not controlled.

Not decisive.

Just close.

She rested her forehead against his chest.
His heart was not racing.
Steady.
He wrapped his arms around her fully this time. His hands slid firmly along her back and settled at her waist. He pulled her in until there wasn't space between them.
She felt the exhale leave him against her hair.
He shifted his weight and rested his chin lightly on the top of her head, then adjusted when it was uncomfortable—small, ordinary correction.
His fingers flexed once at her side.
Then again.
Not to hold her still.
Just because he was there.
She listened.
His breathing changed as he stood there, not slower, not calculated—just syncing unconsciously with hers.
After a moment, he kissed the top of her head. Not performative. Not urgent. A quiet, absentminded press of lips like he had done for years.
She felt it.
Felt the weight of him.
Felt the heat through his shirt.
Felt the faint scratch of his stubble when he tipped his head down and brushed her temple.
"You're shaking," he said softly.
"I'm not," she said.
"You are."
There was warmth in it. Teasing. Familiar.
She let out a breath that sounded closer to a laugh.
He shifted again, sliding one hand up her spine until his thumb pressed lightly between her shoulder blades—the spot he always found when she was thinking too hard.
"That thing you do," he said quietly.
"What thing?"
"Tensing."
She pulled back enough to look at him.

He was watching her with clarity. Recognition.
"You always do that when you're stressed," he added.
She swallowed.
"And what do you do?" she asked.
He tilted his head slightly.
"I do this," he said.
No philosophy.
No thesis.
He just leaned in.
He brushed a loose strand of hair away from her face with the back of his fingers. The gesture was careless, intimate, unmeasured.
Then he leaned down and kissed her—slow, deliberate, not to interrupt her sentence this time. Just to seal something. They stayed perfectly connected and aligned like that for a time; with him pulling at her just above what she found detectable.
When he pulled back, his eyes held hers for a beat too long to be accidental.
He smiled.
It was uneven.
Alive.
"Hey," he said.
She blinked.
"Hey."
They stood like that for several seconds.

He didn't break eye contact.
He leaned down and kissed her again.
Soft at first.
Slow.
Intentional.
The kind of kiss that lingers long enough to communicate what cannot be said.
His hand slid from her waist to the small of her back and drew her closer.
She felt the shift in him — not urgency yet, but certainty.
She answered the kiss.
Not tentative.
Not analyzing.

Just meeting him.

His other hand came up to cradle her jaw, thumb pulling down on her chin. The kiss deepened and kept building. He wasn't rushed.

Then something in him tipped on the counter.

He walked her backward.

One step.

Then two.

Until her shoulders met the nearest flat surface — the hallway wall — and he followed her in, closing the space completely.

The kiss changed.

Less careful. Then messy.

More intent.

His hands moved with vigor — waist, ribs, chest, and back again — as if acquainting himself with her for the first time. She felt the shift in pressure, the edges of his hunger pressing into every part of her that contoured.

She made a sound against his mouth one parts surprise, and two parts invitation.

"Adrian—"

He kissed her again before she could shape the rest of it. Slower this time, then deeper, then breaking just long enough to look at her before going back in.

The sentiment dissolved into heat.

Then into something thicker and messier again.

Less symmetrical.

He kissed the corner of her mouth. Missed. Laughed softly against her lips. Tried again. She tilted her head and their teeth clicked lightly.

That made it worse.

He grinned into the kiss.

It turned playful without losing the charge.

He kissed her cheek, her jaw, then returned to her mouth but off-center; exaggerated, cinematic and ridiculous.

She pushed at his shoulder.

"Hey—" she tried again.

He kissed her quickly. Then again. Rapid. Almost ticklish.

"Adrian."

He kissed her nose. And then opened his mouth wide and latched on; a perfectly formed seal around the center region of her face.
She laughed, inadvertently blowing her nose hard into his mouth.
"Eww," he said.
"*You* Eww…Doofus," she said.

He recoiled like he'd just bitten into something sharply sour.
"Oh, whatever. You love it," she said.
He clutched his throat dramatically and crossed his eyes.
She tried to hold her composure. Failed.
They both broke.

The kind of laugh that comes when tension has nowhere left to hide.
She shoved him lightly.
"Hey," she said, breath uneven but smiling, "I didn't say we need to start right now, mister."
He froze for half a second, then blinked.
"Start what?" he asked, feigning innocence badly.
She lifted an eyebrow. "You know exactly what."
He leaned in like he was going to kiss her again. "You started it," he said.
"I literally didn't do anything."
He kissed her once — sharp, quick, cutting off whatever was coming next.
She stared at him.

"This is assault," she said dryly.
He grinned. "You love it."
She tried not to smile.
Failed.
He kissed her again — slower this time, but not escalating. Just sealing the silliness back into warmth.
When he pulled back, his forehead rested against hers.
"Not right now," he said softly.
She studied his face. "Oh, no?"
"No," he said. "Right is better."
The playfulness didn't leave his eyes.
But neither did the intention.

He brushed his thumb along her lower lip, then stepped back just enough to give her space.
But he was still there.
Entirely there.

Then she stepped back.
"We'll schedule an appointment," she said.
"With?"
"OB."
He nodded.
"And if something looks off?" she asked.
"Then we'll deal with it," he said.
No dramatics.
No speech.
Just that.
She reached for her phone, opened the clinic directory, found a name, and booked the consult.

Confirmation appeared on screen.
June 14 — 09:00.

She turned the phone toward him.
He looked at the date.
Then at her.
He smiled.
Not wide.
But real.
The appointment was set.

Chapter 22
Baseline

Toronto — 2050
The OB clinic was on the other side of the city, tucked into a bright medical building that smelled like citrus cleaner and overheated carpet.
Nadia arrived ten minutes early.
Adrian arrived five minutes after her, wind-touched, hair damp at the temples, carrying two coffees like an apology.
"I got you the one you like," he said.
She took it.
"Thank you," she replied.
He stood close enough that their shoulders brushed as they checked in at the front desk.
The receptionist slid a clipboard toward Nadia without looking up.
"Forms," she said. "Fill these out and bring them back."
Nadia set the clipboard on her lap and began.
Insurance. Family history. Allergies.
Adrian sat beside her, knee bouncing once, then settling when he noticed it.
"You okay?" she asked quietly.
"Yeah," he said. "It's just… this feels very… real. Very adult."
"It is," she said.
He nodded and watched the waiting room like he was trying to memorize it: the aquarium in the corner, the children's books with bent spines, the soft loop of daytime news on mute.
Nadia turned the page.
Routine medications.
Prior procedures.
Then a new section header, printed in the same bland font as everything else:
NEUROREGULATORY EXPOSURE
Her pen paused.

A list of checkboxes followed.
ARC / Eirenex exposure (past or current)
— Patient

— Partner
If yes: date of initiation
If discontinued: date of discontinuation
Dosing interval (if applicable)
Clinic site

Nadia stared at the words long enough that her hand stopped moving entirely.
Adrian leaned closer.
"What?" he asked.
She angled the clipboard so he could see.
His eyes tracked the section.
He blinked once. "That's… them," he said.
"Yes," Nadia replied.
His voice dropped. "Why is that on an OB form?"
Nadia didn't answer immediately.
She looked up at the reception desk.

The receptionist was scrolling on her monitor, expression neutral, a practiced stillness.
Nadia returned her gaze to the form.

ARC / Eirenex exposure.
Past or current.
Partner.
She felt a small coldness behind her ribs that had nothing to do with the air conditioning.
Adrian sat back.
"Should we say yes?" he asked.
Nadia looked at him.
"We should tell the truth," she said.
He nodded once, then hesitated.
"I only dosed briefly," he said.
"I know."
"And that was years ago."
"I know," she said.
She checked the box.

Partner — Yes

Her pen hovered over the date fields.
She wrote it in clean numerals, the way she wrote everything when she didn't want her hand to show.
Adrian watched her write.
"Do you think it matters?" he asked.
"I don't know," she said.
He absorbed that without argument.
She finished the rest of the form.
When she stood to return the clipboard, her coffee sat untouched on the armrest.

At the desk, she slid the papers forward.
"Excuse me," she said, polite, quiet.
The receptionist looked up.
"Yes?"
Nadia tapped the neuroregulatory section lightly with one finger.
"This question," she said. "Is it new?"
The receptionist glanced at it like it was a grocery list.
"Pretty standard," she said.
"Since when?" Nadia asked.
The receptionist shrugged. "Couple years? Maybe longer."
Nadia kept her face neutral.
"And what do you do with it?" she asked.
The receptionist's eyes flicked to the line again.
"It goes in your intake," she said. "Doctor sees it."
"Does it trigger anything?" Nadia asked.
"Like what?"
"Additional screening," Nadia said.
The receptionist gave a small, bored shake of her head.
"Just history," she said. "Lots of people have it now."

Lots of people.

Nadia nodded once.
"Thank you," she said.

She returned to the chair.
Adrian was watching her closely.
"What did she say?" he asked.
"It's standard," Nadia replied.
He frowned faintly. "Standard for who?"
Nadia didn't answer.

A door opened down the hall and a nurse called a name.
A couple stood up together, hands brushing, then separating as they followed.
Adrian's hand found Nadia's.
He laced their fingers without asking.
The contact was warm.
Present.
She held on.
"You're doing it again," he said softly.
"What?"
"That thing," he said. "Going somewhere else."
She looked at him.
His eyes were steady.

"Sorry," she said.
He squeezed her hand once.
"Stay," he said.
She nodded.
"I'm here," she said.

He watched her for a beat, then leaned over and kissed her temple—small, unperformative, familiar.
The nurse called another name.
Time moved in quiet increments: a page turning, a child's cough, the aquarium filter humming.
Nadia's gaze drifted back to the desk.
A stack of the same clipboards sat in a tray.
The same forms.
The same checkbox.
ARC / Eirenex exposure.

She looked away before Adrian could catch her staring.
When their name was finally called, they stood together.
The nurse led them down the corridor.
At the threshold to the exam hall, the nurse smiled.
"First appointment?" she asked.
"Yes," Nadia said.
"Congratulations," the nurse replied.
Nadia's mouth formed the right expression automatically.
"Thank you," she said.

They were shown into a room with a papered exam table and a poster of fetal development stages—weeks labeled in calm pastel colors.
Adrian sat in the chair by the wall, knees spread slightly, hands folded, trying to look relaxed and failing.
Nadia perched on the edge of the exam table.
The nurse took vitals and asked routine questions.
Then she glanced at the intake form.
Her finger paused at the neuroregulatory section.

"Oh," she said lightly. "ARC exposure."
Adrian's jaw tightened.
"Yes," Nadia said.
The nurse nodded once, like she was checking off a grocery item.
"Okay," she said. "Doctor will review."
No follow-up.
No caution.
No explanation.
Just a click of the pen and the smooth continuation of the script.
When the nurse left, the room held its quiet.
Adrian exhaled.

"Weird," he said.
Nadia stared at the closed door.
"Yeah," she said.
He stood and came closer.
He rested a hand on her knee—grounding, familiar pressure.

"Hey," he said.
She looked up at him.

She covered his hand with hers.
"I'm okay," she said.
He nodded once, believing her because he wanted to.
A knock sounded.
The doctor entered.
Introductions, smiles, routine warmth.
Nadia answered questions, gave dates, kept her tone steady.
But the checkbox stayed in her peripheral vision like a small stain.
When the appointment ended, they walked back into the June air.
On the sidewalk, Adrian tilted his head toward her.
"So we're doing this," he said.
"Yes," she replied.
He smiled—not wide, but real.
"Okay," he said.
They walked home together.

Later that night, after Adrian fell asleep, Nadia opened her private log. She wrote a single line:
OB intake now includes ARC/Eirenex exposure for patient and partner. Marked "standard."
She saved it.

Chapter 23
Birth

Toronto — 2051

The hospital room was too bright.

Nadia had asked for the lights lowered twice. They'd dimmed them once. The overhead panel still hummed faintly, a steady electrical note that threaded through the air between contractions.

Adrian stood at her left side, one hand braced against the bedrail, the other wrapped around her forearm. He wasn't speaking. He'd tried that earlier. Now he just stayed.

"Breathe with me," the nurse said. Her badge read **MARTA IONESCU**. Her voice was even, measured. "In through the nose. Slow."

Nadia inhaled. The breath caught halfway down and broke apart.

"Again," Marta said.

Adrian leaned closer. "I'm here," he said.

"I know," Nadia replied through her teeth.

Another contraction took her. Not abstract. Not cinematic. A clean, physical force that folded her forward and dragged sound out of her throat without asking permission.

Marta checked the monitor.

"Progressing," she said. "You're doing what you're supposed to do."

Nadia almost laughed at that. Doing what you're supposed to do.

Across the room, a second nurse adjusted the fetal monitor. The rapid, steady rhythm filled the space—small, fast, undeniable.

Adrian's grip tightened when it dipped for half a beat.

"It's fine," Marta said without looking up. "She's tolerating it."

She.

They'd stopped saying "the baby" weeks ago.

Another contraction. Nadia's fingers dug into Adrian's wrist.

He didn't flinch.

"Look at me," he said quietly.

She did.

His face was pale, focused, eyes fixed on hers like he was trying to anchor her to something solid.

"You're almost there," he said.

"Don't estimate," she snapped.

He swallowed and nodded. "Okay."

Marta moved between Nadia's knees and checked again.

"Full," she said. "We're ready."

The word landed.

Ready.

The room shifted. More hands. A tray rolled closer. The hum of movement tightened.

"On the next one, you push," Marta said.

Nadia nodded once.

The contraction built without asking her first.

"Now," Marta said.

Nadia pushed.

There was no elegance in it. No metaphor. Just effort and sound and the blunt fact of her body working.

Adrian leaned over her shoulder. "You're doing it," he said. "You're doing it."

She pushed again.

Something changed.

A pressure that had been abstract became directional. Marta's voice sharpened slightly.

"I see her," she said.

Adrian froze.

"What?" he asked.

"I see her head," Marta replied.

Nadia pushed again.

And then—

A break in the pressure. A shift. A release that wasn't relief yet but promised it.

A thin, startled sound filled the room.

Not loud.

Just present.

The nurses moved quickly. Efficient. The baby lifted, turned, suctioned in practiced motions.

Adrian's face changed before Nadia saw her.

It wasn't joy exactly. It was shock. Recognition.

"She's here," he said.

They placed her on Nadia's chest.

Warm.

Heavy.

Small.

Her skin was mottled, eyes squeezed shut, mouth open in an indignant protest at the temperature of the world.

Nadia's hands came up automatically.

She didn't think.

She just held.

The crying softened to a wet, uneven breath.

Adrian leaned over them both.

He didn't touch the baby at first.

He touched Nadia's face.

"You did it," he said, voice breaking cleanly in the middle.

Nadia looked down.

Lila.

The name moved through her without resistance.

Lila's fingers flexed once against Nadia's skin. Tiny nails. Perfect.

Adrian finally reached out and touched her foot.

"She's real," he said.

"Yes," Nadia replied.

The word was barely audible.

Marta moved closer. "We'll take her for weight and measurements in a moment."

"Not yet," Nadia said.

Marta paused. Then nodded. "One minute."

Adrian bent and pressed his forehead to Nadia's.

He was crying openly now. No attempt to control it.

"I can't believe she's here," he said.

Nadia felt the heat of her daughter against her chest.
Felt the weight.
Felt the fragile, undeniable proof of future.
Lila opened one eye.
Dark.
Unfocused.
Alive.
Nadia let out a breath she hadn't known she'd been holding for months.
"She's perfect," Adrian said.
Nadia didn't answer immediately.
She was watching Lila's mouth move, the small searching motion.
"She's here," Nadia said instead.

Marta stepped forward gently. "Okay. We need to check her."
Adrian hesitated before lifting Lila from Nadia's chest.
He held her awkwardly at first, then adjusted instinctively, hand behind her head, thumb steady against her back.
The nurse took her and moved to the warmer.

Weight called out.
Apgar score.
Numbers entered into a chart.
All within range.
All clean.
Adrian stood beside the warmer, eyes tracking every movement.
"Everything looks good," Marta said.
Nadia watched him from the bed.

The nurse wrapped Lila and handed her back.
This time, Adrian took her first.
He cradled her against his chest.
She fit there.
He looked down at her with the kind of attention that did not calculate.
"Hi," he said softly.
Lila blinked once, then closed her eyes again.
Nadia felt tears move across her temples into her hair.
Adrian turned and brought Lila back to her.

Together, they leaned over the small, wrapped body between them.
The room had quieted.
Machines still hummed. Paper still moved. But the center had shifted.
Marta made one final note in the chart.
"Congratulations," she said.
The word sounded almost formal.
Adrian didn't look up.
He was counting fingers.
All ten.
Nadia rested her hand over Lila's back.
The baby's breathing was irregular at first. Then steadier.
Then steady.

Outside the window, late afternoon light cut across the neighboring buildings. Traffic moved. A siren sounded somewhere distant and faded. Inside, Lila made a small, soft sound and settled deeper into Nadia's chest.
Adrian leaned down and kissed Nadia's forehead.
"We did this," he said.
"Yes," she replied.
He kissed Lila's head next.
Not urgent.
Not messy.
Just certain.
Nadia closed her eyes.
The future was not abstract anymore.
It had weight.
And a heartbeat.

Chapter 24
Optimization

Toronto — 2052
The sirens were fewer.
Nadia noticed it first on a Tuesday.
She was halfway down Spadina with Lila strapped against her chest, the stroller folded under one hand, when she realized she could hear individual conversations across the street.
A man laughing.
A dog collar jingling.
The hum of the streetcar cables.
No sirens cutting through it.
She stopped walking.
A cyclist swerved slightly around her and muttered something under his breath. She adjusted the carrier and kept moving.
It could have been coincidence.

That afternoon, at the pediatric clinic, the waiting room television played muted footage of a city council press conference. A caption crawled along the bottom:
VIOLENT CRIME RATES DOWN 18% YEAR-OVER-YEAR
EMERGENCY PSYCHIATRIC ADMISSIONS DECLINE

The nurse called, "Hale?" and Nadia stood.
Inside the exam room, Lila kicked against the paper lining on the table, fascinated by the crinkling sound. Her fists opened and closed with clumsy determination.
"She's thriving," the pediatrician said. "Weight's excellent. Tone's good."
Nadia nodded.
Outside, someone laughed again in the hallway.
Not loud.
Just present.

When she left the clinic, her phone buzzed.
Adrian:
Did you see the news?

She typed back:
Which part?
Three dots appeared immediately.
Crime drop. They're saying mental health stabilization is working.

Working.

She slid the phone into her pocket without answering.

That night, Adrian sat on the couch with Lila asleep against his shoulder.
The television played a segment on ARC — no, not ARC.
The new branding.
Eirenex.
The logo was softer. The color palette warmer.
A headline floated behind the anchor:
RELIEF, REFINED — NATIONAL EXPANSION CONTINUES

Adrian shifted slightly to keep Lila from sliding.
"They rebranded," he said.
"I saw," Nadia replied from the kitchen.
"Sounds cleaner."
"It is cleaner."
He looked at her.
"You don't like it."
She didn't answer.

On the screen, a panel of commentators discussed public health savings.
Reduced hospitalization costs.
Fewer crisis interventions.
Lower incarceration rates.
A bar graph appeared behind them.
Steady decline.
One of the commentators said, "When large populations experience reduced distress load, you see downstream stabilization across systems."
Nadia turned off the stove.

Reduced distress load.

Adrian muted the television.

"She slept five hours straight this afternoon," he said, as if that was the part that mattered.

Nadia crossed the room and took Lila from him carefully.

The baby stirred once, then resettled.

"She's easy," Adrian said.

Nadia looked at him.

"Yes," she said.

He watched her face.

"You're doing it again," he said.

"Doing what?"

"Looking for something."

She adjusted Lila's blanket.

"Habit," she said.

Two weeks later, Nadia met Min-Jae Kwan for coffee.

He looked older.

Not physically.

Quieter.

"You left at the right time," he said without preamble.

She stirred her drink once. "Did I?"

He glanced around the café before answering.

"They're celebrating metrics," he said. "Across provinces."

"What metrics?"

"Hospitalizations. Domestic disturbances. Self-harm admissions."

"And?" she asked.

"And they're trending down."

He said it like a fact.

Not like a victory.

Nadia held his gaze.

"That's good," she said.

"Yes," he replied.

They sat there for several seconds.

A couple at the next table spoke in low, even voices. No sharp edges. No raised tone.
Kwan leaned back slightly.
"There's less volatility," he said.
"In patients?" she asked.
"In cities."
She didn't respond.
He watched her carefully.

He tapped his fingers once against his cup.
"Eirenex is entering corporate wellness contracts," he said. "Optional screening incentives. Stress mitigation packages."
She looked up.
"Corporate?"
"Yes."
"Screening is medical."
"They're calling it resilience optimization."
She let out a small breath through her nose.
"That's not Phase II," she said.
"No," he agreed.
He didn't add anything else.
Outside the café window, traffic moved smoothly through the intersection. No honking. No sudden braking.
Nadia's phone vibrated in her bag.
She ignored it.
Kwan watched her.
"They're not slowing down," he said.

That evening, she walked home instead of taking the streetcar.
The air was warmer than it should have been for early April. Snow had vanished from the curbs. Sidewalks were clear.
Two teenagers passed her, arguing softly about something on a phone. Their tone never rose.
She crossed Queen Street.
A police cruiser idled at the corner.
No lights on.
No urgency.

Just parked.
She adjusted Lila's blanket again.

A billboard loomed above the intersection.
EIRENEX
Feel Steady.
Below it, a smaller line:
Now Available Nationwide.
She stopped under it.
The image showed a woman standing in a bright kitchen, sunlight behind her, a child at her hip.
The woman's face was calm.
Not ecstatic.
Not grieving.
Just steady.
Nadia stared at the child in the image.
The baby's mouth was open in something like laughter.
Lila stirred in the carrier, then went still again.
A bus pulled up beside her, brakes sighing.
The doors opened.

At home, Adrian had the news on again.
"They're talking about it everywhere," he said. "It's not just Toronto."
"What are they saying?" she asked.
"That emergency response budgets are shrinking."
He sounded impressed.
"They're reallocating funds."
"To what?" she asked.
"Education. Infrastructure."
He looked at her like this was obviously good.
She set Lila in her bassinet.

On the screen, a public health official said, "We are witnessing sustained stabilization across multiple regions."

Stabilization.

The anchor nodded solemnly.
A ticker crawled along the bottom:
NATIONAL CRISIS LINE CALL VOLUME DECLINES 22%
Adrian muted it again.

"You think this is because of the program?" he asked.
"I think the program is being widely used," she replied.
"That's not an answer."
She sat down.
He studied her. "Do you miss it?" he asked.
"The work?" she asked.
"Yes," he said.
She considered.
"No," she said.
He looked surprised.
"I miss knowing what's happening," she added.
He leaned back. "You always know what's happening."
"Not anymore."
Silence settled between them.
Not tense.
Just present.
Lila made a soft noise in her sleep.
Adrian stood and adjusted the bassinet slightly so it was closer to the couch.
He did it without comment.
Without drama.
Just moved it.

Nadia watched him.
"You're happy?" she asked.
He looked at her.
"Yes," he said.
No hesitation.
No flicker.
She nodded.

Outside, somewhere in the distance, a siren began.

It lasted less than three seconds before fading.
Nadia held still, listening for it to return.
It didn't.

On the television, the headline changed:
EIRENEX APPROVED FOR ADDITIONAL EXPANSION ZONES
Adrian reached for the remote.
She didn't stop him.
The screen went dark.

In the quiet, the apartment felt contained.
Predictable.
Lila's breathing was steady.
Adrian's breathing matched it without thinking.
Nadia stood and walked to the window.
The street below moved in smooth lines.
No shouting.
No flashing lights.
Just cars.
People.
A city operating within limits.

Her phone buzzed again in her pocket.
This time she looked.
Unknown number.
She answered.
"Yes?"
A pause.
Then a woman's voice.
"Dr. Serrano? My name is Callie Lucas. I'm working on a piece about Eirenex. I was told you might be willing to talk."
Nadia didn't answer immediately.
Across the room, Adrian looked up.
The woman continued, calm, professional.
"I'm specifically looking at second-order effects," she said. "Things that don't show up in press releases."
Nadia's grip tightened slightly on the phone.

"Who told you to call me?" she asked.
"I'm not at liberty to say."
Silence.
The city outside remained steady.
Callie Lucas spoke again.
"I think something is missing from the public conversation," she said.
Nadia looked at Lila.
At Adrian.
At the quiet room.
"What do you think is missing?" Nadia asked.
There was a small inhale on the other end of the line.
"I can't say yet," Callie said. "That's why I'm calling."
Nadia didn't hang up.
But she didn't agree either.
Across the apartment, Adrian stood slowly.
"Who is it?" he asked quietly.
Nadia kept her eyes on the window.
"A journalist," she said.
The word settled into the room like a foreign object.
Callie waited.
Nadia finally said, "I'm not part of the program anymore."
"I know," Callie replied.
Another pause.
Then:
"That's exactly why I'd like to speak with you."
Nadia closed her eyes briefly.
When she opened them, the city outside looked the same.
Controlled.
Contained.
She pressed the phone closer to her ear.
"When?" she asked.
Callie didn't hesitate.
"Tomorrow."
The line went silent.
Nadia ended the call.

Behind her, Adrian was still watching.

"About what?" he asked.
She turned toward him.
"I don't know," she said.
But she did not look uncertain.
Outside, no sirens cut the air.
The city held.

Chapter 25
Visitor

Toronto ARC Clinical Network — 2050
The lobby had changed.
Not visibly.
The intake board still pulsed in clean white numbers.
The security desk still required badge scans.
The elevators still opened with the same hydraulic sigh.
But Nadia no longer belonged to the flow.
She stood in line with the visitors.
Her badge did not open the staff lane.
When her turn came, the security guard asked for identification.
She handed over her driver's license.
"Purpose of visit?" he asked.
"Records request," she said.
He typed her name.
Paused.
Looked at his screen again.
"You were staff?" he asked.
"Yes."
He nodded once and printed a temporary pass.
VISITOR.

She clipped it to her coat.
The elevator ride felt shorter than she remembered.
On the administrative floor, the carpet muted her steps.
Her office had been at the end of the hall.
The placard outside the door no longer held her name.
Dr. Priya Raman.
She stopped.
Inside, through the narrow glass pane, she could see the same desk.
The same chair.
The thin plant that never died.
The door opened.
A woman in her early forties stepped out, tablet in hand.
She recognized Nadia immediately.

"Oh," she said. "Dr. Serrano."
Nadia nodded.
"You're looking for someone?" Dr. Raman asked.
"No," Nadia said. "I was just passing through."
Dr. Raman adjusted the tablet against her hip.
"They reassigned most offices last year," she said.
"I see that," Nadia replied.
A pause.
"We're at regional scale now," Dr. Raman added, as if offering explanation.
"I know," Nadia said.
Dr. Raman's eyes flicked briefly to Nadia's visitor badge.
"If you need archives," she said, "records are centralized now. Third floor."
"Thank you."
Dr. Raman stepped back into the office and closed the door.
Through the glass, Nadia watched her sit at the desk.
Open a dashboard.
The plant sat beside the monitor, leaves angled toward light.
Alive.
Nadia turned away.

The third floor smelled like toner and dust.
A receptionist behind reinforced glass slid a form toward her.
"Request scope?" the receptionist asked.
"Phase II variance documentation," Nadia said.
The receptionist typed.
"That requires authorization," she said.
"I submitted a review request three years ago," Nadia said.
The receptionist did not look up.
"All Phase II variance materials are restricted under Senate protection."
"I worked on Phase II," Nadia said.
The receptionist finally looked at her.
"File access of that nature expires upon resignation."
Nadia held the glass with her fingertips.
"I need cohort divergence reports from the first year of scale," she said.
The receptionist turned her monitor slightly.

The screen displayed a stamped header.
PROTECTED INTERVENTION
AUTHORIZED DISTRIBUTION ONLY

"I can submit a formal petition," the receptionist said.
"Processing time?" asked Nadia.
"Six to eight weeks."
Nadia stared at the words.
Six to eight weeks.
Outside the building, intake numbers continued.
"How many active patients?" Nadia asked.
The receptionist blinked.
"That information is public."
"Current count," Nadia clarified.
The receptionist typed once more.
"Toronto network: 312,447 active."
The number landed without ceremony.
Three hundred twelve thousand.
Nadia felt the scale of it move through her body.
"And continuation rate?" she asked.
"Eighty-one percent," the receptionist said.
Nadia nodded once.
"Thank you."
She stepped away from the desk.

In the main atrium, a promotional banner hung above the escalators.
EIRENEX
RELIEF, REFINED.
A video screen played silent testimonials.
A woman smiling at her kitchen table.
A man tying his daughter's shoes.
A headline:
Sleep Restored Across Ontario.
Nadia watched the loop repeat.

On the lower level, a screening group was being guided toward intake.

Seven people.
Coats folded.
Forms in hand.
One of them laughed at something the nurse said.
The laugh was small.
Contained.
Nadia stepped closer to the railing.
Below, a clinician explained dosing intervals.
The word continuation floated upward.
A man nodded eagerly.
She felt it then — not panic.
Momentum.
The system did not need her to validate it.
It did not need her to question it.
It had moved from intervention to infrastructure.

Her phone vibrated.
Adrian.
She answered.
"Hey," he said.
"Hey."
"You at the clinic?" he asked.
"Yes."
A pause.
"For what?"
She looked at the banner again.
"Nothing," she said.
Silence on the line.
"I had my consult today," he said.
Her grip tightened slightly.
"And?" she asked.
"They extended my interval," he said. "Quarterly now."

Quarterly.

She closed her eyes briefly.
"That's good?" she asked.

"Yeah," he said.
His voice was even.
Calm.
Untroubled.
"They said long-term stability's strong."
Nadia watched the intake group disappear through the doors.
"That's what they're saying," she replied.
He didn't notice the difference in wording.
"You okay?" he asked.
"Yes."
A beat.
"I'll be home soon," she said.
"Okay."
The call ended.

Nadia walked toward the exit.
As she passed the security desk, the guard held out his hand.
"Visitor badge," he said.
She unclipped it and gave it back.
He dropped it into a tray without looking at her.
The doors opened.
Cold air hit her face.

Across the street, a bus rolled past with a full-length advertisement.
EIRENEX
NOW PROVINCE-WIDE.
The doors closed behind her.
Inside, the intake board refreshed.
Outside, snow began again.
Thin.
Sideways.
Relentless.

Chapter 26
Signal

Toronto — 2052
Rain made the streetcars sound tired.
Nadia stood under the shallow awning outside a corner café near College, watching water thread down the glass and collect at the curb in rippling bands. A delivery bike cut through it and left a brief hiss behind. The air smelled like wet concrete and espresso.
She hadn't chosen this place for comfort. She'd chosen it because it was public. Because there were windows. Because she could leave fast if she needed to.
Inside, a woman at the counter argued gently with the barista about oat milk. The barista kept smiling. Everyone in the room looked evenly tempered. Not joyful. Not distressed. Just—contained.
Nadia took a table near the back wall and set her phone face down.

A few minutes later, Callie Lucas walked in shaking rain from her hair. She wore a dark coat and carried a thin laptop sleeve under one arm like it was fragile.
She spotted Nadia and didn't wave. She crossed the room in a straight line and slid into the chair opposite her.
"Thanks for meeting," Callie said.
Nadia nodded once. "You said forty minutes."
"I did," Callie replied, already opening the sleeve. "I'll be fast."
She placed a small voice recorder on the table but didn't turn it on.
Nadia looked at it anyway.
Callie noticed. "It's off."
"Keep it off," Nadia said.
Callie's mouth tugged slightly, like she wanted to push and decided not to spend the first minute doing it.
"Okay," she said. "No recording."
She opened her laptop. The screen lit her face a faint blue.

On the table, the rain kept tapping at the window like someone testing patience.
Callie slid the laptop slightly toward Nadia.

"I've been tracking secondary strain," she said.

Nadia didn't touch the laptop. "On what?"

"Systems that change when bodies change," Callie said.

Nadia waited.

Callie clicked twice. A spreadsheet filled the screen—columns, dates, service codes, counts. Nothing dramatic. Nothing labeled *fertility* in bold, nothing written to scare a reader.

Nadia leaned forward anyway.

"What am I looking at?" she asked.

"Referral volumes," Callie replied. "Reproductive endo. Urology. Assisted conception consults. Mostly billed through public systems. It's not the content. It's the shape."

Nadia's eyes moved down the rows. Toronto Central. North York. Scarborough. A neat distribution until—then not.

A spike.

Then another.

Not huge. Not cinematic. Just enough to notice if you were looking.

Nadia sat back.

"This could be seasonal," she said.

Callie nodded immediately, like she'd been waiting for that sentence. "Could be," she agreed. "Could be backlog. Could be a policy change. Could be a coding revision. So I checked."

She clicked into another tab.

A timeline.

A line graph that rose subtly, then held.

Beside it, a separate line for Eirenex uptake by postal code.

The lines didn't mirror each other cleanly—nothing that tidy—but they leaned in the same direction.

Nadia felt her throat tighten in the way it did when her mind tried to build ten models at once.

She forced herself to stay in the room.

"What's your source?" Nadia asked.

"Public billing aggregates," Callie replied. "Freedom-of-information. Slow, annoying, incomplete. But real."

"And you want what?" Nadia asked.

Callie closed the laptop halfway, just enough to break the glow between them.

"I want names," Callie said.

Nadia stared at her.

Callie held steady. "I want a clinician who will go on record. Someone who can say: yes, we're seeing a pattern. Yes, it's new. Yes, it's connected to the protocol."

Nadia's jaw tightened.

"And you don't have that?" Nadia asked.

"I have two physicians who won't speak," Callie replied. "And one clinic administrator who told me—off record—that they were asked to 'plan capacity' for an increase that hadn't happened yet."

Nadia kept her voice flat. "That's not evidence."

"It's a direction," Callie said.

Nadia glanced down at her own hands. Her wedding ring caught a thin strip of café light and looked too bright.

"You said this was about relief," Nadia said.

"It is," Callie replied. "Because relief is everywhere now. Which means whatever comes with it is everywhere too."

Nadia looked up. "Don't say it like that."

Callie didn't flinch. "How should I say it?"

Nadia exhaled once.

Outside, the streetcar bell rang—a bright, clean sound that didn't match the weather.

"You don't get to pull a thread like this and pretend you know what it's attached to," Nadia said.

Callie leaned forward, voice lower. "That's why I'm here. You do."

Nadia almost laughed. It came out as air.

"I left," she said.

"I know," Callie replied. "Which is why you might still be able to see it."

Nadia's phone vibrated once against the tabletop.

She didn't look at it.

Callie watched her not look.

"Your husband was on it," Callie said, careful. Not soft. Measured.

Nadia's eyes sharpened. "Don't."

Callie raised a hand slightly, palm outward. "I'm not trying to bait you. I'm trying to explain why you're the only person who didn't come to this as a brand-new story."

Nadia sat very still.

The barista called out an order. Someone laughed once, quiet and contained.

Callie reopened the laptop fully and scrolled.

"This is only Toronto," she said. "When I look at the provinces with earlier saturation, the curve is cleaner."

"You don't have enough controls," Nadia said.

"I know," Callie replied. "That's why I want you."

Nadia stared at the graph again.

It wasn't proof.

It wasn't even accusation.

It was a gentle slope. A faint misalignment. The kind of thing you could miss if you weren't trained to care.

The kind of thing a system could call noise until it wasn't.

Nadia tapped once on the table, a small, involuntary motion.

Callie's gaze locked onto it like she'd heard a decision being made.

"No," Nadia said immediately.

Callie didn't speak.

"I'm not giving you names," Nadia continued. "Not patients. Not clinicians. Not anyone."

Callie waited.

Nadia kept going, because silence was how people got convinced.

"But," Nadia said, and felt the word leave her like it had weight, "I will tell you where to look."

Callie's expression didn't change much. But her attention sharpened, like a lens turning.

Nadia reached into her bag and pulled out a folded appointment card. The edges were soft from being handled too many times.

She slid it across the table.

Callie looked down at it.

A clinic name. A building address. A specialty stamped in small letters.

Reproductive Endocrinology — Intake.

Callie looked up.

Nadia's voice stayed even. "If there's a capacity memo, it came from somewhere. That clinic will have it. Or they'll have the absence of it. Either way, you'll get a response."
Callie didn't touch the card yet.
"You've been there," she said.
Nadia didn't answer that directly.
Callie's eyes moved over Nadia's face, searching for confirmation without asking for it.
Nadia felt her stomach tighten.

The door opened and a gust of rain-cooled air swept across the café floor.
For a moment, Nadia smelled wet asphalt again and remembered the clinic atrium from two years ago—numbers, banners, calm bodies moving through doors that didn't close.
Callie finally picked up the card.
"Are you coming with me," she asked.
"No," Nadia said.
Callie's mouth tightened. "Then why hand me this."
Nadia didn't look away.
"Because you're going to do it anyway," she said. "And I'd rather you do it pointed."
Callie nodded once, small.
She slid the card into her sleeve with care.
Then she reached into her coat pocket and set something else on the table.
A plain USB drive. No logo. No label.
Nadia looked at it without touching it.
"What's that?" she asked.
"A FOI packet that didn't come through FOI," Callie said.
Nadia's eyes lifted.
Callie met her gaze. "Someone inside sent it to me. They didn't want their name attached. It's not a smoking gun. It's worse."
Nadia held still.
"What," she said.
Callie's voice stayed low. "It's policy language. New 'privacy protections' being drafted. Not about patients. About linkages."

Nadia felt the café narrow.

Callie pushed the USB across the table, just an inch. Not forcing it. Offering it.

Nadia stared at it.

The rain hit the window harder for a few seconds, then eased.

Her phone vibrated again.

She flipped it over.

Adrian.

Running late. Lila won't nap.

Nadia stared at the message until the screen dimmed.

She looked back at the USB.

Callie didn't move.

Nadia reached out and took it.

Her fingers closed around the plastic like it might be warm.

Callie exhaled through her nose, almost like relief, but her eyes stayed sharp.

Nadia slid the USB into her bag and stood.

"You said forty minutes," she said.

Callie checked her watch. "Thirty-four."

Nadia nodded once and walked toward the door.

At the threshold, she paused just long enough to look back.

Callie was already closing her laptop. Already leaving no trace.

Outside, the rain had thinned into mist.

Nadia stepped into it anyway.

Chapter 27
Removed

Toronto — 2052
The update arrived as a newsletter.
Nadia saw it in the morning light between a daycare email and a grocery coupon. No alert tone. No red badge icon. Just a subject line written to sound harmless.
Ministry of Health — Privacy Harmonization Bulletin (Q2)

She opened it with one hand while Lila ate yogurt at the table, a spoon gripped in her fist like a tool she hadn't mastered yet.
The bulletin began with the usual language—patient dignity, modernization, trust.
Halfway down, a subheading:
Cross-Domain Data Linkage Restrictions — Effective Immediately
Nadia's thumb stopped scrolling.

To protect sensitive reproductive outcomes from misuse and inference, the Ministry is implementing a firewall preventing linkage between neuroregulatory treatment histories and reproductive health records. This applies to all research portals, academic registries, and provincial billing aggregates.
Requests for exception require approval by the Reproductive Safeguards Division.

Reproductive Safeguards.

The phrase sat on her screen like it had always existed.
Lila dropped her spoon. It clinked against the plate. Yogurt splattered in a small white fan.
"Uh-oh," Lila said, pleased with herself.
Nadia set her phone down carefully.
"No uh-oh," she said, and wiped the table.
Her hands moved automatically. Her attention did not.
She picked the phone up again and reread the paragraph.
Firewall.

Not a guideline. Not a reminder.
A barrier.
She pushed her chair back and opened her laptop.
The browser loaded to the University research portal she still had access to through an adjunct appointment—thin affiliation, kept alive by one colleague who still answered her emails.
The portal had never given her ARC charts. It never could. It had given her what it was allowed to give: de-identified aggregates, time-lagged billing summaries, and exposure flags folded into anonymous categories.
Enough to see shape.
Enough to suspect.
She logged in.
The dashboard populated.
She clicked into the query she'd saved two nights ago:
ENDO_REFERRAL_VOLUME (Toronto) — by quarter
overlay: **Neuroregulatory exposure prevalence — postal code**
The page loaded, then stalled.
A gray overlay appeared.
NOTICE: DATA LINKAGE DISABLED
Cross-domain correlation functions have been removed under Ministry directive 2052-17.
Removed.
Not restricted.
Not pending.
Removed.

She clicked into the raw export.
Columns appeared—dates, clinic codes, volumes.
No exposure flag.
She scrolled.
The field that used to sit there—small, unremarkable—was gone.
She tried another dataset.
Same result.
Another.
Same.
She leaned back, breathing slow.

Behind her, Lila babbled at a stuffed rabbit, offering it a smear of yogurt. Nadia closed the laptop gently, like the sound might wake something.
Her phone buzzed.
A text.
Kwan: You seeing the bulletin?
Nadia stared at his name for a moment before replying.
Nadia: Yes. When did this happen?
Three dots appeared.
Then:
Kwan: Overnight. Committee vote was sealed. Staff got the memo at 06:00.
Nadia: Reproductive Safeguards Division?
Kwan: New. Not new, technically. Renamed. Reorganized. More authority now.
Nadia's throat tightened.
Nadia: Authority from where?
A longer pause.
Kwan: Senate liaison. Mercer's people aren't saying it out loud, but they're relieved.
Relieved.
Nadia looked at Lila.
Her daughter's cheeks were flushed from the effort of chewing. Her eyes bright. Her body busy, unafraid of the day.
Nadia's phone buzzed again—another message from Kwan.
Kwan: You can't correlate anymore from the outside. Internally, it's now Tier-5.
Tier-5.
She almost smiled at the absurdity of the number. Almost.
Nadia: Does Tier-5 exist?
Kwan: It does now.
Nadia's fingers curled around the edge of the phone.
Lila reached toward her, palm open.
"Up," she said.
Nadia lifted her. Lila's weight settled against her like certainty. Her small hand pressed into Nadia's collarbone and stayed there.
Nadia held her for a moment longer than necessary.
Then set her down and stood.

She went to the kitchen counter and opened a drawer.

Inside, beneath a rubber band and a dead pen, was a small folder she'd started keeping after Adrian withdrew—paper copies of things that weren't supposed to matter.

Appointment cards.

Consent language screenshots.

A printout of a public health graph that had vanished from a government page two days after it went up.

She slid the folder out and laid it flat.

Her phone buzzed again.

Adrian.

Adrian: Running late. Lila wouldn't nap. You okay?

Nadia stared at the question.

You okay?

She typed:

Nadia: Yes. Traffic.

She sent it. It wasn't true. But it was usable.

She opened her laptop again, not to query the portal—there was nothing left to query—but to open her private log.

Personal Log — Variance Event.

The cursor blinked in a clean white document.

She typed one line:

Ministry implemented cross-domain firewall: neuroregulatory exposure ↔ reproductive outcomes. Safeguards Division now gatekeeper. Correlation tools removed from academic portals.

She saved it.

Then she opened her email and searched for the old FOI results Callie had shown her—referral volumes, clinic capacity notes, the gentle slope that wasn't proof until you could anchor it to something.

The folder was there.

She clicked.

A message appeared at the top of the inbox:

This content is no longer available.

Nadia stared.

She clicked again.

Same message.

She checked the trash.

Nothing.

She checked the archive.

Nothing.

The deletion hadn't been done by her.

She sat very still.

In the living room, Lila laughed at her rabbit again, the sound bright and immediate.

Nadia looked toward the noise as if verifying it was real.

Her phone vibrated.

Unknown number.

She answered without thinking.

"Dr. Serrano?" Callie Lucas's voice said.

Nadia didn't speak.

Callie continued, low and quick.

"They just cut the linkages," she said. "Publicly."

"I saw," Nadia replied.

"And they just pulled my FOI packet access," Callie said. "Not a denial. A removal."

Nadia's stomach tightened.

Callie's voice sharpened.

"Someone anticipated correlation," Callie said. "This isn't cleanup. This is preemption."

Nadia looked at the folder on her counter.

Paper.

The only version that couldn't be quietly unmade.

"What do you have left?" Nadia asked.

Callie exhaled once.

"A source," she said. "Inside. They want to meet."

Nadia's grip tightened on the phone.

"When?" she asked.

"Tonight," Callie said. "They won't wait."

Nadia glanced at the clock.
Adrian would be home in twenty minutes.
Daycare pickup in an hour.
Dinner after.
A normal day.
A normal life.

"Where?" Nadia asked.
Callie gave an address.
Nadia repeated it once to lock it in.
When the call ended, she stood at the counter, staring at the saved document on her laptop and the paper folder beside it.
Lila called from the living room, impatient now.
"Mommy!"
Nadia picked up the folder and slid it into her bag.
Not the laptop.
Not the phone.
The paper.
She zipped the bag closed.
Then she walked into the living room and lifted her daughter, pressing her face briefly into Lila's hair.
Warm. Sweet. Real.

Adrian's key turned in the lock.
The door opened.
He stepped in, damp from rain, cheeks pink from cold.
"Hey," he said, and smiled when he saw them.
Nadia smiled back automatically.
"Hey," she said.
Adrian shook water from his jacket.
"Everything okay?" he asked again, casual.
Nadia held Lila a little tighter.
"Yeah," she said.
Lila rested her head on Nadia's shoulder.
Outside, rain tapped against the windows.

Chapter 28
Confirmed

Toronto — 2052

The clinic walls were painted the same pale gray as every other medical building in the city. The color was meant to calm.

It didn't.

Nadia sat with Lila in her lap, fingers resting lightly over the child's ribs as if counting breath. Lila swung her legs against the vinyl chair and watched a fish tank in the corner. The tank light flickered faintly at the top seam.

Adrian stood near the window, arms crossed.

He had not sat down.

The consultation room door opened.

Dr. Hye-Jin Park stepped in, tablet in hand. She closed the door behind her with a soft click.

"Thank you for waiting," Dr. Park said.

Nadia nodded.

Adrian didn't move.

Dr. Park sat across from them and rested the tablet flat on her knee.

"We've completed the imaging and endocrine panels," she said. "I'd like to go over the findings."

Nadia adjusted Lila slightly so she could see Dr. Park clearly.

Lila reached for Nadia's necklace.

Adrian stepped closer to the chair but remained standing.

Dr. Park did not soften her tone.

"There are structural differences in Lila's ovarian development," she said. "Specifically, absence of viable follicular formation."

Nadia did not blink.

Adrian's arms tightened across his chest.

"Explain," Nadia said.

Dr. Park angled the tablet toward them.

An image filled the screen—two small structures outlined in clean white against darker tissue.

"These should contain visible follicular clusters," Dr. Park said. "They do not."

Adrian leaned in.

"So what does that mean?" he asked.

Dr. Park looked directly at him.

"It means there is no projected pathway for oocyte maturation."

Silence.

Lila laughed softly at something only she could see in the fish tank.

Nadia's hand stilled on her daughter's back.

"You're saying she won't be able to conceive," Nadia said.

Dr. Park held her gaze.

"Correct."

Adrian blinked once.

"At what age does that become relevant?" he asked.

Dr. Park didn't hesitate.

"It's relevant now."

Adrian shook his head faintly, as if adjusting a frequency.

"She's two," he said.

"Yes," Dr. Park replied.

Lila twisted in Nadia's lap and reached toward the tablet screen.

"Fish," she said.

Nadia shifted the device out of reach.

"Is this reversible?" she asked.

"No."

"Is it progressive?"

"No."

"So it's fixed," Nadia said.

"Yes."

Adrian finally sat down.

The chair creaked beneath him.

"What causes that?" he asked.

Dr. Park folded her hands.

"Developmental irregularity," she said.

"From what?" Nadia asked.

"There are multiple possibilities," Dr. Park said.

"List them," Nadia said.

Dr. Park nodded.

"Genetic mutation. Early gestational exposure to endocrine disruptors. Rare spontaneous anomaly."

"Test for mutation?" Nadia asked.

"We did. No identifiable pathogenic variant."

"Environmental exposure?" Nadia asked.

"None documented in your file."

Adrian looked between them.

"In our file?" he asked.

Dr. Park met his eyes.

"Maternal records indicate no flagged exposure."

"And paternal?" Nadia asked.

Dr. Park hesitated just long enough to be seen.

"Paternal history is not typically correlated with this presentation," she said.

"Not typically," Nadia repeated.

"No."

The fish tank filter hummed.

Lila slid off Nadia's lap and walked toward the glass, pressing her hands against it.

Adrian watched her.

"So what now?" he asked.

Dr. Park's voice remained even.

"There is no medical intervention indicated at this time. We recommend long-term counseling resources when appropriate."

"When appropriate," Adrian repeated.

"Yes."

Nadia stood.

The movement was slow and controlled.

"Print the report," she said.

Dr. Park nodded.

A printer whirred in the corner. Paper slid out.

Adrian stared at the floor.

Nadia took the pages without looking down.

"Is this isolated?" she asked.

Dr. Park paused.

"I am not at liberty to discuss other cases," she said.

"So there are others," Nadia said.

Dr. Park did not respond.

Adrian's head lifted.

"What do you mean?" he asked.

Dr. Park looked at him, then at Nadia.

"My obligation is to your daughter's care," she said.

"Answer the question," Nadia said.

Dr. Park's jaw tightened slightly.

"I cannot comment on aggregate trends," she said.

"Aggregate trends," Adrian repeated quietly.

Nadia stepped closer to the desk.

"Has the Ministry issued any advisory regarding pediatric reproductive irregularities?" she asked.

Dr. Park did not blink.

"No."

"Has ARC?" Nadia asked.

"ARC does not oversee pediatric reproductive care," Dr. Park said.

The distinction hung in the room.

Adrian stood again.

His hands were shaking now.

He pressed them against the back of the chair to still them.

"You're telling us," he said slowly, "that our daughter will never have children."

"Yes," Dr. Park said.

Lila laughed at the fish again.

Nadia felt the sound move through her like a fracture.

"Is she otherwise healthy?" she asked.

"Yes."

"Development normal?"

"Yes."

"Cognitive?"

"Yes."

Adrian exhaled sharply.

"So everything's fine," he said.

Dr. Park didn't answer.

Nadia placed a hand on his arm.

"Adrian," she said quietly.

He pulled away without meaning to.

"She's two," he said again.

"Yes," Nadia said.

Dr. Park slid a card across the desk.

"Follow-up imaging in twelve months," she said. "If you have additional questions, you can contact my office."
Nadia picked up Lila.
Lila wrapped her arms around Nadia's neck.
Warm. Certain. Alive.
Adrian stared at the printed report in Nadia's hand.
The top line read:
REPRODUCTIVE NON-VIABILITY — CONFIRMED
Black text.
Clinical font.
No emotion.
Nadia looked at Dr. Park one last time.
"If this presents again," she said, "you'll notify us."
Dr. Park held her gaze.
"I am not authorized to initiate external notifications," she said.
"Authorized by who?" Adrian asked.
Dr. Park did not answer.
The silence stretched long enough to define itself.
Nadia turned toward the door.
Adrian followed.

In the hallway, the fluorescent lights felt harsher.
Parents sat with toddlers. A woman bounced a baby on her knee. A boy played with a plastic stethoscope.
Normal sounds.
Normal rooms.
The world unchanged.
Adrian stopped walking halfway down the corridor.
Nadia turned.
He was staring at Lila.
Not at her face.
At her small body, her hands gripping Nadia's collar.
"She won't—" he started.
He couldn't finish.
Nadia didn't help him.
The elevator doors opened at the end of the hall.
No one moved.

Adrian swallowed.

Nadia looked at him.
There was something sharp and vertical rising behind his eyes.
The elevator doors began to close.
Nadia stepped forward before they could.
Adrian followed.
As the doors sealed, Lila rested her head on Nadia's shoulder and closed her eyes.
The building descended.

Chapter 29
Inevitable

Toronto — 2052

The kitchen light hummed faintly.
Lila's chart lay open on the table.
Non-viable reproductive pathway.
Follicular development absent.
Congenital, non-correctable.
Adrian stood at the counter, hands flat against the edge, staring at nothing in particular.
Nadia sat with her laptop open.
A spreadsheet filled the screen.
Rows.
Ages.
Parent exposure status.
Treatment history.
No internal ARC portal.
No badge-level access.
Just public health releases, anonymized registry data, and three datasets Kwan had sent her through an encrypted academic channel labeled: "aggregate only."
She sorted again.

Parent participation in ARC Phase II — Yes / No.
Birth year cohort — 2049–2052.
Reproductive anomaly flag — Present / Absent.
She recalculated.
The ratio shifted.
She recalculated again.
Adrian turned.
"Are you doing that again?" he asked.
"Yes," Nadia said.
He walked to the table and looked down at the screen.
"I don't want this to become a project," he said.
"It isn't," she replied.
"It sure looks like one."

She didn't answer.

The cursor blinked at the bottom of the column.

She highlighted a subset: children born to at least one ARC participant.

Then another subset: children born to non-participants.

She ran the comparison.

The percentage difference populated.

Adrian leaned closer.

"What does that mean?" he asked.

"It means the rate isn't even," she said.

"Even how?"

"Across exposure."

He stared at the numbers.

"How uneven?" he asked.

She didn't look at him.

"Statistically significant," she said.

He laughed once. "That's not an answer."

"It is," she said.

He pulled a chair out but didn't sit.

"So say it like a person," he said.

She scrolled.

Another dataset.

Another city.

Same age range.

Same flag.

She merged the tables.

Ran it again.

The screen paused.

Then populated.

The percentage tightened.

Adrian watched her face.

"What?" he asked.

She swallowed once.

"If it were random," she said carefully, "the distribution would scatter."

"And?"

"It isn't scattering."

He pulled the chair closer and sat. "So what does that mean?"

"It means the probability of coincidence drops," she said.

"To what?"
She hesitated.
"I'd need more longitudinal data."
"That's not what I asked," he said.
She closed her eyes briefly, then opened them.
"It means this cluster isn't noise."
Silence.

The refrigerator motor clicked on.
Adrian stared at the rows again.
"So you're saying," he began slowly, "that kids like Lila—"
"Don't," Nadia said sharply.
He stopped.
She steadied her voice.
"I'm saying the anomaly correlates with ARC exposure," she said.
He sat back.
"Correlates," he repeated.
"Yes."
"That's not causation."
"No," she said.
"But it's not random either," he said.
"No."
The word landed heavy.
He looked at the chart again.
"How many?" he asked.
"In this subset? Thirty-two percent," she said.
He blinked. "And baseline?"
"Under three."
His mouth opened slightly.
"That can't be right," he said.
"It is," she said.
He stood abruptly and paced toward the window.
"You're using public data," he said. "That's incomplete."
"Yes."
"You don't have internal—"
"No," she said.
"You don't have full—"

"No."

"So this could be sampling error," he said.

She didn't answer immediately.

"It could," she said finally.

He turned. "But you don't think it is."

"No."

Silence stretched between them.

He walked back toward the table.

"Show me again," he said.

She rotated the screen.

He leaned in.

She reran the formula in front of him.

Same result.

He stared at it like it might rearrange itself if he watched long enough.

She held his gaze.

"Do you think it's accidental?"

"Of course it is," she said again.

He laughed, but it wasn't humor. "You always know."

"I mean… not this," she admitted.

He pushed the laptop slightly away from him.

"So what happens now?" he asked.

"I get more data."

"And if it holds?"

She looked at Lila's chart on the table. "Then it holds."

"That's not an answer," he said.

"It's the only one I have."

He stared at her.

"So our daughter," he said quietly, "is part of a statistical pattern."

"Yes," she said.

"And that pattern is tied to something I did."

Her voice remained level.

"Exposure," she said.

He stepped back like the word had force.

"I did that," he said.

"You didn't know."

"That doesn't change it."

She closed the laptop halfway but didn't shut it.
"We don't have proof of mechanism," she said. "Only correlation."
"That's enough," he said.
"For what?"
"For me."
She looked at him carefully. "For you to do what?"
He didn't answer.
Instead, he walked into the hallway.

Lila's bedroom door was open. Nightlight on. Soft breathing audible.
He stood in the doorway for several seconds.
Nadia remained at the table.
The spreadsheet still visible in the gap of the half-closed screen.

After a moment, Adrian returned.
"Tell me something," he said.
"What?" she asked.
"If the probability of coincidence drops far enough—" he paused, "—what does it become?"
She held his eyes. "It becomes inevitability."
The word stayed in the air.
Not accusation.
Not conspiracy.
Just mathematics.
Adrian's jaw tightened. "So this isn't bad luck."
"No."
"And it's not one doctor's error."
"No," she said.
"And it's not one batch," he said.
"No."
He nodded slowly.

Then:
"Then someone should know," he said.
"They do," she said quietly.
He looked at her sharply. "You think they've seen this?"
"Yes."

"And nothing is being done?"
She didn't answer.
He stepped back as if the room had shifted.

"And you think this is random?" he said.
"No," she said.
He laughed again, harsher now. "Then what is it, Nadia?"
"It's an outcome."
The words were colder than she intended.
Adrian stared at her like she had struck him.

"An outcome," he said.
"Yes," she said.
Silence.
Then he nodded once.
Slow.
Deliberate.

"Okay," he said.
The word was not agreement.
It was distance.
He walked past her toward the bedroom without touching her shoulder.
Nadia remained at the table.
She reopened the laptop.
Ran the formula one more time.
Same result.
She saved the file under a new name:
Cohort Exposure — 2052 Cross-City Aggregate
Then she closed it.

In the bedroom, Adrian lay down beside Lila's bed instead of in theirs.
Nadia stood in the kitchen doorway, watching the hallway light spill under the door.
The pattern had not accused anyone.
It had not revealed a villain.
It had only refused to be random.
And that was enough.

Chapter 30

Logged

Toronto — 2052

The kitchen light was too white for the hour.

It laid itself across the counter like a sheet, making every crumb visible, every fingerprint on the stainless sink. Outside the window, the building across the street held its own square of blue-black night. A few rooms were lit. Most weren't.

Nadia sat at the table with her laptop open.

The screen glow made her hands look paler than they were. Her fingers hovered above the trackpad, then moved again, then stopped.

On the table beside the laptop: a folded discharge summary, a pediatric consult printout, and a pen that had leaked slightly into the grain of the wood.

Across the room, Adrian stood with his back against the fridge.

He had a glass of water in his hand that he wasn't drinking.

"You're still doing this," he said.

Nadia didn't look up. "I'm still awake," she said.

"You know what I mean."

She clicked into the browser again. The page refreshed: a public health portal login screen with a clean government crest, a rotating "system maintenance" banner, and a narrow line of text at the bottom about new privacy compliance.

She typed her university credentials. The password field filled with dots. Adrian laughed once without humor. "You're going to log your way into grief."

Nadia hit enter.

The screen accepted her and loaded a dashboard—population tiles, anonymized trend charts, controlled categories with locked icons. The section she needed sat there like a sealed drawer.

REPRODUCTIVE OUTCOMES — RESTRICTED (FIREWALL ACTIVE)

She clicked it anyway.

A dialog box opened.

Access Denied.

Reason: Cross-domain linking prohibited under the Reproductive Data Protection Framework.

Below it, a small line:

All access attempts are logged.

She stared at that line until the letters stopped looking like letters.

Adrian pushed off the fridge. He set his glass down too hard on the counter. Water trembled in it.

"Good," he said. "Good. That's your answer."

"It's not," Nadia said.

"It is. It's literally a door. It's closed."

Nadia closed the dialog box and opened her notes. A plain text file. No header. No formatting. Just dates and short lines—clinic names, age ranges, sample sizes she could infer, a few numbers she'd written down in the margins of someone else's paper.

Adrian's voice tightened. "Nadia."

She looked up.

He wasn't yelling. That was the problem. He was careful. He was trying to be careful, like careful could keep something from breaking further.

"You left," he said. "You left that building. You said we were done being watched."

"I said I was done being inside," she replied.

"That's the same thing."

"It isn't," she said.

He shook his head once, slow. "You're going to make it the same thing."

Nadia lowered her gaze back to the table. Her hands found the discharge summary again, thumb flattening the crease where she'd folded it too sharply earlier.

She could see the phrase without reading it. She could feel it in her body like a bruise.

Adrian stepped closer. His feet made almost no sound on the floor. He stopped behind her chair, close enough that she could feel the heat of him without him touching her.

"You think if you find a spreadsheet," he said, "it will turn into something you can fix."

Nadia swallowed.

"I think if I don't look," she said, "it stays allowed."

Adrian exhaled hard through his nose. "Allowed?"

Nadia turned in the chair to face him fully.

His eyes were bright in a way she didn't trust. Not with tears—just intensity. A kind of focus she had seen in him before, years ago, when he'd been bracing for nights and counting hours and calling it living.

"You want to know what I think?" he said.

Nadia didn't answer.

He kept going anyway.

"I think you want a villain," he said. "Because if there's a villain, then there's a reason. And if there's a reason, then this"—his hand moved once, a sharp motion toward the papers—"isn't just... what happens."

Nadia held his gaze.

"I don't want a villain," she said. "I want an explanation that fits the numbers."

Adrian laughed again—shorter this time. "You hear yourself?"

Nadia turned back to the laptop.

The cursor blinked in an empty email draft.

Recipient field empty.

Subject empty.

The cursor was the only moving thing in the room.

Adrian's hand came down on the back of her chair. Not hard. Not gentle. Claiming the space.

Nadia's fingers paused over the keys.

Nadia's throat went tight. She let the silence sit long enough to become a choice.

Then she typed a name into the recipient field.

KWAN, J.

An old address autofilled beneath it.

Adrian's grip on the chair tightened slightly. "Nadia."

Nadia kept typing.

Subject line:

Question about the firewall

No. Too obvious.

She backspaced until it was blank again.

Then she wrote:

Need help finding a denominator

Adrian's voice dropped. "Nadia."

She didn't look at him.

She wrote the message in short lines, like notes she might take in a meeting, like procedure.

Not a confession.

Not a theory.

Just a request.

I'm outside the system.

I'm seeing clinic-level anomalies that won't resolve as noise.

The public firewall went up before any public controversy existed.

I need to know what they were linking before they stopped letting anyone link it.

If you can't talk on record, tell me where to look without you.

She stopped.

Added one more line, because her hand moved without asking her permission:

It's my daughter.

Adrian made a sound—small, involuntary, like air hit a sore place. "Don't," he said. "Don't use her like that."

Nadia's jaw clenched.

"I'm not using her," she said. "I'm refusing to pretend she's a coincidence."

He stepped around the chair until he was in her line of sight. He crouched slightly so he could see her face.

His voice softened into something almost pleading.

"Please," he said. "Please stop. Just—stop. For one night. For one week. For—"

Nadia looked at him.

She saw what he was asking for: not ignorance. Not peace. Just delay. A small pocket of time where their lives didn't become another kind of life.

Nadia's hand rested on the trackpad.

The send button sat there, bright, waiting.

She could feel her pulse in her fingers.

"Adrian," she said quietly.

He flinched at his name, like it came with history attached.

"I can't," she said. "If I stop, it means I accept it."

His eyes held hers. "And if you don't stop," he said, "it means you set a fire in our house, knowingly."

Nadia didn't answer right away.

Then she said, evenly, "If the house is already burning, I want to know who locked the exits."

Adrian's face changed. Not anger. Something else. Something that made his mouth go still.

He stood up.

"Okay," he said.

It was not agreement.

It was the sound of someone stepping away from a cliff edge and letting another person stand there alone.

Nadia turned back to the laptop.

Her thumb hovered.

She pressed **Send**.

For a second, nothing happened.

Then the message left the draft pane. The screen flashed a small confirmation.

Sent.

Immediately after, another banner slid down across the top of the portal window she'd left open:

NOTICE: Unauthorized access attempts may trigger credential review.

If you believe this is an error, please contact Compliance.

Nadia stared at the banner.

Adrian didn't move.

The kitchen light hummed.

Outside, a streetcar rattled along the avenue, bright and ordinary, as if the city had not just shifted under their feet.

Nadia closed the laptop.

The click of it sounded final.

She sat there with her hands flat on the table, papers between her palms like an offering and a weapon at the same time.

Adrian's voice came from behind her, quiet.

"If they answer," he said, "they'll know you asked."
Nadia didn't turn.
"I know," she said.
And that was the decision.

Chapter 31
ES-47

Toronto — 2053
The email arrived at 02:14.
No subject line.
No greeting.
Just a string of characters and a Toronto Public Health footer that looked almost legitimate.
Nadia didn't open it immediately.
The apartment was dark except for the kitchen under-cabinet light she had left on hours ago. Lila's room door was closed. Adrian was asleep on the couch, one arm over his eyes, television muted but still glowing faintly.
Nadia sat at the kitchen table with her laptop open and the fertility export sheet still on the screen.
Thirty-seven cases.
All children.
All non-viable reproductive pathways.
All with at least one ARC-exposed parent.
The pattern no longer trembled.
It held.

Her phone vibrated again.
Same sender.
She opened it.
Inside the body of the email:
You're pulling the wrong dataset.
Stop querying clinic-level reproductive reports.
They locked the cross-domain join last week.
If you want to see what matters, you need pre-rollout modeling.
Call me from a clean line.
No name.
But the cadence was unmistakable.
Min-Jae Kwan.
Nadia stood very still.

She closed the laptop first.
Then deleted the message.
Then emptied the trash folder.
Then checked the header trace.
It routed through a municipal health relay, but the originating server pinged an internal ARC subnet.
He hadn't left.

She didn't call from her phone.
She didn't call from the apartment.
She walked.
Two blocks east, then south, then into a twenty-four-hour pharmacy where the fluorescent lights flattened everyone's face into the same exhausted tone.
She bought a prepaid phone with cash.
No loyalty number.
No email.

She stepped back outside into the cold.
Snow threatened but didn't fall.
She dialed the number embedded in the email signature.
It rang twice.
"Don't say my name," he said immediately.
His voice was lower than she remembered.
"Okay," she replied.
"You're escalating your queries," he said.
"You're blocking them," she answered.
Silence.
"I didn't," he said.
"But someone did."
"Yes."
A car passed behind her, tires hissing on wet pavement.
"What did you see?" he asked.
"Correlation," she said. "Early-stage. Not noise."
"How tight?"
"Too tight."
Another silence.

"You can't prove intent," he said.
"I'm not trying to prove intent," she replied. "I'm trying to understand mechanism."
He exhaled slowly.
"They moved the firewall up two tiers," he said. "Reproductive registries can't be linked to ARC participant IDs anymore."
"I noticed."
"That wasn't administrative," he said.
"No," she said.
Wind pushed at her coat.
"Why are you calling me?" she asked.
"You already know why."
She waited.
"Because if you keep querying fertility outcomes directly," he said, "you'll trigger oversight."
"I probably already have."
"Yes."
A beat.
"Then why help me?" she asked.
His answer came without pause.
"Because I was in the room before Phase I."
Nadia didn't speak.
"I wasn't in the rollout," he continued. "I was in the modeling."
Her fingers tightened around the prepaid phone.
"What modeling?" she asked.
"Pre-launch viability simulations," he said. "Long-horizon projections."
"For distress reduction?"
"That's what we were told."
"And?"
Another pause.
"And the simulations included demographic variables that weren't clinically necessary."
The streetlight above her hummed faintly.
"What variables?" she asked.
"Birth-rate elasticity. Intergenerational transmission probability. Cohort attrition."
Her pulse slowed instead of quickening.

"Why would that be in a distress-regulation model?" she asked.

"I asked that," he said.

"And?"

"They said it was exploratory."

She said nothing.

"Exploratory for what?" she asked finally.

"Population stability modeling," he said.

The words hung between them.

Nadia's breath left her body slowly.

"You're telling me," she said carefully, "that before rollout, someone simulated long-term demographic effects."

"Yes."

"And those files are where?"

"Not on the clinical server," he said. "Not on the public research archive."

"Where?" she asked.

"In the archive tier," he said. "Buried in legacy."

"Legacy what?"

"Environmental Systems."

She closed her eyes briefly.

Environmental Systems.

"That's not psychiatry," she said.

"No," he said.

"That's ecological modeling," she said.

"Yes."

A car door slammed somewhere behind her.

"What exactly did the simulations show?" she asked.

"They showed," he said slowly, "that under certain exposure thresholds, the second-generation reproduction rate declines."

Her throat tightened.

"How much decline?"

"Enough to bend the curve."

She leaned against the brick wall of the pharmacy. "Bend it how?"

"Gradually," he said. "Not collapse. Not extinction. Slope correction."

Her breath fogged in front of her.

"You're certain?" she asked.

"I ran some of them," he said.

Silence.

"You ran them," she repeated.

"Yes."

"And you didn't tell me."

"I didn't understand what I was looking at," he said. "Not fully."

"And now?" she asked.

"I understand the math," he replied.

A long pause.

"Correlation is not design," she said.

"No," he agreed.

"But you think it might be."

He did not answer directly.

"They didn't remove the models," he said instead. "They just hid them."

"Why tell me now?" she asked.

"Because you're already looking," he said. "And because if you request the archive without knowing what you're asking for, they'll shut you down."

"So what do I ask for?" she said.

"Legacy Environmental Systems modeling archive," he said. "Pre-Phase I. File tree begins with ES-47."

She memorized it.

"Access level?" she asked.

"Academic collaborator request might pass," he said. "You still have external researcher privileges through the university."

"Limited," she said.

"Limited is enough if you ask for the right thing."

"And if they deny it?"

"They probably will," he said. "They should."

She swallowed.

"Then what?"

"Then I send you one file," he said.

Her heart rate changed at that.

"You'd risk that?" she asked.

"I already have," he said.

Silence stretched.

Across the street, a streetcar glided past, windows bright.

"You think this was intentional," she said.

He did not respond immediately.
"I think," he said carefully, "that the outcome was modeled."
"That's not the same."
"No, It's not the same."
She pressed. "And?"
"But I think outcomes that are modeled are rarely accidental," he said.
The wind shifted again.
She looked up at the dark sky.
"Why are you still inside?" she asked.
"Because someone has to be," he said.
A beat.
"If you access ES-47, don't download everything," he added. "Just the demographic sensitivity tables."
"Why those?"
"They show threshold inflection points," he said.
She memorized that too.
"Min—" she started.
He cut her off gently.
"Don't," he said.
Silence.
"If I'm wrong," she said, "I burn my credibility chasing ghosts."
"If you're right," he replied, "you already lost it."
The line clicked.
Call ended.

Nadia stood in the cold for a long time after that.
Environmental Systems.
Birth-rate elasticity.
Cohort attrition.
Bend the curve.
She walked home slowly.

Inside the apartment, Adrian hadn't moved.
Lila's door remained closed.
Nadia sat at the kitchen table again.
She opened her laptop.
She didn't reopen the fertility sheet.

Instead, she opened the university research portal.
External collaborator login.
Username accepted.
Password accepted.
She typed:
Legacy Environmental Systems Archive
Pre-Phase I Modeling
File Tree: ES-47
She hesitated only once.
Then pressed enter.
The screen loaded.
A directory appeared.
Restricted.
Request access?
Yes / No
Nadia clicked:
Yes.

Chapter 32
Threshold

Toronto — 2053

The request did not approve immediately.
The university portal spun once, then froze on a neutral gray screen.
REQUEST SUBMITTED
Estimated review time: 24–72 hours.

Nadia stared at it.
Twenty-four to seventy-two hours meant routing. Routing meant visibility.
She logged out.
Then logged back in.
Same screen.
She closed the browser entirely and reopened it through a different network path.
External collaborator access verified.
Pending archive authorization.
She did not try a third time.
Instead, she opened a new tab and searched the public metadata index for Environmental Systems.
Most entries were climate resilience studies. Urban heat modeling. Watershed recovery projections.
Then she found it.
ES-47 — Demographic Stability Modeling Framework
Access: Restricted
Classification: Cross-Domain Simulation Archive

Cross-Domain.

She copied the file ID into her private document.
Then she waited.
Her phone vibrated.
Min-Jae.

Denied yet? the message read.

Pending, she typed.
Good.
Good?
If it's instant, it's monitored. If it's delayed, it's routed quietly.
She didn't like that distinction.
What am I looking for exactly? she typed.
A pause.
Then:
Open sensitivity tables first. Not executive summary.
Why?
Because summaries are curated.
She stared at that.

Curated.

The portal pinged.
ACCESS GRANTED — LIMITED VIEW
Archive Tier: ES-47
Download Disabled
Print Disabled
Session Logged

Session logged.

She inhaled slowly and clicked open.
The interface was older than the clinical portal.
Gray menus. Thin fonts. Folder trees nested deep enough to discourage curiosity.
She navigated:
ES-47
→ Simulation Models
→ Phase Pre-Launch
→ Demographic Projections
Three files.
Baseline Stability Projection
High-Exposure Scenario
Elasticity Threshold Sensitivity

She opened Baseline first.
A population curve appeared—smooth, gradual decline beginning two decades out, then leveling into stability.
Axis labels:
Projected Reproductive Viability Index
Cohort Continuity Rate
Exposure Density (%)
She scrolled.
Assumptions listed in bullet points.
Voluntary enrollment.
Urban distress clusters.
No direct fertility intervention.

No direct fertility intervention.

She moved to High-Exposure Scenario.
The curve dipped more steeply.
Projected second-generation reproduction rate: 0.61
Baseline replacement threshold: 1.00
Her mouth went dry.

She opened Elasticity Threshold Sensitivity.
The screen filled with a grid.
Exposure density on the horizontal axis.
Intergenerational transmission probability on the vertical.
Cells shaded in gradients from pale to deep blue.
A note at the bottom:
Inflection point observed at exposure density > 0.38 with transmission probability > 0.72.
She froze.

0.38.

She switched tabs and opened the revised Phase II adoption curve from Mercer's update.
Projected plateau: 0.44.

Above threshold.
She stared at the number.

Above threshold.

Her heart rate slowed instead of accelerating.
She typed into her private log:
ES-47 — Elasticity Threshold Sensitivity
Inflection > 0.38 exposure density
Revised Phase II plateau: 0.44
Correlation visible at model level.
She stopped before writing the next word.
Design.
She deleted the line.
Rewrote:
Projected adoption exceeds modeled demographic inflection threshold.
Her phone buzzed again.

You see it, Min-Jae wrote.
Yes.
Long pause.
You understand what that means?
It means if adoption holds at revised projection, second-generation reproduction declines below replacement, she typed.
Another pause.
And?
She stared at the screen.
And that outcome was modeled pre-launch.
Three dots appeared immediately.
Yes.
Her breath fogged against the window beside her.
The apartment was silent except for the faint hum of the refrigerator.
Lila was asleep down the hall.
Adrian shifted on the couch but did not wake.

Nadia clicked deeper into the archive.
Subfolder: Stakeholder Review — Restricted.

Denied.
She returned to the sensitivity table.
Scrolled further down.
A comment embedded in the margin:
Environmental Load Reduction Curve Stabilizes Within 30–40 Years Under High-Exposure Scenario.

Environmental load reduction.

She felt something inside her chest go cold.
She copied the comment into her private document.
Then stopped.
Session logged.

She minimized the browser and opened a blank text file offline instead.
Handwritten notes only.
ES-47 modeling includes environmental load reduction metric.
High exposure scenario bends demographic curve within 30–40 years.
No direct fertility intervention required.
Outcome emergent from distress-regulation adoption density.

She looked back at the grid.
The inflection cell was dark blue.
Below it, pale gray.
Just a few percentage points.
A small difference in enrollment.
She checked the retention rate from last week.
Seventy-four percent continuation consult.
If continuation held, exposure density would not just plateau.
It would compound.

Her phone vibrated.
You need to stop logging into the archive for tonight, Min-Jae wrote.
Why?
Because your session duration is being tracked.
How long is safe?
Under twenty minutes.

She checked the timestamp in the corner of the portal.
Eighteen minutes.
She closed the browser immediately.
Logged out.
Cleared history.
Powered down the laptop entirely.
Then sat still.

Across the room, Adrian's breathing remained steady.
Manageable.
She looked at his chest rising and falling in the dim light.
He had taken one dose.
One.
Exposure density > 0.38.
How many doses did it take to count as exposure in the model?
She reopened her notebook.
Under assumptions:
Exposure defined as ≥1 completed initiation.
Her stomach tightened.

One.

She stood and walked quietly to the window.
Toronto at night was a field of small lights—condos, traffic, hospital towers in the distance.
Somewhere inside those towers, the intake board was still refreshing.
New screenings.
New doses.
New exposure density.
Her phone vibrated again.

Last message tonight, Min-Jae wrote.
Okay.
There's a second dataset.
Her pulse flicked.
Where?
Not in ES-47.

Where then?
Off-ledger modeling.
Her fingers tightened around the phone.
What does it show?
Longer horizon.
How long?
He didn't answer immediately.
Then:
Two generations.
She swallowed.
And?
Silence.
Then:
Call me tomorrow.
The line went quiet.

Nadia stood at the window for a long time after that.
Two generations.
She returned to the kitchen table and reopened her encrypted copy of the private log.
She added one line only:
Modeled demographic inflection confirmed at projected adoption density.
Then she hesitated.
Below it, she typed:
Intent not yet established.
She left it there.

Down the hall, Lila turned in her sleep.
Adrian murmured once, then settled.
Nadia closed the laptop.
The city lights did not flicker.
Somewhere in the system, exposure density ticked upward by one more scheduled intake.

Chapter 33
Suspended

Toronto — 2053
The notice arrived at 08:12.
Not to her phone.
Not to her private inbox.
To her university account.

Subject: Improper Data Access — Advisory Review
Nadia read it standing at the kitchen counter.
Adrian was already gone for work. Lila's backpack was still on the chair where she'd dropped it the night before.
The email was structured cleanly.

Dr. Serrano,
Your recent access to Legacy Environmental Systems Archive (ES-47) has triggered a compliance review under cross-domain statistical privacy protocols.
Access to archive tier materials is hereby suspended pending clarification of research intent and scope.
Please refrain from further attempts to retrieve or analyze demographic sensitivity data.
Failure to comply may result in revocation of collaborator privileges and notification to licensing authorities.

Licensing authorities.

She read that line twice.
No accusation.
No claim of wrongdoing.
Just procedural language.
She opened the portal anyway.
Legacy Environmental Systems Archive
Status: Access Suspended
Below it:
Reason Code: Cross-Domain Reproductive Linkage Risk

She exhaled slowly.
The phrasing was precise.

Reproductive linkage.

Not fertility.
Not population.
Linkage.
Her phone vibrated.

Min-Jae.
You lasted one night, he wrote.
They moved fast.
Yes.
She typed: Licensing authorities.
Pause.
Expected.
Expected?
They can't fire you. You're external.
They can freeze your credentials.
She didn't respond to that.
Instead she opened the metadata index again and searched for ES-47 through a different path.
Nothing.
The entry had been hidden.
She checked her session logs.
Previous access recorded: 19 minutes, 42 seconds.
Under that:
Compliance Flag — Elevated Monitoring
She stared at the phrase.

Elevated.
Not violation.
Monitoring.

Her phone vibrated again.
Don't log in again today, Min-Jae wrote.

I wasn't going to.
Good.

She moved to the dining table and opened her handwritten notes instead.
Inflection point > 0.38
Projected plateau: 0.44
Environmental load reduction curve stabilizes within 30–40 years
She traced the numbers with her finger.
Thirty to forty years.
Lila would be forty-three in thirty years.
She closed the notebook.

Another email arrived.
This one from the College.
Dr. Serrano,
We have received a courtesy notification regarding your recent archive query activity involving restricted demographic modeling frameworks.
At this time no action is required.
However, we remind license holders that cross-domain reproductive analysis involving identifiable exposure cohorts requires prior ethics board clearance.
No action required.
Reminder.

She leaned back in her chair.
The refrigerator hummed.
The apartment was too quiet.
Her phone rang.
Not text.
Call.
She stepped into the hallway before answering.
"Hello."
"You escalated," Min-Jae said without greeting.
"I opened a file," she replied.
"You opened the wrong file first."
"Baseline?"
"Yes," he said. "That's public enough to trigger routing."

Silence.

"Did they contact you?" she asked.

"Not yet."

"Yet."

"They won't," he said. "I'm internal."

"And?" she asked.

"And internal queries are normal."

"Not for you," she said.

He didn't answer that.

Instead:

"They're sealing ES-47," he said.

"I saw."

"They'll relabel it under Environmental Stabilization Annex."

Her pulse ticked once.

"They're burying it," she said.

"They're complying with privacy firewalls," he replied.

"Don't," she said.

He let the word hang.

"You need the raw correlation file," he said finally.

"I already saw the inflection."

"That's modeling."

"Yes," she said.

"You need empirical," he said.

She pressed her palm against the hallway wall. "I know."

Silence.

"Have they contacted you directly?" he asked.

"University compliance. The College."

"Threat level?"

"Procedural," she said.

"That will change if you keep pushing," he said.

"I'm aware."

A pause.

"You understand what this means," he said.

"That the firewall isn't accidental," she said.

"Yes."

"And that they're watching."

"Yes," he said.

"And?" she asked.
"And that I have to decide if I cross the next line," she said.
He didn't speak.
She heard the faint echo of typing on his end.
"I can get you the correlation table," he said.
Her breath slowed. "How?"
"I still have backend analytics access."
"That's traceable."
"Yes," he said.
"Then don't," she said.
"You just said you need empirical."
"I do."
"Then you need me," he said.
The refrigerator kicked louder for a moment, then settled.
"If you pull it," she said, "they'll see the query."
"They'll see *a* query."
"And you?"
"I'm allowed to audit," he said.
"Not that table," she said.
He didn't answer.
"You'd be flagged," she said.
"Yes."
"And?"
"And I'm already in too deep," he said.
Silence stretched between them.

Across the hall, Lila's door remained closed.
Nadia lowered her voice.
"What would the file show?" she asked.
"Participant exposure ID cross-referenced with live birth registry," he said.
"Identifiable?"
"Hashed."
"And?" she asked.
"And reproductive outcome marker," he said.
Her jaw tightened.
"Binary?"

"Yes."
Viable / non-viable.
"You've run it," she said.
Pause.
"Once," he said.
"And?" she asked.
"It's not noise."
She closed her eyes briefly.
"How wide?" she asked.
"Wider than your thirty-seven," he said.
"How much wider?"
"National."
The word landed without drama.
Just scale.

She pressed harder.
"Show me," she said.
Silence.
"You understand that if I send it," he said carefully, "I can't undo that."
"I know."
"And if you act on it publicly?"
"I haven't decided that," she said.
"That's not an answer," he said.
"No," she said. "It isn't."
A long pause.
"I'll call you tonight," he said.
The line went dead.

Nadia stood in the hallway for a long time after that.

National.

She walked back to the kitchen and opened her laptop again.
The portal remained suspended.
She opened her private log instead.

She typed:

Archive access suspended within 12 hours.
College notified.
Firewall justification: reproductive linkage risk.
Then she stopped.
Her fingers hovered.
She added:
Empirical correlation exists at national scale (per Kwan).
Not yet verified independently.
She saved the file.

Across the room, Lila's backpack sat open, contents partially visible.
Nadia crossed the room and zipped it closed.
Her phone buzzed again.
Unknown number.

She hesitated before answering.
"Yes."
"Dr. Serrano?" a woman's voice said. Controlled. Professional.
"Yes."
"This is Compliance Oversight for the University Research Consortium. We're conducting a brief clarification regarding your archive query last night."
Nadia walked to the window.
"Clarify what?" she asked.
"The scope of your intended analysis," said the woman.
"I was reviewing environmental modeling history," said Nadia.
"Specifically reproductive elasticity variables."
"Yes."
"For what purpose?" asked the woman.
"Scholarly interest," said Nadia.
A pause.
"Do you currently hold ethics board approval for cross-domain fertility analysis involving ARC exposure cohorts?"
"I do not."
"Then you understand why the firewall engaged," said the woman.
"I understand the policy," she Nadia.
Silence.

"We're not alleging misconduct," the woman continued. "However, further attempts to access restricted demographic models may result in formal review."
"Understood."
Another pause.
"Dr. Serrano," the woman said, voice still level, "are you currently collaborating with any internal ARC personnel?"
Nadia did not answer immediately.
"No," she said.
"Thank you. That's all."
The call ended.
Nadia lowered the phone slowly.

Are you currently collaborating with any internal ARC personnel?

She stood at the window again.
Below, traffic moved steadily along the street.
People crossing. Buses braking. Ordinary movement.

Inside the system, the firewall had moved.
Her access was cut.
Her license was tagged.
Min-Jae was considering pulling national-level correlation data.

She opened her private log once more.
Under the previous entry, she typed:
Compliance inquiry escalated to direct phone contact.
Question re: internal collaboration.
Then she added one final line:
They know I'm not done.
She saved the file.

Her phone vibrated again.
A text from Min-Jae.
Tonight, he wrote.
Nadia stared at the word.
Tonight meant action.

Not modeling.
Not suspicion.
Data.
She set the phone down carefully.
Then opened a new encrypted folder on her desktop.
And waited.

Chapter 34
Proof

Toronto — 2053
The file arrived at 22:17.
No attachment.
No text.
Just a link.
One-time access.
Expires in 14 minutes.
Nadia stared at it without touching the screen.
Her apartment was dark except for the desk lamp. Lila's door was closed. The dishwasher hummed in the kitchen.

Her phone vibrated.
Min-Jae:
Open it on something that's not yours.
She closed her laptop immediately.
Powered it down.
Then reached for the prepaid phone still wrapped in pharmacy plastic in her drawer.
She stepped into the hallway, coat over her shoulders, and left the apartment without turning on any additional lights.
Two blocks west, the all-night café was half full.
Students with headphones. A man asleep over a newspaper. Espresso machine hissing like breath.
Nadia ordered tea with cash and sat near the back wall, where the security camera faced the counter instead of her.

She powered on the prepaid.
The link was still active.
13 minutes remaining.
She opened it.
A plain-text interface loaded.
No logos.
No headers.
Just a directory listing.

ARC_EXPOSURE_NATIONAL
LIVE_BIRTH_REGISTRY_CROSSREF
HASH_KEY_V2

Her throat tightened.

Min-Jae's message appeared beneath the directory:

Download only the merged output. Do not open the raw tables online.

She clicked:

MERGED_OUTPUT_CORRELATION.csv

The file began downloading.

A progress bar crept across the screen.

She watched the door of the café instead of the phone.

No one looked at her.

No one moved toward her.

The download completed.

12.4 MB.

She opened the file offline.

Rows filled the screen.

Columns labeled:

Participant_ID (hashed)

Exposure_Status

Offspring_Count

Offspring_Reproductive_Viability

She scrolled.

Hundreds.

Thousands.

She filtered:

Exposure_Status = TRUE

Offspring_Count $\geq$ 1

Rows collapsed.

She filtered again:

Offspring_Reproductive_Viability = NON-VIABLE

The number in the corner updated.

2,184.

Her pulse slowed.

She changed the filter.

Exposure_Status = FALSE
Offspring_Count ≥ 1
Offspring_Reproductive_Viability = NON-VIABLE
The number updated again.
    47.
She stared at it.
2,184.
Versus 47.
Same time window.
Same birth registry.

She exported both subsets into separate files.
Saved them to the prepaid's encrypted storage.
Her phone vibrated.

Min-Jae:
Close the link.
She looked at the top of the screen.
6 minutes remaining.
She exited the browser.
The link expired on its own.
The café noise continued around her.
Milk steaming.
Chair scraping.
Someone laughing too loudly.
She reopened the merged file.
Sorted by region.
The pattern didn't cluster randomly.
Urban Phase II sites were darker.
High-density enrollment corridors.
She zoomed out.
A percentage column caught her eye.
Second-Generation Reproductive Failure Rate (Exposed Cohort): 71.3%
Non-Exposed Baseline: 2.1%
Her hands went cold.

Seventy-one percent.

Not blip.
Not anomaly.
Not noise.

She opened a new document on the prepaid.
Typed:
National cross-reference confirms severe second-generation reproductive non-viability in exposed cohort.
She stopped.
Deleted severe.
Retyped:
National cross-reference confirms second-generation reproductive non-viability rate dramatically exceeds baseline in exposed cohort.
She saved the note.

Her phone vibrated again.
Min-Jae:
Did you see it?
Yes.
Long pause.
Then:
It gets worse.
Her breath slowed further.
Explain.
The failure rate increases with cumulative dosing.
Her chest tightened.
Dose count variable?
Yes.
Filter ≥3 initiations.
She did.
The number shifted.
Failure rate: 84.9%.
Her jaw set.
And one dose? she typed.
Filter ≥1 initiation only.
She adjusted.

Failure rate: 63.2%.
Still catastrophic.
Still above threshold.
She leaned back in the café chair.
The espresso machine screamed again.
Her tea sat untouched in front of her.

Min-Jae sent one final message.
They knew before Phase II expansion.
She didn't respond.
Instead, she opened the file's metadata.
Created: 2048-09-12
Modified: 2048-10-03
Two years before Lila's diagnosis.
She copied the metadata into her notes.
Her pulse did not spike.
It narrowed.
She encrypted the downloaded files.
Then duplicated them onto a cloudless storage partition inside the prepaid.
Then she powered the device down.
Sat still.
The café clock ticked audibly above the pastry case.
Ten twenty-nine.
Ten thirty.
Her tea had gone cold.

She stood, threw it away untouched, and left without looking at anyone.
Outside, Toronto air was sharp and metallic.
Traffic lights shifted red to green.
A streetcar passed.
She walked home without touching her phone.

Inside the apartment, the dishwasher had stopped.
Lila's door was still closed.
Nadia went to the desk and turned on her primary laptop.
She did not connect the prepaid.

Instead, she opened her encrypted local drive and created a new folder.
Title:
EVIDENCE — CORRELATION CONFIRMED
She stared at the blank folder for a long time.
Then reached into her coat pocket.
The prepaid felt heavier than it had an hour earlier.
She connected it.
Transferred the files.
Watched the progress bar move.
2%.
17%.
49%.
83%.
100%.
Transfer complete.
She ejected the device.
Powered it off again.
Then opened the correlation file on her own machine.
The numbers did not change.
2,184.
Versus 47.
Seventy-one percent.
Eighty-four percent at three doses.

Her phone vibrated.
A message from Min-Jae.
Delete it.
She typed back:
No.
Three dots appeared.
You cross this line, he wrote, there's no return.
I know.
Another pause.
Then:
They'll call it terrorism.
She didn't answer that.
Instead, she opened a new document.

She typed:
ARC exposure correlates nationally with second-generation reproductive non-viability at statistically catastrophic levels.
Cumulative dosing amplifies failure rate.
Data timestamp predates public fertility anomaly awareness.
She saved it.
Her hands were steady.

In the bedroom, Lila turned once in her sleep.
Nadia looked toward the hallway.
Then back at the screen.
She renamed the folder.
PROOF.
And began drafting the next move.

Chapter 35
Case #2186

Toronto — 2053
The message arrived through the encrypted form at 01:42.
Subject: My son.
No greeting.
Just this:
You're collecting ARC cases.
My son is five.
They told us he has no viable germline development.
His father completed Phase II in 2048.
We were told this is "rare."
Is it?
Nadia read it once.
Then again.
Five.
That tracked.
She replied at 01:47.
I can't provide medical advice.
If you're willing to meet and share records, I can review them.
The response came three minutes later.
Yes.

They met at SickKids.
Public corridor. Neutral ground. Too many witnesses for anyone to escalate.
The father arrived first.
Early thirties. Construction jacket. Sleeves dusted with drywall powder he hadn't noticed.
He stood when Nadia approached.
"Dr. Serrano?"
"Yes."
"I'm Marco Alvarez."
They didn't shake hands.
They sat on opposite sides of a narrow bench outside Pediatric Endocrinology.

Through the glass wall, children moved in slow loops—stickers in hands, parents bent at the waist to listen.

"Where is your son?" Nadia asked.

"In for imaging," Marco said.

His voice was tight, but contained.

"They found it during a developmental panel," he said. "He wasn't hitting certain markers."

"What markers?" she asked.

"Pubertal hormone baselines," he said. "Even though he's five."

Nadia nodded.

"They ran genetic screens," Marco continued. "Everything normal. Chromosomes normal."

"And then?" she asked.

Marco reached into his jacket and pulled out a folded packet.

"They said his germline precursor cells never formed," he said.

Nadia opened the report.

Gonadal tissue present.

Precursor germ cells: absent.

Etiology: indeterminate congenital failure.

Recommendation: future reproductive viability unlikely.

Age: 5 years, 3 months.

Her pulse stayed level.

"When did you complete ARC?" she asked.

Marco didn't hesitate.

"Started March 2048. Stayed on it about a year."

"How many doses?"

"Initial plus four follow-ups."

Five total.

"And your partner?" Nadia asked.

"She never took it."

Silence settled between them.

Through the glass, a nurse walked past with a sticker sheet.

Marco looked down at his hands.

"They told us it's rare," he said. "One in thousands."

Nadia held his eyes.

"It's not one in thousands," she said.

His jaw tightened.
"How many?" he asked.
She chose carefully.
"High enough to show up in national cross-reference," she said.
He stared at her.
"You're sure?" he asked.
"Yes."
He nodded once.
No visible anger.
Just recalibration.

Inside the imaging room, a small boy's voice rose in protest.
Marco turned instinctively toward the sound.
"That's him," he said.
The protest faded.
"Does he know?" Nadia asked.
"He's five," Marco said. "He knows he doesn't like needles."
Silence again.
Marco leaned forward, elbows on knees.
"I took it so I wouldn't lose my job," he said. "I was spiraling. Couldn't focus. Couldn't sleep. It helped."
Nadia didn't respond.
"It helped," he repeated, as if that still mattered.
"It can help and still have consequences," she said.
He swallowed.
"Did they know?" he asked.
Nadia held the question.
"I have evidence the demographic outcome was modeled," she said.
"Modeled before?" he pressed.
"Yes."
His breathing changed.
He looked back through the glass.
His son sat on an exam table now, legs swinging, distracted by a plastic dinosaur the nurse had handed him.
Small.
Alive.
Oblivious.

Marco stood abruptly.
"I want his file included," he said.
Nadia looked up.
"Included where?" she asked.
"Wherever you're taking this." He met her eyes.
"You said national," he said. "Then add him."
She nodded.
"I'll need full records," she said.
"You'll have them," he replied.
"And your consent in writing."
"You'll have that too."

A nurse opened the imaging door.
"Mr. Alvarez?" she called.
Marco straightened.
He looked at Nadia one last time.
Then he walked into the room.
The door closed.

Nadia remained seated.
She opened her encrypted file.
Filtered by birth year: 2048.
    2049.
    2050.
The numbers adjusted.
Children under six.
Confirmed non-viable germline development.
The total ticked upward.
2,186.
She typed:
Case #2186 — Male — Age 5 — Germline precursor absence — Paternal ARC exposure (5 doses, 2048–2049) — Maternal non-exposed.
She saved.
Then added one more line:
Direct pediatric confirmation.

Her phone vibrated.

Min-Jae.
You met one in person, he wrote.
Yes.
Pause.
And?
Nadia watched through the glass as Marco lifted his son down from the table and held him close for just a second longer than necessary.
It's not theoretical, she typed.
No, Min-Jae replied.
It's not.
Nadia closed the laptop.
And made a decision.
She would not anonymize the next release.

Chapter 36
Projected

Toronto ARC Clinical Network — 2053
The access request was denied at 08:12.
No explanation.
Just a red banner across Nadia's university portal screen:
REQUEST DECLINED — ARCHIVE RESTRICTED
Legacy Environmental Systems (Pre-Phase I)
Contact Administrator for Inquiry.

She did not contact anyone.
Instead, she forwarded the denial notice to a new encrypted thread.
Subject line: ES-47.
Min-Jae responded twelve minutes later.
You asked too cleanly.
She typed back:
Academic collaborator credentials are the only ones I have.
Pause.
Then:
You're requesting the wrong layer.
Explain.
Another pause.
The typing indicator appeared, disappeared, returned.
The demographic models were not filed under ARC.
She leaned back in her chair.
Where?
Environmental Systems archived under Resource Stabilization.
Her fingers stopped moving.

Resource Stabilization.

That phrasing did not belong to psychiatry.
Send path, she typed.
There was no response for a full minute.
Then:
ES-47 → RS-Demographic Elasticity → Long Horizon Simulation Batch.

Her pulse slowed.
Access?
You won't get it through the portal.
Then how?
Another delay.
They mirrored part of the archive during the federal firewall transition.
Mirrored where?
Public health redundancy node.
She stared at the screen.
That's still protected.
Less protected, he replied.

Her phone vibrated.
Unknown number.
She stood immediately and left the apartment.
Two blocks. Then three.
She did not answer until she was outside a construction site where jackhammers made conversation unintelligible.
"Yes," she said.
"Don't say names," Min-Jae said.
"Fine."
"You can't pull the full simulation batch," he continued. "It's flagged."
"I don't need full," she said. "I need proof of pre-rollout modeling."
Silence.
"You're certain you want that?" he asked.
"Yes."
Another silence.
Then:
There's a summary layer. Executive digest. It survived the mirror.
Her jaw tightened.
Send it.
If I send it, he said, it's traceable.
Then don't send it.
Another pause.
There's a terminal access point at the Public Health redundancy wing.
Basement level. Kiosk labeled Climate Modeling Archive.
She almost laughed.

Climate.

That's where they buried it, he said.

"What's the window?" she asked.

Maintenance block tonight. 22:00–23:00. Limited oversight.

"You're still inside?" she asked.

Someone has to be.

The line went dead.

—

22:11.

Toronto Public Health building.

The lobby was dimmer than the hospital. Fewer cameras. Older tile.

Nadia walked past a wall display about urban tree canopy restoration and followed signage toward Records & Archive.

Basement air smelled like dust and overheated wiring.

A corridor ended in a small public workstation alcove.

Three terminals.

One flickering fluorescent light.

A printed sign taped above the middle monitor:

CLIMATE MODEL ARCHIVE ACCESS — PUBLIC VIEW.

She sat.

The login screen did not require credentials.

Search field blinking.

Her fingers moved carefully.

RS-Demographic Elasticity.

The system hesitated.

Then loaded.

A file tree appeared.

Batch Simulation Overview

Executive Summary — Restricted

Elasticity Threshold Tables

Projection Visualizations

Her breathing remained level.

She clicked:

Executive Summary — Restricted.

A warning appeared:

Viewing logged.

She did not hesitate.
Open.
The document loaded in plain text.
Header:
Resource Stabilization Initiative
Demographic Elasticity Forecasting
Pre-Implementation Modeling — 2046

2046.

Before intake surge.
Before caps lifted.
Before Adrian.

Her eyes moved line by line.
Objective:
Assess long-horizon ecological stabilization impact of distress-regulation pharmacology.
Not psychiatric outcomes.
Ecological stabilization.
She continued.
Modeled Variable:
Projected reduction in second-generation reproductive viability under cumulative exposure thresholds.
There it was.
Projected reduction.
Not discovered.
Projected.
She scrolled.

Simulation Outcome (Median Projection):
Exposure uptake ≥ 38% adult urban population → 55–70% second-generation fertility decline within 25-year horizon.
Ecological rebound markers initiate at population contraction inflection.

Inflection.

Her throat tightened.
Further down:
Enrollment targeting sensitivity analysis indicates: Higher uptake probability among high-distress economic cohorts.
Elevated participation likelihood in populations demonstrating chronic affective volatility and reduced long-term optimism metrics.
Enrollment saturation strongest in regions with multigenerational instability indicators (housing, employment, relational continuity).
Predictive modeling confirms voluntary adoption correlates with persistent psychological burden clusters rather than demographic identity markers.
Projected elasticity amplification highest where baseline dissatisfaction and stress-reactivity indexes exceed national mean.

Her hand went still on the mouse.

They had modeled who would volunteer.
Not just what would happen.

She scrolled further.
Ethical review note:
Intervention framed as voluntary distress relief.
Secondary demographic impact classified as non-primary objective outcome.

Non-primary objective outcome.

She read it twice.
Not accident.
Not oversight.
Classified.

At the bottom:
Implementation Recommendation:
Proceed with Phase II expansion.
Monitoring language to emphasize mental health stabilization.
Demographic variables remain internal.

Remain internal.

Her reflection in the dark monitor glass looked older than it had that morning.
A footstep sounded in the hallway behind her.
She did not turn.
She clicked open the Projection Visualizations.
Graphs populated.
Blue lines bending downward across a 25-year span.
Birth cohort slope gradually correcting.
Correcting.
A small note beneath one graph:
Threshold 3 cumulative dosing increases elasticity effect by +12%.
Three doses.
She saw Marco's son in her mind.
Five doses.
Lila.
Her daughter.
Her stomach dropped but her hands stayed steady.
The fluorescent light flickered once.

She navigated back to the summary.
At the very bottom:
Approval Pathway:
Multinational Ecological Advisory Board — Consensus Authorization (2038)
    2038.
Nine years before ARC rollout.
Nine years before Adrian ever heard the word.
A chair scraped faintly somewhere down the corridor.
She closed the document.
Returned to the file tree.
Opened Elasticity Threshold Tables.
Rows of percentages.
Exposure bands.
Urban density overlays.

The math was explicit.
If uptake reached 50% in dense corridors, second-generation reproduction would fall below replacement in twenty-three years.
It was not speculative.
It was calibrated.

She reached into her pocket and removed the prepaid device.
Connected it via cable to the public terminal.
The screen flashed:
External storage detected.
She selected:
Download — Executive Summary
Download — Elasticity Tables
A progress bar appeared.
4%.
17%.
She watched the hallway.
No one approached.
49%.
73%.
91%.
Complete.
She ejected the drive.
Disconnected it.
Cleared the terminal history.
Closed the file tree.
Returned to the main search screen.
Her heart rate had not spiked once.
She stood.
Walked back down the corridor.
Up the stairs.
Out into Toronto night air.
Cold.
Sharp.
Unmoved.

On the sidewalk, she opened the prepaid.

The files were there.
She opened the Executive Summary again under streetlight.
Read the line once more:
Projected reduction in second-generation reproductive viability.
Projected.
Not emergent.
Not unexpected.
Modeled.

Her phone vibrated.
Min-Jae.
You saw it, he wrote.
Yes.
Long pause.
And?
She looked up at the city skyline.
Condominium lights. Traffic signals. Steam rising from grates.
It was built in, she typed.
Another pause.
Then:
Yes.
She powered off the prepaid.
And began planning who would see it next.

Chapter 37
Selection

Toronto Public Health Redundancy Wing — 2053
The executive summary was not the worst file.
The appendix was.
Nadia sat at her desk with the mirrored archive open on her primary machine and the stolen national correlation dataset layered beside it.
Two windows.
Two timelines.
One equation.
She dragged the enrollment sensitivity appendix into view again.
Sub-variable Weighting — Predictive Uptake Model
— Economic precarity index
— Housing instability frequency
— Mental health utilization density
— Chronic stress biomarker overlays
— Educational non-completion clustering
— Violence exposure probability
— Reported dissatisfaction metrics
Weight multipliers populated in a narrow right-hand column.
Not moral judgments.
Just coefficients.
She opened the national exposure dataset.
Sorted by postal code.
Then overlaid the city's public distress density map—an old public health dashboard she'd saved years ago when she still believed dashboards were neutral.
The colors matched.
High enrollment corridors.
High distress corridors.
High cumulative dosing corridors.
The map didn't accuse.
It aligned.

Her phone buzzed.
Min-Jae.

You're looking at geography, he wrote.
Yes.
You see it.
Yes.
Pause.
It wasn't racial modeling, he added.
I know.
It was volatility modeling.
She read that twice.

Volatility.

She typed back:
Distress volatility predicts voluntary uptake.
Yes.
And cumulative uptake drives elasticity effect.
Yes.
She leaned back.
On her screen, she filtered the national file by cumulative dosing ≥ 3.
The urban clusters darkened.
Postal codes with multi-dose concentration correlated directly with second-generation non-viability rates.
She ran the regression.
Exposure density vs reproductive failure.
The line didn't wobble.
It held.

She switched back to the appendix.
A paragraph she had skimmed earlier now sat differently.
Projected participation clusters overlap with individuals reporting low perceived life-trajectory mobility and persistent affective burden.
She cross-referenced that against the enrollment demographic sheet.
Age bands.
Income tiers.
Education levels.
It wasn't random.
It wasn't universal.

It was concentrated where the future already felt thin.
Her throat tightened once—then steadied.

Her laptop chimed.
An encrypted file from Min-Jae.
No message.
Just data.
She opened it.
Enrollment Funnel Model — Internal Use Only
Columns:
Initial Distress Index
Enrollment Probability
Continuation Likelihood
Projected Offspring Count Adjustment

Projected Offspring Count Adjustment.

She stared at that phrase.
It wasn't labeled sterilization.
It wasn't labeled suppression.

Adjustment.

She sorted by highest distress index.
Continuation likelihood increased.
Projected offspring count decreased.
She sorted by lowest distress index.
Enrollment probability dropped sharply.
Continuation likelihood minimal.
Projected offspring count unchanged.
The math was not cruel.
It was directional.

She typed into the secure thread.
They didn't target genes.
No.
They targeted likelihood.

Likelihood of what?
Raising a hand.
She stared at the screen.
Across the room, Lila's homework lay open on the dining table.
Multiplication sheets.
Seven times eight.
Simple, linear math.
Her phone vibrated again.
They couldn't mandate reproduction control, Min-Jae wrote.
No.
They couldn't sterilize by law.
No.
They could only offer relief.
Yes.
And relief would cluster where pain clustered.

She looked back at the enrollment funnel model.
A final line at the bottom of the sheet:
Voluntary distress-regulation adoption expected to concentrate among populations demonstrating sustained environmental stress load.
Secondary demographic contraction emerges from saturation threshold.

Emerges.

She closed her eyes briefly.
When she opened them, she pulled up Marco Alvarez's file.
Five doses.
Construction corridor postal code.
High stress density zone.
She overlaid his region against the predictive uptake map.
The model had forecast 63% adoption saturation there within five years.
Actual adoption: 67%.
Above projection.
Her chest felt tight but her hands stayed still.

She opened a blank document.
Title:

TARGETING PATTERN — CONFIRMED
She typed:
Enrollment probability weighted toward high-distress density populations.
Continuation likelihood increases proportionally with distress index.
Projected offspring count adjustment modeled as emergent outcome of voluntary saturation.
No identity-based targeting variables required.
She stopped.
Then added:
Distress = selection mechanism.
She read the line again.
It did not accuse.
It did not editorialize.
It described.

Her phone rang.
Not encrypted.
Unknown number.
She hesitated.
Then answered.
"Yes."
"Dr. Serrano?" a woman's voice asked.
"Yes."
"This is Callie Lucas. I was given your contact information."
Nadia stood slowly.
"Given by whom?" she asked.
"Someone who said you're about to cross a line," Callie replied.
Nadia looked at the document on her screen.
Targeting Pattern — Confirmed.
"What line?" Nadia asked.
"The one where this stops being internal," Callie said.
Silence.
"You've seen something," Callie added.
"Yes," Nadia said.
A beat.
"Is it design?" Callie asked.

Nadia watched the cursor blink at the end of her last sentence.
Distress = selection mechanism.
"Yes," she said.
The word left her mouth without hesitation.
Across the table, Lila's crayon rolled slowly off the edge and hit the floor.
The sound was small.
But final.

Chapter 38
Design

Toronto — 2053

Callie Lucas did not meet in public.

The address she texted was a coworking floor above a bakery on Dundas. No signage on the street. A keypad at the door. Nadia entered the code and climbed one flight.

Inside: exposed brick, long tables, two people in headphones pretending not to listen.

Callie stood at the far end of the room, sleeves rolled, recorder already on the table between them.

"You brought it?" she asked.

"Yes," Nadia said.

They did not shake hands.

Nadia placed the prepaid drive on the table.

Callie looked at it without touching it.

"Before I open anything," Callie said, "I need you to say it."

Nadia held her gaze.

"Say what?" she asked.

"That this isn't a correlation you're misreading," Callie replied. "That this isn't grief distorting math."

Nadia did not flinch.

"It's design," she said.

Callie nodded once, almost imperceptibly.

"Show me."

The Executive Summary opened first.

Callie read quickly, lips barely moving.

She did not interrupt.

She scrolled to the section header:

Demographic Elasticity Forecasting — Pre-Implementation Modeling (2046)

She looked up. "Pre-Implementation," she said.

"Yes," said Nadia.

"Before Phase I."

"Yes."

Callie returned to the screen.
Her finger traced one line.
Projected reduction in second-generation reproductive viability under cumulative exposure thresholds.
She exhaled through her nose.
"They modeled offspring sterility before rollout," she said.
"Yes."
Callie scrolled further.
Enrollment targeting sensitivity analysis indicates higher uptake probability among high-distress density cohorts.
She stopped.
"Explain that," she said.

Nadia opened the second file.
Sub-variable weighting tables populated across the screen.
Economic precarity index.
Housing instability frequency.
Mental health utilization density.
Chronic stress biomarker overlays.
Reported dissatisfaction metrics.

"They didn't target identity," Nadia said. "They targeted probability."
"Probability of what?" asked Callie.
"Voluntary enrollment."
Callie leaned back slightly. "And voluntary enrollment clustered where distress clustered," she said.
"Yes," said Nadia.
"And distress clustered where?" Callie asked.
Nadia didn't answer philosophically.
She turned the screen toward Callie and opened the national exposure map.
Urban cores darkened.
High-stress corridors saturated.
"Where the future already felt thin," Nadia said.
Callie stared at the map.
"And they knew that?" she asked.
"They modeled it."

Callie's eyes flicked back to the Executive Summary.

Another line caught her.

No viable moral solution exists for population correction without concentrated demographic impact. Relief-first enrollment provides dual-function pathway.

Callie read it aloud quietly.

"Dual-function pathway."

Silence sat between them.

"Relief," Callie said.

"And elasticity adjustment," Nadia replied.

Callie looked at her sharply. "So this wasn't a side effect."

"No."

"It wasn't a miscalculation."

"No," said Nadia.

"It wasn't discovered later?" asked Callie.

"No."

Callie closed the laptop slowly.

She did not speak for several seconds.

Outside, someone dropped a tray in the bakery below. The sound traveled upward, dull and distant.

"You understand what this is," Callie said.

"Yes."

"This isn't corporate misconduct," Callie continued. "This is policy."

"Yes," said Nadia.

Callie tapped the table once with her knuckle. "They'll call it conspiracy," she said.

"It isn't," Nadia replied.

"They'll call it terrorism if anyone reacts."

Nadia didn't answer that.

"And you're sure," Callie said, "that the reproductive failure rate we're seeing now matches the projection?"

"Yes," said Nadia.

"How sure?"
"I ran the regression twice."
"And?" asked Callie.
"The line holds," said Nadia.
Callie nodded slowly.
"So the math was right."
"Yes."
Silence.

The hum of laptops around them continued as if nothing had shifted.
Callie reached for her recorder.
"I need one clean statement," she said. "No metaphors."
Nadia didn't hesitate.
Callie held her gaze.
"They built predictive models showing cumulative exposure would reduce second-generation reproductive viability," she said. "They weighted enrollment toward populations statistically most likely to self-select under distress. They identified the demographic outcome as acceptable within their modeling framework. They expanded anyway."
Callie stopped the recorder.

Outside, a siren moved down Dundas and faded.
"What happens if I publish?" Callie asked.
"They will deny design," Nadia said. "They will call it predictive modeling misinterpreted."
"And you?"
"I will release the raw files."
"They'll freeze your license," said Callie.
"Yes," said Nadia.
"They'll investigate you."
"Yes."
"They'll call it destabilization," said Callie.
"Yes," said Nadia.

Callie leaned back in her chair.
"Why are you doing this?" she asked.
Nadia thought of Lila.

Five years old.

Sleeping without knowing her future ended at her.

"They built a world that improves," Nadia said. "They just didn't tell anyone what it cost."

Callie nodded once.

"And the cost?" she asked.

Nadia's voice did not rise.

"Lineage."

Silence again.

Callie picked up the drive and slipped it into her bag. "If I run this," she said, "there's no going back."

Nadia stood. "I know."

Callie watched her carefully. "You're crossing into exposure," she said.

"Yes."

"And exposure triggers containment."

"I know," said Nadia.

Callie held out her hand finally.

This time, Nadia took it.

"Then we don't wait," Callie said.

Nadia released her hand.

Outside, the city moved without pause.

Inside, the decision had been made.

And could not be undone.

Chapter 39
Containment

Toronto — 2053

The bakery smelled like sugar and heat.

Nadia stood outside for a full minute before going in.

Inside, a rack of cooling bread blocked the stairwell. A handwritten sign taped to the wall read:

CO-WORKING — UPSTAIRS

No logo.

No branding.

Just an arrow.

She climbed.

The coworking floor was the same as before—exposed brick, long tables, three people in headphones, posture too still.

Callie Lucas stood at the far end with her sleeves rolled. A small pouch sat on the table beside a paper cup of coffee.

Nadia set her bag down. She stayed standing.

Callie tapped the pouch once with two fingers—an unspoken confirmation that the drive was still here, still shielded.

"I made two calls," Callie said. "One to an analyst I trust. One to a lawyer I don't like."

Nadia's eyes stayed on her hands.

"And?" Nadia asked.

Callie slid a folded sheet of paper across the table.

Not a contract. Not a release.

A timeline.

Verification Window
Publication Window
Legal Response Window

Nadia read without moving her mouth.

"Verification," Callie said, "can't be a week. Not if they decide to move first."

Nadia looked up.

Callie held her gaze. "They'll try to bury it in process."

"And you won't let them," Nadia said.

Callie nodded once, like that was the only reason Nadia was here.

"What do you need from me?" Nadia asked.

Callie opened her laptop. No files. No archive. Just a blank document with three headings.

Chain of Custody
Authenticity
Redundancy

"I need you to behave like someone who expects to be cut off," Callie said.

Nadia didn't respond.

Callie typed without looking at the keys.

"Where did you pull the raw files from?" Callie asked.

Nadia answered. "Internal archive. Legacy sim folders. Kwan gave the access path."

Callie typed. "Did you export from a secure terminal or personal device?"

"Secure terminal," Nadia said.

"Encrypted in transit?"

"Yes."

"Any copies in your possession right now?" asked Callie.

Nadia hesitated a fraction.

Callie's eyes flicked up.

"Yes," Nadia said. "One."

"Where?"

Nadia didn't answer immediately.

Callie waited.

"Not here," Nadia said.

Callie's fingers stopped.

"Good," Callie said. "Because they will take whatever is closest."

Nadia felt her throat tighten and kept her voice flat.

"They'll come for you too," Nadia said.

Callie's mouth twitched once—almost a laugh, but not.

"They'll try," Callie said. "But it's harder to stop a publication than it is to stop a person."

Callie clicked into a new line under **Redundancy**.

"You said you'll release raw files if they deny design," Callie said.

"Yes," said Nadia.

"How fast can you do that?" Callie asked.

Nadia answered without thinking. "Minutes."

Callie's gaze stayed steady. "Show me the minutes."

Nadia opened her bag and removed her phone.

She didn't hand it over.

She unlocked it and held it at an angle Callie could see.

A draft email, unsent.

Recipients hidden under a distribution label.

Attachments: encrypted package, checksum file, a short readme.

Callie's eyes moved once across the screen.

"Dead-man?" Callie asked.

Nadia nodded.

"If I don't check in," Nadia said, "it sends."

Callie's face didn't soften. "Where is it scheduled?" Callie asked.

Nadia said, "Nowhere fixed."

Callie looked up sharply.

Nadia corrected herself. "It sends on a trigger. I can initiate. Or it initiates if I don't respond to the check."

Callie exhaled through her nose. "Set it to something that doesn't depend on your calm."

Nadia watched her.

Callie pointed at the phone. "If you're panicking, you'll delay it. If you're bargaining, you'll delay it. If you're telling yourself you can still work this through channels—"

"I won't," Nadia said.

Callie's eyes didn't move.

Nadia didn't repeat herself.

Callie leaned back slightly and said, "They're going to try three things first."

Nadia waited.

"First: they will isolate you," Callie said. "Freeze license. Freeze access. Make you look unstable."

Nadia didn't blink.

"Second: they will make you the story," Callie said. "Not the files. Not the modeling. You."

Nadia felt the heat rise in her cheeks and forced it down.

"Third," Callie continued, "they will offer you something quiet. A settlement disguised as compassion."
Nadia's hands curled and uncurled once. "They won't," Nadia said.
"They will," Callie corrected. "Because it works on most people."

Nadia stared at the blank document on Callie's screen, the headings clean and clinical, like a case file.
"You're not scared?" Nadia asked.
Callie's jaw shifted. "I'm not the one who has a child."
Silence sat between them.

The coworking floor continued its soft hum—keyboard taps, ventilation, the distant muffled thud of trays downstairs.
Callie glanced past Nadia, toward the windows.
"Someone's watching," Callie said, voice lowered.
Nadia didn't turn.
"You saw them?" Nadia asked.
"I didn't have to," Callie said. "The coworking guy who's been 'on a call' for twenty minutes stopped pretending when you walked in."
Nadia's eyes stayed on Callie.
"Then we end this now," Nadia said.
Callie nodded once.
She reached for the Faraday pouch and slid it into her own bag with a movement that looked casual. Then she picked up her keys.
"Walk out separately," Callie said. "Five minutes."
"I can't—" Nadia began.
Callie cut her off. "You can. And you will."
Nadia swallowed.

Callie stood. "I'm going to verify fast," she said. "If I can authenticate signatures and timestamps, I publish with your clean statement and the smallest excerpt that forces them to respond."
Nadia's voice stayed controlled. "You'll need more than an excerpt."
"I'll have more," Callie said. "Not all at once."
She stepped closer.
"And Nadia," Callie added, "do not try to warn people inside."
Nadia stared at her.

Callie's tone didn't change. "They're already choosing. Let them choose with consequences."

Nadia's breath came shallow for a second, then steadied.

Callie walked away first, down the corridor toward the stairs, moving like she belonged in the space.

Nadia stayed.

She sat for the first time.

Her legs felt distant, like they belonged to a different day.

She set her phone on the table and opened her draft again.

She added one line under the attachment list:

Checksum verified — publishable as-is

Then she opened her contacts and scrolled to Kwan's name.

She didn't press call.

She typed a single message.

They know. Burn your access. If you can't, leave your devices.

She didn't send it.

Her thumb hovered.

She could feel Callie's warning in her body like a hand on her wrist.

Nadia locked the screen instead.

She stood.

She waited four minutes and then walked toward the stairwell.

At the top of the stairs, she paused and listened.

No footsteps behind her.

Downstairs, the bakery was busy—people in coats, a woman holding a box tied with string, a man paying with his phone.

Nadia kept her face neutral and walked out onto Dundas.

Cold air hit her.

She didn't look around quickly. She didn't scan.

She walked east.

Half a block later, her phone vibrated.

Unknown number.

She kept walking.

It vibrated again.

She stopped beside a lamppost with a peeling poster wrapped around it.
She answered.
No greeting.
Just a voice—male, unfamiliar, controlled.
"Dr. Serrano," it said evenly.
Nadia didn't speak.
"You moved something that does not belong to you," the voice continued.
Nadia's hand tightened around the phone.
A pause.
Then, quieter, almost polite:
"We'd like to discuss containment."
The line went dead.
Nadia lowered the phone slowly.
Her reflection in the dark glass of a storefront looked calm. Her eyes were not.

Across the street, a car idled at the curb with its headlights off.
It didn't move.
Nadia turned and walked again, faster now but not running, the phone still in her hand like a weight she couldn't put down.
At the next corner, her device lit with a new notification.

AUTHENTICATION ALERT
Attempted sign-in — ARC Clinical Network Portal
Location: Unknown
Action: Blocked

A second notification arrived before she could lock the screen.

SECURITY NOTICE
Your credentials may be subject to review.
Nadia kept walking.

The city moved around her without pause.
Behind her, the idling car's engine started.
And eased into traffic, one lane behind.

Chapter 40
Injunction

Toronto — 2053
The article went live at 06:12.
Callie texted only one word.
Published.
Nadia was already awake.
She opened the link without sitting up.
The headline did not use the word conspiracy.
It used the word **modeled**.
ARC Phase II Deployment Included Pre-Implementation Demographic Impact Forecasting
Below it: scanned internal projections. Cohort targeting tables. A paragraph describing second-generation reproductive viability thresholds.
No adjectives.
Just structure.
Nadia read the clean statement she'd given:
"They built predictive models showing cumulative exposure would reduce second-generation reproductive viability," she said. "They weighted enrollment toward populations statistically most likely to self-select under distress. They identified the demographic outcome as acceptable within their modeling framework. They expanded anyway."

Her phone began vibrating before she reached the end.
Unknown number.
She let it go.
Then another.
Then a message.
ARC Legal Affairs: Please contact us immediately.
Adrian stood in the doorway of the bedroom.
"You did it," he said.
"Yes."
He crossed the room and took the phone from her hand.
"It's already everywhere," he said.
On his screen, social feeds were splitting into two currents:

— whistleblower
— destabilization
He refreshed.
A third appeared:
— misinterpreted modeling scenarios
Nadia sat up.
"Time?" she asked.
"06:19," he said.

Her email populated in waves.
Subject lines stacked faster than she could read them.
CEASE AND DESIST
IMMEDIATE LEGAL NOTICE
Breach of Data Security Act
Defamation Warning

Her university account logged her out automatically.
She tried again.
Access Denied.

She moved to her licensing portal.
The page hung.
Then:
Account Under Review.

Adrian lowered the phone slowly.
"That's fast," he said.
"Yes."
Her banking app sent a notification.
Temporary Account Restriction Pending Identity Verification.
Adrian looked at her.
"They froze it?"
"Not yet," she said.
He opened their joint account.
Balance visible.
Then refreshed.
Processing Hold — Regulatory Inquiry.

He looked up. "They froze it."

At 06:32, her phone rang again.
This time the caller ID showed a name.
ARC Governance Office.
She answered.
"Dr. Serrano," a woman said calmly. "This is Mara Ellison, Senior Compliance Director for ARC International."
Nadia stood and walked into the kitchen.
"Yes," she said.
"We are aware of the material published this morning," Ellison continued. "We need to clarify whether you transmitted proprietary modeling archives."
"I released documentation verifying pre-implementation forecasting," Nadia said.
"That was not authorized."
"It was accurate."
There was a brief pause.
"Accuracy is not the issue," Ellison said.
"It is for me," said Nadia.
"Dr. Serrano," Ellison replied, still calm, "you are currently under investigation for unlawful dissemination of protected institutional material. Effective immediately, your clinical research privileges are suspended pending review."
"I'm not employed by ARC," Nadia said.
"You hold active licensure under its network accreditation," Ellison replied. "That accreditation is now frozen."
Nadia looked at Adrian across the room.
He was very still.
"Additionally," Ellison continued, "we are filing for an emergency injunction to prevent further distribution of archive files."
"They're already distributed," Nadia said.
"Not legally," Ellison replied.
Silence.
"Your financial institutions have been notified of regulatory inquiry," Ellison said. "This is standard containment procedure during breach review."

Containment.

Nadia did not speak.
"You may retain counsel," Ellison added. "We recommend it."
The line went dead.

Adrian exhaled once.
"They're trying to box you," he said.
"Yes," said Nadia.

Her phone vibrated again.
A message from Kwan.
They're locking internal archives. Air-gapping entire 2046 directory. You triggered emergency protocol.
She typed back.
Expected.
Three dots appeared.
Then:
Be careful. This escalates beyond PR.

Before she could respond, her screen flickered.
Cellular signal dropped to one bar.
Then none.
Adrian checked his own phone.
"Mine's fine," he said.
He handed it to her.
Her number wouldn't dial.
Blocked.
She tried Wi-Fi.
Connected.
She opened the article again.
The page stalled.
Then loaded.
But the downloadable archive links had been replaced with:
FILE REMOVED PENDING LEGAL REVIEW.

Callie called from a private line.

"They filed within twenty minutes," Callie said.

"I know."

"They're claiming the projections were hypothetical scenario planning."

"They weren't," said Nadia.

"I know that," Callie said. "But they're moving to classify the original simulation environment as incomplete modeling."

Nadia leaned against the counter. "Will you retract?" she asked.

"No," Callie said immediately. "But we need redundancy."

"I released raw files."

"They'll challenge authenticity," Callie replied. "We need independent verification."

"They're sealing access," Nadia said.

"Then we move faster," Callie replied.

A pause.

"They're not treating this as a story," Callie said quietly. "They're treating it as infrastructure damage."

"Yes."

Adrian was watching her carefully.

Callie lowered her voice further. "There's something else," she said.

"What?" asked Nadia.

"They've requested a national security consult."

Silence.

"On what grounds?" Nadia asked.

"Population destabilization risk," Callie said. "If the public believes reproduction was deliberately compromised."

Adrian stepped closer.

"What does that mean?" he asked, loud enough for Callie to hear.

"It means," Callie said evenly, "they're reframing you as a destabilization vector."

Nadia closed her eyes briefly. "When do they move beyond financial pressure?" she asked.

"They already have," Callie said.

"What?"

"You're trending on three international feeds," Callie replied. "Half calling you a terrorist."

Adrian's jaw tightened. "Let them," he said.

Callie continued. "They're requesting expedited review from the federal medical board."

"For suspension?" Nadia asked.

"Yes."

"And travel?" she asked.

A pause.

"They haven't restricted movement yet," Callie said. "But if this escalates to federal injunction—"

Nadia understood.

She looked at Adrian.

His face had shifted.

Not panic.

Not fear.

Focus.

"Forty-eight hours ago," Callie said, "this was a data story."

"And now?" Nadia asked.

"It's geopolitical."

The call ended.

The apartment felt smaller.

Adrian walked to the window and pulled the curtain aside.

Outside, Toronto moved normally.

Streetcars.

Commuters.

Delivery trucks.

Nothing looked paused.

Her phone buzzed again.

This time, a formal notification.

Emergency Petition Filed — Ontario High Court

Plaintiff: ARC International Governance

Defendant: Serrano, Nadia

Motion: Injunctive Relief / Asset Preservation / Digital Containment

Asset preservation.

Adrian laughed once, without humor.

"They're freezing you like you're laundering money," he said.

Nadia opened the attached PDF.

The language was clean.

Neutral.

Technical.

Alleged dissemination of incomplete modeling materials likely to induce public panic and destabilize essential health infrastructure.

She closed it.

"They moved fast," Adrian said.

"Yes," said Nadia.

He turned from the window. "They're scared."

"No," Nadia said.

He looked at her.

"They're structured," she said.

Her laptop chimed.

A new headline appeared.

ARC Responds to Mischaracterized Modeling Leak

She opened it.

The statement was signed by:

Helena Voss

Chief Executive Officer

ARC International

Adrian leaned over her shoulder.

"Who's that?" he asked.

Nadia read the statement silently.

The language was measured.

Measured enough to feel practiced.

ARC modeling included a wide range of hypothetical demographic scenarios in compliance with international health forecasting standards. Any suggestion of intentional reproductive suppression is categorically false. ARC remains committed to voluntary relief and transparent oversight.

Adrian's voice hardened. "She's lying."

Nadia looked at the name again.

Helena Voss.

The signature felt deliberate.
Public.
Centered.
"She's not lying," Nadia said quietly.
Adrian turned to her sharply.
"She's reframing," she said.

The article refreshed.
A banner appeared across the top.
LEGAL REVIEW IN PROGRESS — CONTENT MAY BE TEMPORARILY RESTRICTED.

Adrian's phone buzzed.
A message from his employer.
We need to speak with you today.
He stared at it.
"They're coming through me now?" he asked.
"Yes," said Nadia.
He looked at her. "This doesn't stop with freezing accounts?"
"No."

Another notification.
Ontario College of Physicians and Researchers
Expedited Review Hearing — 14:00 Today
Her breath steadied automatically.
"They're not waiting," Adrian said.
"No."
He stepped closer.
"What do we do?"
Nadia looked at the frozen bank screen.
At the locked research portal.
At the name Helena Voss repeating across news feeds.
"They're trying to isolate me," she said.
Adrian nodded.
"So we don't isolate," he replied.
She met his eyes.
"How?" she asked.

His answer came clean. "We don't let this stay about modeling."
Silence.
"You want escalation," she said.
"I want them to feel pressure," he replied.
Nadia looked back at the injunction notice.
At the word containment.

Her phone vibrated once more.
This time from Kwan.
They're scrubbing internal cross-links. If this goes to Voss publicly, she'll have to respond in person.
Nadia typed back:
Public forum?
Three dots.
Then:
Global Health Summit — three weeks. Toronto. She's keynote.
Adrian saw the message.
He looked at her.
Three weeks.
The apartment felt very small.

Outside, a siren passed in the distance.
Inside, Nadia locked her phone screen.

Chapter 41
Voss

Toronto — 2053

The article went live at 06:12.
Callie Lucas did not wait for a full rollout cycle.
She published with documents embedded.
Redactions minimal.
Archive signatures intact.
The headline did not use the word genocide.
It did not use conspiracy.
It did not use catastrophe.
It used one word.
Modeled.

By 06:20, the ARC Clinical Network homepage was inaccessible.
By 06:24, the public-facing Eirenex site redirected to a holding page:
SYSTEM MAINTENANCE IN PROGRESS
By 06:31, Nadia's inbox received its fourth legal notice.
Unauthorized dissemination of proprietary modeling frameworks.
Violation of federal biosecurity statutes.
Cease contact with media immediately.
She did not respond.

Her phone buzzed.
Not Kwan.
Not Adrian.
Unknown number.
She declined it.
The television was already on.
Adrian stood in front of it, barefoot, volume too high.
A news anchor filled the screen.
"…internal modeling projections dating back to pre-implementation phases—"
Cut.
Another anchor.
"…documents suggest demographic elasticity modeling—"

Cut.
Then a third feed.
Live press conference.
EIRENEX GLOBAL.
A white backdrop.
The logo centered.
A podium.
Empty.
Adrian turned up the volume further.
"They're moving fast," he said.
Nadia did not sit.

The podium filled.
A woman stepped into frame.
Late forties.
Dark suit.
No jewelry.
Hair pulled cleanly back.
Posture still.
Not rushed.
Not defensive.
Calm.
The chyron appeared beneath her.
HELENA VOSS — CEO, EIRENEX GLOBAL
Nadia felt something in her chest settle into alignment.
There.
Not a board.
Not a spokesperson.
Not a committee.
A single steward.

Voss adjusted the microphone once.
Then looked directly into the cameras.
"My name is Helena Voss," she said.
Her voice did not strain.

"Eirenex Global has been made aware of documents released this morning suggesting intentional demographic design within ARC Phase II modeling."
She paused.
No denial yet.
"We take these concerns seriously," she continued.
"Our mission has always been relief-first intervention for individuals experiencing debilitating distress."
Relief-first.
The phrase from the archive.
Voss continued.
"The documents referenced represent exploratory modeling frameworks conducted during early research phases."

Exploratory.

Not predictive.
Not operational.
"Those models examined numerous possible long-term social outcomes," she said.
"Not directives."
Adrian let out a sharp breath.
Nadia watched Voss's face.
No tremor.
No glance offstage.
No flicker.
"The ARC compound was approved based on safety and efficacy data," Voss said.
"Any suggestion that demographic outcomes were a primary objective is categorically false."
Categorically.
The word landed hard.
Behind Voss, a slide appeared on a side screen.
EARLY SAFETY DATA CONFIRMED
NO EVIDENCE OF REPRODUCTIVE INTENT

Intent.

Not effect.
Voss clasped her hands lightly on the podium.
"We have initiated an internal review to ensure full transparency," she said.
"We are cooperating with regulatory partners."

Regulatory partners.
Not investigators.

"We remain committed," she said,
"to stabilizing lives."
Adrian stepped closer to the screen.
"She's not denying the modeling," he said.
Nadia did not answer.

The press conference opened to questions.
A reporter stood.
"Ms. Voss, were demographic projections part of your Phase II expansion calculus?"
Voss met her gaze.
"All major medical interventions undergo predictive modeling," she said.
"That does not equate to intention."
Another reporter.
"Did you know second-generation fertility decline was projected?"
Voss did not blink.
"We model risk ranges across all possible physiological domains," she said.
"We do not design for harm."

Not design for harm.
Careful.

Another reporter.
"Are you saying the sterility correlation is incidental?"
Voss paused.
A half-second.

Enough to register.
"We are saying," she replied evenly,
"that correlation does not prove design."
Adrian turned toward Nadia.
"She's threading it," he said.
Yes.
She was.
Voss lifted her chin slightly.
"We will continue serving patients who seek relief," she said.
"We will not suspend access based on misinterpretation."
There.
Not pause.
Not investigate.
Not suspend.
Continue.
A final statement.
"We cannot allow fear to destabilize effective care."

Fear.

The room buzzed as reporters began shouting follow-ups.
The feed cut.
Back to studio.

Adrian turned off the television.
Silence filled the apartment.
"She's lying," he said.
Nadia stared at the blank screen.
"She's not panicking," she said.
Adrian looked at her.
"Why would she?"
Nadia didn't answer immediately.
Because she expected this.
Because she prepared for it.
Because she is not reacting.
She is executing.

Her phone buzzed.

Not unknown this time.

Kwan.

She answered.

"What's happening internally?" she asked.

"They consolidated," he said immediately.

"Board emergency session. Authority centralized."

"Under who?" she asked.

Silence.

Then:

"Voss."

"How centralized?" Nadia asked.

"Full stewardship declaration," Kwan said.

"She's assuming direct oversight of Phase II global operations."

Adrian heard enough to understand.

"She's taking control," he said.

"Yes," Nadia replied.

Kwan continued.

"They're framing this as external destabilization," he said.

"Security posture elevated."

"How elevated?" she asked.

"Your access is permanently revoked," he said.

"Mine is being audited."

A beat.

"And Nadia," Kwan added,

"She's not just the CEO."

Nadia felt it before he said it.

"What is she?" Nadia asked.

"She signed the expansion authorization," he said.

"Phase II scale shift? Her signature."

The room went still.

Not Mercer.

Not Duarte.

Not a board vote.

Voss.

"She wasn't just steward," Nadia said.

"No," Kwan replied.
"She executed it."
The line crackled.
"They're preparing litigation," he added.
"Against Callie. Against you."

"Let them," Nadia said.
There was a pause on the other end.
"She's consolidating authority," Kwan added. "Full executive control. Security clearance tightened. No external meetings."
"None?" Nadia asked.
"Not without legal counsel present," he said. "And not with you."
The line went quiet.
"They've flagged your name in the escalation brief," Kwan said. "You're categorized as hostile."
Adrian looked up sharply.
"Hostile?" he repeated.
"Yes," Kwan said. "Security posture is elevated. Executive floor restricted. Badge-only access. Temporary lockdown."
Temporary.
Nadia absorbed it.
"Where is she?" Nadia asked.
"Eirenex Tower," Kwan replied. "Financial District. Forty-third floor. Private elevator."
"And public access?"
"Lobby only."
The call ended.

The apartment was silent.
Adrian stared at her.
"So that's it?" he asked. "She hides behind glass and lawyers?"
Nadia didn't answer immediately.
On the television, a replay of the press conference ran in the corner of the screen.
Voss standing steady.
Unmoved.
"She's not hiding," Nadia said quietly.

Adrian waited.

"She believes she's right," Nadia continued.

Adrian's jaw tightened. "So what do we do?"

Nadia looked at the frozen image of Helena Voss on the screen. Then she said:

"We go to her."

Chapter 42
Inflection

Toronto — 2053

The apartment was quiet.
The television was off.
Adrian sat at the kitchen table with her laptop open in front of him.
He didn't look up immediately.
"You left it unlocked," he said.
Nadia closed the door slowly.
"What are you doing?" she asked.
He rotated the screen toward her.
A projection curve filled it.
Second-generation viability index.
Cumulative exposure threshold.
Inflection point marked in red.
"You ran it again," he said.
"Yes."
He looked back at the screen.
"I wanted to see it," he said.
Nadia stepped closer to the table.
"You don't need to," she said.
"I do."
He enlarged the graph.
The bend in the curve sharpened.
"Explain it again," he said.
"You've heard it," she replied.
"Explain it like I'm not in it," he said.
Silence.
She pulled out the chair opposite him and sat.
"The model tracks exposure saturation," she said. "Once a certain percentage of the reproductive cohort is dosed, downstream viability declines even if enrollment stops."
"How much?" he asked.
She tapped the axis.
"We crossed the threshold two years ago."
He stared at the date.

December 2051.
Lila was three.
"So even if they stop today," he said.
"Yes."
"It doesn't change her," he finished. "It doesn't change anything."
"No."
He leaned back in the chair.
The wood creaked.
"And if they halt continuation dosing?" he asked.
"The cohort already exposed carries it forward," she said.
"How?" he asked.
"Epigenetic pathway disruption," she said.
He didn't blink.

He turned the laptop back toward himself.
Scrolled down.
Enrollment projections.
Geographic clustering.
Distress-density overlays.
"They weighted who would say yes," he said.
"Yes."
"They knew who would enroll," he said.
"Yes."
"And they knew what would happen after," he said.
"Yes."
The word stopped landing between them.
It just accumulated.
He shut the laptop.
Not violently.
Deliberately.
"So exposure doesn't fix it?" he said.
"No."
"It just proves it."
"Yes."
"And they get to keep going," he said.
"They've paused intake," she replied.
"That's not stopping," he said.

"No."
He stood.
Walked to the sink.
Hands on the counter.
He wasn't shaking.
He wasn't pacing.
He was still.
"When she said correlation doesn't prove design," he said, not turning around, "was that a lie?"
"I'm not sure."
He nodded once.
Small.
"Then Voss, she's choosing this," he said.
Nadia didn't answer.
He turned around slowly.
"She believes it's necessary," Nadia said.
Silence filled the space between them.

In the hallway, Lila's door was closed.
Her nightlight glowed faintly under it.
Adrian looked toward it.
"She doesn't get a child," he said.
"No."
"Our line ends," he said.
"Yes."
He exhaled once through his nose.
Not grief.
Not disbelief.
Calculation.
"Voss gets to stand at a podium and say it's modeling," he said.
"Yes."
"And we get this," he said.
Nadia held his gaze.
"What do you want?" she asked.
The question was clean.
He didn't answer immediately.
He walked back to the table.

Picked up the laptop.
Opened it again.
The curve returned.
He stared at the red inflection point.
He looked at her.
Something aligned behind his eyes.
Not volume.
Direction.
"She runs it," he said.
"Yes," said Nadia.
Silence again.
Then:
"Then she needs to explain it. How any of it was justified." he said.
Not a question.
Nadia watched him carefully.
The words did not rise.
They settled.

In the hallway, Lila turned in her sleep.
The apartment stayed quiet.
Nadia looked at the closed door.
Then back at Adrian.

Chapter 43
Breach

Toronto — 2053
EIRENEX GLOBAL — Executive Tower
The building faced University Avenue in sheets of glass.
No barricades. No visible guards outside.
That was the point.
Adrian stood beside Nadia at the corner.
"You're sure she's here?" he asked.
"Yes."
"You're sure about the floor?"
"Twenty-seven," Nadia said. "West corridor. Executive suite."
Kwan's message replayed in her head.
Board review ended at 14:10. She stays in-office after. Private access elevator restricted to executive badge class.
Adrian studied the façade.
"How do we get past the lobby?" he asked.
"We don't use the lobby."

They entered through the side entrance marked:
SERVICE — AUTHORIZED PERSONNEL
A delivery truck idled beside the curb. Two uniformed contractors rolled crates through the open bay.
Nadia timed the gap.
When the contractors badged in, the door held for six seconds.
She stepped through on three.
Adrian followed before it sealed.

Inside: concrete floor. Fluorescent lights. Freight elevator bank.
No reception.
A security camera angled toward the loading dock. Another toward the elevator.
Adrian glanced at it.
"We're on camera," he said.
"Yes." She pressed the freight elevator call button.
It lit red.

"Badge required," Adrian muttered.
Nadia removed her phone from her coat pocket.
Kwan's forwarded credential token blinked on-screen.
Temporary contractor clearance — maintenance tier.
Valid: 12 minutes.
"You're kidding," Adrian said.
"No."
She held the phone near the reader.
Green.
The elevator doors opened.

Inside, the panel displayed floor access limits.
1–12 accessible under maintenance clearance.
27 grayed out.
Adrian looked at her.
"That doesn't reach her."
"No," Nadia said.
She pressed 12.
The elevator moved.

Floor 12 opened to a mechanical corridor.
Server rooms. HVAC access. Restricted signage.
The air smelled metallic.
Kwan's second message had been shorter:
Executive floors connect through internal stairwell — north maintenance spine. No badge scan. Emergency use only. Alarm delayed 90 seconds.

Adrian found the stairwell door.
It was marked:
EMERGENCY ACCESS ONLY
ALARMED

He looked at her.
"If that triggers—"
"It will," she said.
He pulled the handle.

The door opened.
No immediate siren.
They stepped inside.
The stairwell was narrow concrete. No windows.
Adrian closed the door behind them.
"Timer?" he asked.
"Ninety seconds," she said.
They climbed.
    23.
    24.
    25.
Adrian's breathing grew louder but steady.
    26.
On the landing before 27, Nadia stopped.
Above them, faint voices.
She pushed the door open.

The executive corridor was carpeted.
Quiet.
Glass walls. Framed landscape photographs.
A woman in a navy suit stood at the far end, speaking into a headset.
She turned.
Saw them.
Paused.

"Excuse me," she said. "This floor is restricted."
Nadia walked forward.
"Oh, We know."
The woman stepped sideways, blocking the glass double doors behind her.
"Badge access required."
"We don't have one," Adrian said.
Two security officers rounded the corner behind them.
Not sprinting.
Not shouting.
Moving quickly, controlled.
Adrian tensed.

"Stay behind me," he said to Nadia.
"No," she replied.
The security officer closest to them spoke evenly.
"You need to return to a public access floor."
"We're here to see Helena Voss," Nadia said.
"Do you have an appointment?"
"No."
"Then you'll need to leave."
The second officer reached for his radio.
Nadia stepped forward again.
"She knows who I am," she said.
The first officer studied her face.

"Tell her Dr. Nadia Serrano is here."
The officer hesitated.
"Spell it," he said.
"S-E-R-R-A-N-O."
He spoke into the radio.
"Executive level, we have two unauthorized individuals requesting access. Name given: Dr. Nadia Serrano."
Static.
A pause that stretched just long enough to feel deliberate.
Adrian watched the officer's posture change.
Not alarm.
Adjustment.
The radio clicked.
"Stand by. Allow."
The officer lowered it slowly.
He studied Nadia.
"She'll see you," he said.
Adrian turned to Nadia. "Did you plan that?"
"No," she said.
And that was true.

The navy-suited assistant stepped aside from the glass doors.
"Follow me," she said.
The stairwell door behind them opened.

A distant alarm began to pulse somewhere below.
Security had logged the breach.
The assistant did not look concerned.

They passed conference rooms.
Closed doors.
Muted conversations inside glass.
The skyline widened ahead.
Lake Ontario flat and gray beyond the window wall.
The assistant stopped at a frosted door.
CEO — HELENA VOSS
She opened it without knocking.

Helena Voss stood near the window.
Hands clasped behind her back.
She did not turn immediately.
The assistant closed the door behind Nadia and Adrian.
A soft magnetic seal engaged.
Adrian heard it.
Click.
He turned toward the sound.
There was no handle on the inside.
He looked back at Nadia.
Her expression did not change.

Helena Voss turned.
"Dr. Serrano," she said.
Her gaze shifted.
"And Mr. Hale."
Adrian took one step forward. "You knew we were coming?"
Voss nodded once.
"You triggered the north maintenance alarm," she said. "It's a distinctive sound."
Nadia did not sit. "We accessed your demographic modeling," she said.
"I know," Voss replied.
"You projected generational decline before rollout."
"Yes."

Adrian's jaw flexed.

"You crossed the elasticity threshold knowingly?" Nadia said.

Voss met her eyes. "We projected adoption behavior," she said.

"That's not what I asked."

Outside the glass wall, security moved back into position.

Logged.

Contained.

Inside the sealed office, three people stood.

No podium.

No press.

No witnesses beyond whatever recording system was active.

Voss stepped away from the window.

"You broke into my building," she said calmly.

"You built something that ends our lineage," Adrian replied.

The air shifted.

Voss looked at him fully for the first time. "That is not how we framed it," she said.

Adrian stepped closer. "But, that's how it works."

Behind them, a red light above the internal panel illuminated.

SESSION RECORDING ACTIVE

Nadia saw it reflected faintly in the glass.

She did not turn.

"Good," she said.

Voss's expression did not change.

"Since you've forced access," she said, "we might as well speak clearly."

The door remained sealed behind them.

No one else was entering.

Security would not intervene without instruction.

They had crossed the line.

And Helena Voss had allowed it.

Chapter 44
Yes

Toronto — 2053

SESSION RECORDING ACTIVE glowed above the internal panel.
Nadia kept her eyes on Voss.
"You projected generational decline before rollout," she said.
"Yes," Voss replied.
"You modeled offspring non-viability," Nadia said.
"Yes."
Adrian exhaled through his nose.
"You crossed the elasticity threshold knowingly?" Nadia asked.
Voss folded her hands loosely.
"We modeled adoption curves against planetary strain indicators," she said. "When uptake exceeded projections, we recalibrated distribution."
"That's not what I asked," Nadia said.
"You're asking whether we understood reproductive impact before Phase II scaling," Voss replied.
"Yes," said Nadia.
"We did," said Voss.

Adrian took one step closer.
"And you deployed anyway."
"Yes," said Voss.
Nadia's voice did not rise.
"You flagged demographic contraction as a design constraint."
Voss held her gaze. "It was not labeled as primary intent."
"Constraint," Nadia repeated.
"Yes."

Outside the glass wall, two security officers shifted position. They did not enter.
Nadia stepped forward.
"You targeted high-distress regions," she said.
"We prioritized relief access where distress metrics were highest," said Voss.
"Urban density overlays matched your fertility modeling," said Nadia.

"They correlated," said Voss.

"They were selected."

"They were approved."

Adrian moved closer to the desk. "You built a filter," he said.

"We built a treatment," said Voss.

"You built a filter," he repeated.

Voss looked at him directly. "Relief was voluntary," she said. "The demographic result was mathematics."

The red recording light reflected in the glass.

Nadia did not blink. "You could have disclosed generational impact."

"We disclosed known risks."

"You buried it in secondary modeling."

"It was statistically emergent," said Voss.

"It was consistent," Nadia said.

"Yes."

Adrian's hands flexed at his sides. "You ended our bloodline," he said.

"You chose participation," Voss replied.

"We chose relief," he snapped.

"And received it."

Nadia spoke before he could continue. "Children of participants cannot reproduce."

"Yes," said Voss.

"You confirmed that internally."

"Yes."

"You suppressed it," said Nadia.

"We restricted premature release pending regulatory review," said Voss.

Nadia took another step. "You prevented linkage across reproductive databases."

"We complied with privacy frameworks," said Voss.

"You initiated those frameworks."

Voss did not answer immediately.

Then:

"We supported them."

The lake beyond the windows remained flat.

"You calculated long-term population stabilization curves," Nadia said.
"Yes," said Voss.
"You compared them against freshwater decline."
"Yes."
"Crop volatility," said Nadia.
"Yes," said Voss.
"Climate migration projections."
"Yes."
"And ARC adoption lowered those curves," said Nadia.
"It reduced projected strain," said Voss.
"At the cost of lineage," Adrian said.
"At the cost of growth," Voss replied.
"Human growth," he said.
"Yes."

Nadia's breathing stayed even. "You framed this as relief."
"It is relief," said Voss.
"For who?"
"For those in distress."
"And their children?" asked Nadia.
Voss did not look away. "They inherit a stabilized system."
"They inherit sterility," Adrian said.
"They inherit survivability."
Adrian let out a short, disbelieving sound. "You don't get to decide that trade."
"No individual does," Voss replied.
"Then who?" Nadia asked.
Voss answered without pause. "Civilization does."
Silence filled the room.

Nadia stepped closer until only the desk separated them. "You never intended reversal," she said.
"No," said Voss.
"You never built an off-switch."
"No."
"You planned contraction," said Nadia.
"Yes," said Voss.

The word settled.
Not defensive.
Not rushed.
"Yes."
Adrian's jaw tightened. "You call that stewardship?"
"Yes," said Voss.
"Of what?" he demanded.
"Continuity."

Nadia watched her.
"There were other models," she Voss. "Carbon rationing. Migration redesign. Urban collapse buffering."
"They failed adoption thresholds." She said.
"So you chose fertility," said Nadia.
"We chose voluntary relief at scale," said Voss.
"And accepted sterility."
"Yes."

Adrian moved.
Not toward Nadia.
Toward Voss.
Nadia saw it. "Adrian," she said.
He didn't look at her. "She's saying it," he said.
Voss remained still. "There were, are, and never will be moral solutions to overpopulation," she said. "Only managed outcomes."
The words did not echo.
They landed.

"You decided who ends," Adrian said.
"No," Voss replied. "We selected for individuals in the highest measurable states of distress," she said. "And for those statistically most likely to transmit that distress."

Adrian's breathing shifted.
Nadia stepped between them slightly. "Did you ever consider telling the public?" she asked.
"Yes," said Voss.

"And?"
"We projected adoption collapse."
"So you concealed it," said Nadia.
"We sequenced disclosure," said Voss.
"After contraction was irreversible."
"Yes."

Outside, security remained in position.
Inside, the red light stayed on.
Nadia's voice dropped. "My daughter will never have a child."
Voss held her gaze. "She will live in a world that can sustain her."
Adrian moved before Nadia could speak again.
His hand went inside his coat.
Nadia saw it. "Adrian."

Adrian drew a gun.
The motion was not theatrical.
It was direct.
Security outside the glass shifted.
Too late.
Voss did not step back.
She did not reach for the desk.
She did not call out.
She looked at him.
The red recording light reflected in the window.

Chapter 45
Discharge

Toronto — 2053

The gun was steady for half a second.
Then it wasn't.
"Adrian," Nadia said.
Not loud.
Not a command.
His breathing shifted.
Helena Voss did not move.
Her hands remained loosely folded at her waist.
Security outside the glass noticed the weapon.
A hand went to a shoulder mic.
Too slow.
Adrian's arm straightened.
The sound was not cinematic.
It was blunt.
A single detonation inside glass and drywall.
Voss's body jerked once.
The impact threw her backward into the edge of the desk.
Her shoulder struck first.
Then her head.
She collapsed sideways.
The red recording light continued blinking.
Nadia did not scream.
She turned toward Adrian as if the sound had come from somewhere else.
There was blood on the white wall behind the desk.
Not much at first.
Then more.
Adrian was still holding the gun.
His face was emptied of everything except breath.
Security hit the door.
Locked.
Another shot.
Not at her.

Into the ceiling.
The sprinkler system did not trigger.
The second shot was not aimed.
It was force.
Nadia stepped forward and gripped his wrist.
"Stop."
Her voice broke on the word.
He did not pull away immediately.
Security slammed against the glass panel.
The door mechanism began to override.
Adrian looked down at Voss.
She was on her side.
Eyes open.
Unfocused.
Blood spreading across the floor toward the base of the window.
He lowered the gun.
Not gently.
Just downward.
The door burst inward.
Two officers entered first.
Weapons raised.
"Drop it!"
Adrian turned slowly.
For a second, Nadia thought he would raise it again.
He didn't.
The gun fell from his hand and hit the floor.
An officer kicked it away.
Another drove Adrian face-first into the carpet.
His cheek hit hard.
Hands forced behind his back.
Cuffs ratcheted closed.
Nadia stepped backward.
One officer pivoted toward her.
"Hands where we can see them."
She raised them.
Palms open.
"I didn't—" she began.

"Step back."
She stepped.
Her heel slipped slightly in something wet.
She looked down.
Blood had reached her shoe.
Behind the desk, someone shouted for medical.
Another officer knelt beside Voss.
Pressure applied.
Too late.
The red recording light still blinked.
Adrian was on his knees now.
Breathing fast.
Face pressed into the floor.
His eyes found Nadia's.
There was no triumph.
No clarity.
Only shock settling in.
"You said there was no moral solution," he said toward Voss.
She did not respond.
An officer pulled Adrian to his feet.
He stumbled once.
Caught himself.
Nadia lowered her hands slowly when no one was looking at her anymore.
She looked at Voss.
At the widening red beneath her.
At the clean glass beyond it.
Outside, traffic continued.
The lake was flat.
The officers moved fast now.
Radio chatter.
Medical kit open.
Late.
Adrian was led toward the door.
He did not resist.
As he passed Nadia, their shoulders nearly touched.
He didn't look at her this time.

The hallway filled with more security.
Phones raised.
Someone was already filming.
The red recording light finally went dark.
And Helena Voss did not move again.

Chapter 46
Custody

Toronto — 2053

Adrian was already halfway down the corridor when the first shout broke loose behind him.

"Seal the floor."

The officers did not slow.

His hands were secured behind his back. The cuffs had been locked the moment he crossed the threshold.

The hallway lights were too bright.

Security moved ahead of him, clearing space that had not existed seconds earlier.

"Step back. Phones down."

No one put their phones down.

Nadia remained inside the office doorway for one breath too long.

Then an officer touched her shoulder.

"You're coming."

It wasn't a request.

She turned once — just once — toward the room behind her.

The desk.

The white wall.

The shape beneath the sheet already being pulled across Voss's torso.

Then the door shut.

Adrian walked without resisting.

The rhythm of his steps was steady. Almost measured.

Two officers flanked him. A third walked backward in front, creating distance.

"Head down," one of them said.

Adrian didn't obey.

He kept his gaze level.

Not defiant.

Just forward.

Nadia was directed the opposite way.

"Separate them," an officer said.

"I didn't—" she began.
"You breached executive clearance."
"We had authorization."
"You can explain that downstairs."
Her badge was removed from her coat pocket.
Bagged.
Tagged.

The executive floor elevators required dual clearance.
They overrode it.
A keycard.
A code.
A hard mechanical click.
Adrian was guided inside first.
The doors began to close.
For half a second, Nadia saw him framed in brushed steel and fluorescent light.
He looked smaller in that reflection.
Not broken.
Contained.
The doors sealed.

Inside the elevator, the hum was immediate.
An officer read from memory.
"You are under arrest for the attempted murder of Helena Voss."
Attempted.
The word arrived without drama.
Adrian's breathing remained even.
"You have the right to remain silent."
He did not respond.
The elevator descended.
Floor numbers blinking downward in calm succession.
He flexed his fingers once inside the cuffs.
Stopped.

On a different bank, Nadia descended separately.
An officer stood between her and the control panel.

"You're being detained pending investigation."
"For what?"
"Accessory. Conspiracy. Unauthorized access."
"I did not—"
"You can clarify in interview."
The elevator did not feel like motion.
It felt like compression.

Police vehicles idled outside.
No sirens.
Just light.
The elevator doors opened.
Sound flooded in.
Adrian was moved through the lobby in a tight formation.
He did not resist.
He did not look for Nadia.
A cruiser door opened.
He was guided inside.
The door shut.
Automatic lock.

Across the lobby, Nadia was held at the security desk while officers spoke in low tones over radios.
"Secondary individual detained."
"Yes, same event."
"Unknown coordination."
Her phone was taken.
Powered off.
Placed into evidence packaging.
"Hands visible," the officer repeated.
She kept them visible.

Through the glass façade, the ARC tower reflected the afternoon sky as if nothing had occurred.
Traffic continued.
Streetcars passed.
Pedestrians slowed but did not stop.

The system did not flicker.

In the cruiser, Adrian finally lowered his eyes.
Not to the floor.
To his reflection in the darkened partition glass.
He studied it briefly.
Then closed them.
The vehicle pulled into traffic without activating lights.
Behind them, the ARC tower remained upright.
Untouched.
And operational.

Chapter 47
The Verdict

Toronto — 2053

The courtroom was colder than the hallway outside it.
Adrian stood when instructed.
The cuffs had been removed, but his wrists still bore the faint red indentation where metal had lived for months.
The clerk read the charge clearly.
"Attempted murder resulting in death."
A pause.
"Count One: Second-degree murder of Helena Voss."
The words settled in the room without distortion.
Adrian did not look toward the gallery.
He looked forward.

Nadia sat in the second row behind the defense table.
Her hands were folded.
Not clenched.
Folded.
Callie Lucas sat two seats away, notebook open, pen still.

The prosecutor rose.
"On April 12th," she began, "the defendant unlawfully entered a secured executive office within the ARC Clinical Network and discharged a firearm at close range."
A screen behind her lit up.
Still image.
Helena Voss standing near her desk.
Timestamp in the corner.
Another image.
The gun visible in Adrian's hand.
Another.
The moment of discharge.
The sound did not play.
The silence made it worse.

The prosecutor continued.
"The defendant was not under physical threat. He was not restrained. He was not defending himself."
A click.
Still frame of Voss falling backward.
"The victim was unarmed."

Defense counsel stood slowly.
"Your Honor," he said, "context matters."
The judge did not respond.
The defense continued.
"The defendant's family was directly impacted by the policies overseen by the deceased."
The prosecutor objected.
"Relevance."
"Sustained," the judge said.
Defense counsel lowered his eyes briefly, recalibrating.
"We will demonstrate," he continued carefully, "that Mr. Hale was in an acute emotional crisis."
The prosecutor did not look at him.

Callie's pen began moving.
Across the aisle, a row of ARC legal staff sat in dark suits.
Immovable.

Video resumed.
Audio enabled this time.
Voss's voice, calm.
"…there were no moral solutions."
Adrian's voice, louder than in memory.
"You selected for the most distressed."
The prosecutor paused the recording.
"The defendant engaged in ideological confrontation," she said.
"Then escalated to violence."
She did not raise her voice.
She did not need to.

The judge turned toward Adrian.

"Do you understand the charges against you?"

"Yes," Adrian said.

His voice did not waver.

"Do you plead guilty or not guilty?"

A silence.

One breath.

"Not guilty," Adrian said.

Nadia's jaw tightened.

Not because she disagreed.

Because it meant time.

The prosecutor resumed.

"For the record," she said, "ARC Phase II remains operational."

No objection.

"The defendant's actions did not interrupt clinical services."

Another slide appeared.

Press release headline:

ARC CONFIRMS CONTINUED RELIEF ACCESS

The image disappeared.

"The system did not fail," the prosecutor said.

She did not look at Nadia when she said it.

Defense counsel called Dr. Min-Jae Kwan.

Kwan walked to the stand slowly.

He did not look toward Adrian.

"Dr. Kwan," the defense began, "are you familiar with the ARC enrollment patterns during Phase II?"

"Yes," said Kwan.

"Did internal modeling examine demographic outcomes?"

The prosecutor stood immediately.

"Objection."

"Sustained."

Defense counsel adjusted.

"Did the program anticipate multi-generational impact?"

The prosecutor stood again.

"Objection."

"Sustained."

The judge's patience thinned.

"Counsel," he said, "we are not litigating public health policy."

Kwan remained still on the stand.

He did not volunteer anything.

Callie looked up briefly.

Her pen stopped.

Then resumed.

The prosecution called a forensic specialist.

"Cause of death: gunshot wound to thoracic cavity."

"Immediate fatal trauma."

The word immediate hung in the air.

No one challenged it.

During recess, Nadia stepped into the hallway.

Adrian was led past her by two officers.

Their shoulders did not touch.

He stopped for half a second anyway.

"They won't let it widen," he said quietly.

"I know," she replied.

He searched her face.

"Did it matter?" he asked.

She did not answer.

An officer nudged him forward.

He did not resist.

Closing arguments came faster than expected.

The prosecutor stood centered before the jury.

"This case is not about policy disagreement," she said.

"It is about violence."

She gestured toward the still frame of Voss.

"No citizen may appoint themselves arbiter of public survival."

The phrase landed deliberately.

Public survival.

Defense counsel's response was smaller.
"My client is a father," he said.
"He acted from grief."
The prosecutor did not interrupt.
Grief was not a defense.

The jury deliberated less than two days.
When they returned, the room stood.
"On the charge of second-degree murder," the foreperson said, "we find the defendant guilty."
No one gasped.
Adrian did not move.

Sentencing occurred three weeks later.
The judge spoke evenly.
"Mr. Hale, you deliberately ended a human life."
Pause.
"The court recognizes the emotional distress involved."
Another pause.
"But it cannot sanction private retaliation."
He read the term.
"Life imprisonment with parole eligibility after 25 years."
Nadia did not close her eyes.
Adrian nodded once.
As if confirming an appointment.

In the hallway afterward, Callie approached Nadia.
"They blocked every structural question," she said.
"Yes," Nadia replied.
"You still going forward?" Callie asked.
Nadia looked toward the holding corridor where Adrian had disappeared.
"Yes," she said.
Callie nodded.
"Then we'll need something stronger than grief."
Nadia did not answer.

Adrian was processed into the provincial system two days later.
Intake.
Fingerprints.
Uniform exchange.
Property catalogued.
He did not ask for special placement.
He did not request protective status.
He signed where instructed.
Cell assignment printed automatically.
Unit C-4.
Door closed.
Metal.
Mechanical.
Final.

In her apartment that night, Nadia opened the archived trial footage.
She skipped to the moment Voss's voice played in court.
"There were no moral solutions."
She paused it there.
Her laptop screen reflected her face faintly over Voss's.

Outside, traffic moved.
ARC dosing clinics remained open.
Enrollment continued.
And Adrian Hale began serving his sentence.

Chapter 48
Steward

Toronto — 2053

The prison glass was thicker than Nadia expected.

It distorted the edges of Adrian's shoulders when he leaned forward, the fluorescent light bending slightly at the seam. The receiver in her hand was heavier than it looked.

He watched her through the partition.

"Trial phase two," he said.

She nodded once.

The first hearing had ended weeks ago—verdict secured, sentencing deferred pending procedural review. The state had moved quickly. The building had not.

"They entered additional archival material into record," she said.

Adrian's expression did not change.

"What kind?" he asked.

"Pre-authorization modeling."

He blinked once.

"How pre?" he asked.

She held his gaze.

"Decades."

Silence moved between them.

Behind him, a guard shifted weight from one foot to the other.

"They framed it as background," she said. "Historical environmental projections. Resource depletion curves. Population strain models."

Adrian's jaw flexed once.

"And?" he asked.

"They weren't ARC-branded," she said. "They predate ARC."

He leaned back slightly.

"Who authored them?" he asked.

She shook her head. "Consortium identifiers. Multinational ecological planning boards. Joint task authorities. No single name."

He stared at her through the glass.

"You're saying she didn't design it," he said.

"I'm saying she inherited it."

The guard glanced at them, then away.

Adrian's hand tightened around his receiver.
"So what was she?" he asked.
"A steward," Nadia said.
The word landed cleanly.
He didn't respond immediately.
"She operationalized it," Nadia continued. "Scaled it. Public-facing governance. Senate alignment. Regulatory packaging."
"But the architecture," he said.
"Was already modeled."

The fluorescent hum filled the space between sentences.
Adrian's eyes dropped briefly to the steel table bolted to the floor.
"She said there were no moral solutions," he said.
Nadia did not answer.
"She wasn't improvising," he added.
"No," said Nadia.
He looked up again.
"Does the court care?" he asked.
"They entered it," Nadia said. "They did not center it."
"How was it framed?" he asked.
"As context," she replied.
"For what?"
"For why ARC was 'necessary.'"

The guard stepped closer.
"Five minutes," he said.
Adrian nodded once without looking at him.
"Was it voted on?" Adrian asked.
"Yes," said Nadia.
"How many?" he asked.
She swallowed once.
"Multiple governments. Multi-year consensus drafts."
He let out a breath that did not shake.
"So it wasn't a conspiracy," he said.
"No," said Nadia.

"It was agreement."
"Yes."
The words settled.

On the other side of the glass, another inmate laughed at something unseen. The sound echoed strangely in the room.
Adrian stared past Nadia's shoulder for a second.
He closed his eyes briefly.
When he opened them again, there was no rage.
He nodded once.
The guard cleared his throat softly.
"Last minute," he said.
Adrian leaned closer to the glass.
"Does this change anything?" he asked.
She considered the question carefully.
"It changes scale," she said.
He waited.
"It doesn't change outcome," said Nadia.

His fingers loosened around the receiver.
"Is the data public?" he asked.
"Portions," she said. "Redacted."
"Who's above the boards?" he asked.
She shook her head again.
"There isn't above," she said. "It was distributed."
She let out a breath.
"Consensus, not command."
The words stayed in the air between them.

The guard stepped forward.
"Time."
Adrian held Nadia's eyes for a second longer.
The line clicked dead.

The guard signaled Adrian to stand.
He did.
His posture was straighter than it had been months ago.

He did not look back as he was led through the inner door.
Nadia remained seated for a moment longer, the silent receiver still pressed to her ear.
On the wall behind the glass, a small sign read:
VISITS LIMITED TO APPROVED LIST
She lowered the receiver.

Outside the facility, March wind pushed along the perimeter fence. Snow had melted into gray patches along the curb.
Across the street, a construction crew worked on a new mid-rise. The banner stretched across the scaffolding read:
SUSTAINABLE LIVING — COMING 2055
Nadia stood on the sidewalk and watched traffic move.
No sirens.
No shouting.
Just the ordinary rhythm of the city.

Her phone vibrated.
A notification from the public health registry.
Updated demographic projections available.
She did not open it.
Instead, she turned her face toward the skyline.
And watched cranes move slowly against the sky.

Chapter 49
The Outcome

Toronto — 2083

The ferry terminal was quieter than Nadia remembered.

Not empty.

Just thinner.

The digital departure board cycled through destinations without urgency. No flashing delays. No crowd compression near the gates. People stood with space between them, bags at their feet, and shoulders relaxed in a way that had once required effort.

Outside, the lake was flat.

Ice had not formed this winter.

Adrian stood beside her in a navy coat stamped inside the collar with institutional inventory numbers. Not prison gray. Not civilian either. Transitional.

A plastic ID card hung at his chest on a breakaway lanyard. His name. A barcode. A photo taken under fluorescent light that made him look younger than he was.

His ankle monitor sat above his left boot, matte black, sealed.

Two men in plain clothes waited fifteen feet behind them. One checked a watch. The other stood with his hands clasped in front of him like he was trying not to look like security.

Escorted temporary absence.

Reintegration module.

Four hours.

Adrian had more hair than Nadia expected. More white in it too. His hands were larger than she remembered, or maybe just older.

He did not reach for her.

She did not reach for him.

Across the water, the skyline was visibly different. Not ruined. Not collapsed.

Just changed.

Fewer cranes.

More rooftop gardens.

Three towers had been dismantled entirely, replaced with low, terraced structures covered in vegetation.

"You can see the shoreline now," Adrian said.
His voice had roughened over the decades. Slower. Weighted.
"You could always see it," Nadia said.
"No," he said quietly. "You couldn't."
A family walked past them—two adults, one child. Only one.
The child ran ahead without being called back.
No one shouted.
No one grabbed.
The ferry doors opened.
The escort behind them moved first, a small hand gesture: go.
Adrian stepped forward with Nadia and held his ID out to the scanner at the gate.
A green light blinked.
A soft confirmation tone.
The second escort scanned his own badge.
Another green light.
They boarded.

The island path was wider than it used to be. Less foot traffic had worn the grass back into the soil, exposing older stone beneath.
A sign near the entrance displayed a municipal update:
Urban Wildlife Recovery — Population Index +18% (5-Year Rolling)
Below it, a small graph.
Adrian stopped to read it.
"+18%," he said.
Nadia did not respond.
One of the escorts slowed behind them and pretended to read the same sign.
A fox moved through the brush fifty feet away and did not bolt at the sight of them.
Adrian watched it.
"It doesn't scare easy," he said.
"Less traffic," Nadia replied.
"Less noise," he said.
They kept walking.

The monitor on his ankle made no sound, but Nadia noticed how he shortened his step without meaning to, like his body still expected a boundary.

The city's violence index had dropped steadily for two decades.
That wasn't on a billboard.
It didn't need to be.
Police vehicles were fewer. Their paint had shifted from aggressive striping to muted civic blue. Patrol presence was lighter, redistributed into community service hubs instead of rapid response units.
The sirens that once cut across the lake at night were rare enough now that when one sounded, people paused.
Adrian had paused the first time he heard one from inside the institute's courtyard.
He did not pause anymore.

They reached the old dock.
It had been rebuilt twice. The wood was composite now. Weather-resistant. No visible nails.
Adrian stepped onto it carefully.
One escort stopped at the entrance of the dock and stayed there, arms loose, eyes on the water like he was enjoying the view.
The other remained on the path behind them, not close enough to interrupt, not far enough to disappear.
The lake moved in small, controlled ripples.
Adrian stood at the edge and looked down.
For a long time.
Nadia remained a few steps behind him.
"You don't have to," she said.
"I know," he replied.
He crouched.
Touched the surface.
Cold.
He withdrew his hand and looked at it like he was checking for something that might not be there.
"The storm that night," he said.
Nadia waited.

"I don't hear it the same anymore."
The wind moved through the reeds softly.
Behind them, two cyclists rode past without dismounting.
No one shouted.
No one collided.

Downtown, a former correctional facility had been converted into a training center.
The sign outside read:
Restorative Justice Institute — Toronto
Adrian had transferred there in his twenty-eighth year.
Less barbed wire.
More glass.
Structured mediation.
Long-term accountability review.
Community reintegration modules.
He had resisted the transfer at first.
"I don't want it softened," he had told Nadia during visitation.
She had sat across from him at a narrow table, hands folded.
"It's not softening," she had said. "It's reclassification."
"I don't deserve reclassification," he had replied.
"You don't decide that alone," she had said.
He had refused early reviews for years.
Convinced an appeal would come.
It never did.
Eventually, he stopped saying he would be acquitted.
Eventually, he agreed to mediation sessions.
Eventually, his file qualified him for afternoons like this—four hours outside, watched by men who didn't wear uniforms.

They turned back before the escort's watch hit the next quarter hour.
On the return path, Adrian did not look behind him, but Nadia saw his eyes flick once toward the ferry schedule posted on a pole.
A posted return time.
A fixed window.
The ferry brought them back to the mainland before sunset.
Traffic was light.

The avenue that once carried a constant stream of commuters now held gaps between vehicles large enough for silence to stretch.

In the median, young trees had been planted ten years earlier. They were taller than the traffic lights now.
Adrian noticed.
"They're bigger," he said.
"Yes," Nadia replied.
"How long?" he asked.
"Ten years," she said.
He absorbed that.
Ten years.
A decade used to pass in cycles of urgency.
Now it seemed to pass in restoration.

At an intersection near the hospital where ARC had first expanded, a digital display showed public health metrics.
Emergency psychiatric admissions:
Down 42% over twenty years.
Stress-related workplace claims:
Down 37%.
Domestic violence reports:
Down 29%.
The numbers rotated without commentary.
No slogan beneath them.
Just data.
Adrian stopped walking.
His escort stopped too, close enough now that the distance collapsed into something formal.
Adrian read each line.
"You believe this was worth it?" he asked quietly.
It was not accusation.
It was not approval.
Just a question.
Nadia did not answer immediately.
Across the street, a couple pushed a stroller with no baby inside. Storage only. Groceries.

The sun lowered behind the buildings, casting long vertical shadows across the glass.
"Worth," Nadia said finally, "is not a measurable unit."
Adrian looked at her.
"Then what is?" he asked.
Nadia glanced at the public display again.
"Stability," she said.
The display refreshed.
Air quality index: improved.
Urban heat variance: reduced.
Food insecurity: trending downward.
Adrian inhaled.
The air did feel different. Cleaner. Or maybe that was age. Or the fact that he had spent most of his adult life breathing recycled institutional air.
"You think she knew it would look like this?" he asked.
"Voss?" Nadia said.
"Yes."
"She knew the projections," Nadia said.
"And you?" he asked.
"I know the outcome," she said.

They stood in the cooling light.
No sirens.
No shouting.
No visible collapse.
Just a city that had thinned itself and found equilibrium.
One of the escorts cleared his throat softly—not a command, not loud, just present.
Time.
The crosswalk signal changed.
Adrian stepped forward with Nadia.
His ankle monitor caught the last strip of sun and flashed once.
Behind them, the display continued to cycle.

Chapter 50
Release

Toronto — 2084

The release office did not look like the place he had entered thirty-two years earlier.

No bars on the windows.

No shouting down corridors.

Just glass partitions, pale laminate desks, a soft queue system that pulsed numbers onto a wall display like a clinic.

Adrian sat in a molded chair with his hands folded on his knees, posture too straight for something that was supposed to be over.

A staff member slid a thin tablet across the counter.

"Confirm your current address."

He looked down.

The address was a transitional residence on a side street west of Spadina. Three floors. Shared kitchen. Curfew posted in the common room. A name he did not recognize listed under *Case Supervisor*.

He touched the screen.

The tablet vibrated once.

The staff member did not smile.

"Confirm your conditions."

A new list appeared.

Weekly check-ins.

No contact with former ARC executives or board affiliates.

No weapons.

No travel outside Ontario without approval.

No public statements without counsel notification.

The words were administrative. The weight was not.

He scrolled to the bottom.

Signed.

The staff member took the tablet back and set it beside a stack of identical devices.

"Property."

A clear bin was placed on the counter.

A wallet issued by the institute.

A paper envelope with his old ID card inside—expired by decades, the photo a younger man with dark hair and a face that still believed in outcomes.

A ring he had stopped wearing when swelling made his fingers ache in winter.

A small notebook with a cardboard cover, the edges softened by years of handling.

He picked up the notebook first.

It was heavier than it should have been.

The staff member watched without comment.

A second staff member appeared at the side door and nodded once.

"Final walk-through," she said.

Adrian stood.

His knees complained the way they always did now—quietly, reliably. He followed her down a corridor that smelled faintly of detergent and coffee. Doors closed behind them with controlled clicks.

No slams.

At the end of the corridor, a low alcove held a bench and a wall-mounted device.

Ankle monitor.

The device chirped as the staff member entered a code. A green light blinked. The clasp loosened.

She lifted the band away and set it into a sealed bag.

His sock had an indented line where it had pressed all day, every day, for years.

His ankle felt naked.

The staff member handed him a folded sheet.

"Your reporting schedule," she said. "First check-in is Monday at 09:00."

He nodded.

He did not say thank you.

Another door.

A keypad.

A final buzz that sounded the same as every other controlled access point he'd passed through since 2052.

The staff member opened it and stepped aside.

"Mr. Hale," she said, voice neutral. "You are released."

He took one step.

Then another.

And then he was outside.

The air was colder than the building had been, clean in a way that felt almost chemical after years of recycled ventilation.

Traffic moved on the street beyond the fence, but there were gaps between cars large enough for the city to breathe.

A tree line stood across the road where there had once been a parking lot.

The sky was pale, the light flat, as if Toronto had learned to conserve even its brightness.

He stopped on the sidewalk.

Not because he was overwhelmed.

Because he was recalibrating.

A security camera perched on the corner of the institute tracked him without turning its head. An LED on the housing blinked—recording, as always.

He looked down at his hands.

They were larger than he remembered.

Older.

The staff member remained just inside the threshold, waiting for him to leave the property line.

He walked forward.

The gate clicked shut behind him.

No cheering.

No one waiting with signs.

No reporters.

The story had burned out long ago and been replaced by newer emergencies, quieter ones, systemic ones.

Across the street, Nadia stood near a bus shelter, hands in the pockets of a dark coat.

She did not wave.

She waited like she had waited for decades—without theatrics, without asking the world to validate the cost.

When he reached her, they stopped a careful distance apart.
Close enough to speak.
Not close enough to pretend.
"You're out," she said.
He nodded once.
He looked past her at the street.
A couple crossed the intersection with a grocery cart. No stroller. No second child chasing behind.
A digital billboard above a pharmacy rotated through public metrics without slogans:
Emergency psychiatric admissions — down 44% (20-year trend)
Violent crime index — down 31%
Urban wildlife recovery — stable
The numbers changed. The city kept walking.
Nadia watched him read.
"They approved the final review," she said. "No delays."
He looked at her then.
Her hair had more gray, pulled back tight the way it always was when she needed steadiness.
Her face held the same discipline it had held in court.
He swallowed.
"They don't call it parole anymore," he said.
"Supervised reintegration," she said. "It makes everyone feel cleaner."
He let out a short breath through his nose.
A humor that never fully reached his face.

Nadia shifted her weight once and held out something small.
A phone.
Not new. Not sleek. Functional.
"It has your case supervisor's contact preloaded," she said. "And mine."
He took it.
The device was warm from her pocket.
He turned it over in his hand like it might refuse him.
"I don't—" he started.
Nadia's eyes stayed on him.
"You do," she said. "You just don't want to."
He didn't argue.

He slipped it into the inside pocket of his coat.
For a moment, neither of them moved.

A bus passed, quiet, electric.
Reflections slid across the shelter glass.
Adrian's face appeared for an instant in the window—older, thinner, unrecognizable in the way time could make a person both more himself and less.
He looked down at the folded reporting schedule in his hand.
Then back up.
"Does she know I'm out?" he asked.
Nadia's jaw tightened slightly before she answered.
"She knew the date," she said. "She agreed to meet."
His throat worked once.
He did not ask for details yet, as if saying her name would make her real.
Nadia took a step toward the curb.
"We can walk," she said.
He matched her pace when she moved.

They crossed at the light with the rest of the city—no escort, no hand on his elbow, no metal at his wrists.
Just two people moving through the consequence of what had been done.
On the other side of the intersection, Nadia spoke again, quieter.
"She's not a child anymore," she said.
He nodded.
"I know."
But his hands tightened around the paper anyway, knuckles whitening.
And when Nadia turned down a side street toward a waiting car, he followed—because for the first time in thirty-two years, he could.

Chapter 51
The Meeting

Toronto — 2084

The café was not chosen for symbolism.

It was chosen because it was public.

Large windows. Midday light. Tables spaced far enough apart that voices did not travel easily.

Nadia sat first.

Adrian stood for a moment before sitting across from her, hands resting flat on the table as if waiting for instruction.

"She's on her way," Nadia said.

He nodded.

Outside, traffic moved in steady intervals. A cyclist paused at the light. A delivery van idled without noise.

Adrian adjusted his sleeve once.

"You don't have to say anything perfect," Nadia said.

"I know," he replied.

He did not look at her when he said it.

The door opened.

A woman stepped inside, scanned the room once, and stopped.

Adrian saw her before Nadia did.

He didn't move.

Lila stood still for half a second too long.

She had his eyes.

Nadia's mouth.

Her hair was pulled back loosely, not severe. No wedding band. No ring at all.

She crossed the room without hurrying.

When she reached the table, she stopped at its edge.

"Hi," she said.

Her voice was level.

Adrian stood.

He almost reached for her.

He didn't.

"Hi," he said.

There was no script for this.

Nadia stood too.

"I'll get coffee," she said.

Lila shook her head slightly.

"You can stay," she said.

Nadia remained standing for a moment longer, then sat again.

Adrian lowered himself back into his chair.

Lila pulled out the seat opposite him.

Not beside Nadia.

Opposite him.

The geometry was clear.

For a few seconds, no one spoke.

A server approached, placed three glasses of water down, and left without asking questions.

Adrian looked at her hands first.

No tremor.

He looked at her face.

Much older than the last time he'd seen her.

Not in a photograph but in motion.

"Well, you look—" he began.

He stopped.

"Different," he finished.

She gave a small, dry smile.

"I was six, Dad" she said.

"Yes."

He swallowed.

"I wanted to say—" he started.

She held up one hand, not sharply. Just enough.

"I know what you want to say," she said.

He closed his mouth.

Her eyes held his.

"You asked Mom not to bring me," she said.

"Yes."

"Why?" she asked.

His jaw worked once before sound came.

"I thought I'd be out," he said. "I didn't want you seeing me there if I wasn't going to stay."

"And when you stayed?" she asked.

He didn't answer immediately.

"I thought it would be easier if you remembered me before," he said.

"Before you shot someone?" she asked.

The café did not react.

No one turned.

Adrian did not look away.

"Yes," he said.

Lila nodded once, like she was confirming a data point.

"I watched it in civics class," she said.

His fingers tightened against the table.

"It was in the curriculum," she continued. "Domestic extremism case study."

Nadia's breath shifted almost imperceptibly.

Lila kept her eyes on her father.

"They paused the footage before the shot," she said. "But everyone knew what happened."

Adrian inhaled slowly.

"I'm sorry," he said.

"For what?" she asked.

He opened his mouth.

Closed it.

"For killing her?" she said. "Or for making me live with it?"

He did not hesitate this time.

"For both."

Lila studied him.

"Did you think it would fix it?" she asked.

"No," he said.

"Then why?"

He looked at her directly.

"Because I couldn't accept it," he said.

"Accept what?" she asked.

"That you would never have a child," he said.

The words did not echo.

They settled.

Lila's face did not change immediately.

Then something in her eyes hardened—not anger, not grief. Recognition.

"You think *that's* what I lost?" she asked.

He didn't answer.

She leaned back slightly.

Nadia stayed still.

Lila looked at her mother briefly, then back to Adrian.

The question was clean.

Not defensive.

Not wounded.

Adrian stared at her.

The table was quiet.

He absorbed that.

"You don't feel cheated?" he asked.

"By biology?" she said. "Or by you?"

He didn't speak.

She leaned forward slightly.

"You made a choice because you couldn't tolerate an outcome," she said.

Her tone did not rise.

"I live in a world where fewer people scream at each other," she continued. "Where the air is cleaner, opportunity and choice are abundant, and where my friends don't spiral into panic at twenty-three."

Adrian's eyes flicked toward Nadia and back.

"That doesn't mean it was right," Lila said. "It doesn't mean it was wrong either."

The words sat between them.

He exhaled.

"I told myself I was protecting you," he said.

"I know," she said.

Silence again.

This one softer.

A server passed behind them carrying plates.

The door opened and closed with a light bell.

Adrian looked at his daughter like he was trying to memorize her.

"You don't have to forgive me," he said.

"I'm not here to," she replied.
"Then why are you here?" he asked.
She considered that.
"To see what you look like outside," she said.
He almost smiled.
"And?" he asked.
"You look older," she said.
He nodded.
"So do you," he replied.
For the first time, she let a small real smile through.
Nadia watched it move across both of their faces and then fade.
Lila reached into her bag and pulled out a thin folder.
She placed it on the table.
"I brought something," she said.
Adrian didn't touch it.
"What is it?" he asked.
"My health file," she said.
Nadia's spine stiffened.

Lila kept her eyes on her father.
"I want you to see it," she said.
He placed his hand on the folder but did not open it yet.
"Why?" he asked.
"So you stop imagining something worse than what is," she said.
He opened it.
Lab reports. Imaging summaries. The phrase that had lived in his head for decades in sterile print:
Non-viable reproductive pathway.
No ambiguity.
No poetry.
Just language.
He looked at it.
Then looked at her.
"I'm sorry," he said again.
She nodded once.
"I know," she said.
He closed the folder carefully.

The three of them sat in the quiet of a public place that had no idea what it was holding.

Outside, traffic continued.

Inside, no one raised their voice.

Lila finished her water.

"I have to go," she said.

She stood.

Adrian stood too.

This time, he did reach for her.

Slowly.

Not to hold.

Just to touch her shoulder.

She let him.

For a second.

Then stepped back.

"I'll see you again," she said.

It wasn't a promise.

It was simply a next.

She walked toward the door without looking back.

The bell sounded softly as it opened.

Adrian remained standing.

His hand hovered where her shoulder had been.

Nadia rose and stood beside him.

He did not cry.

He did not collapse.

He watched the door.

And when it closed, he sat down again.

The folder remained between them on the table.

Outside, the light shifted.

And nothing reversed.

Chapter 52
The Trade

Toronto — 2084

The café was small and deliberately quiet.

Not trendy. Not nostalgic. Just practical. Composite tables. Recycled wood paneling. Plants that were real but spaced widely enough that no one brushed against them by accident.

Nadia sat facing the window.

Across from her sat Lila.

Adult. Composed. Shoulders straight in a way that echoed both of them but belonged to neither.

Adrian had not come.

He had asked to.

Lila had said no.

"I want to speak with Mom first," she'd said.

So he had stayed back at the transitional residence, hands folded on his knees the way he had folded them in the release office.

Lila stirred her tea once and set the spoon down precisely.

"You look tired," she said.

Nadia smiled faintly. "I'm seventy-three."

"That's not what I meant."

They held each other's gaze for a moment. The air between them was not hostile. It was calibrated.

Outside, University Avenue moved at a steady, unhurried pace. Fewer cars than decades earlier. More cyclists. A bus passed almost silently.

Lila folded her hands.

"I've reviewed the archival releases," she said.

She didn't say ARC. She didn't say Eirenex.

Archival releases was enough.

Nadia nodded once.

"And?" she asked.

Lila did not answer immediately.

"I've been reading the archival hearings," Lila said.

Nadia nodded once.

"And?" she asked.

"They weren't improvising," Lila said. "The demographic models that predated rollout. The enrollment funnel…"

She didn't lower her voice. She didn't dramatize it.

Nadia held her gaze. "Yes."

"The ecological projections tracked within margin," Lila continued. "Urban heat variance. Wildlife corridors. Food pressure. Atmospheric load."

She paused, but not for effect.

"The models were accurate."

Nadia's hands remained folded in her lap. "Yes," she said.

Lila exhaled once. "And the outcome followed."

A beat.

"It worked."

Across the room, a couple in their thirties shared a pastry without speaking. No stroller beside their table. No second chair pulled out for someone running late.

Nadia watched the condensation slide down her water glass. "It worked," she agreed.

Lila leaned back slightly. "For the planet," she said.

"Yes."

"And not for us," Lila said.

The sentence was clean.

Nadia did not rush to fill it.

"No," she said.

Silence stretched between them.

Not heavy. Just present.

Lila's eyes shifted toward the window.

"I don't feel robbed," she said.

Nadia's head tilted slightly.

"No?" she asked.

Lila shook her head once.

"I never imagined children," she said. "Not instinctively."

Nadia watched her carefully.

"I imagined other things," Lila continued. "Research. Travel. Work that doesn't collapse under population pressure."

She met her mother's eyes again.
"The world I live in is stable," she said.
Nadia felt the word land in her chest.
Stable.

Outside, a delivery drone moved overhead in a straight line, quiet and efficient.
"And you think that matters?" Nadia asked.
"Yes," Lila said.
The answer was immediate.
"It matters that the lake isn't choking," she said. "It matters that emergency admissions are down. It matters that people aren't living in constant volatility."
Her gaze sharpened slightly.
"It matters that climate migration stabilized."
Nadia's throat tightened almost imperceptibly.
"And lineage?" she asked.
Lila didn't look away. "Lineage is biological continuity," she said. "Not moral superiority."
Nadia blinked once. "You're not angry?" she asked.
Lila considered. "I was," she said. "At him."
Adrian.
Nadia nodded.
"He chose violence," Lila said.
"Yes."
"It didn't stop anything," she said.
"No."
Lila's hands tightened once around her mug, then relaxed again.
"But I understand why he did it," she said.
Nadia's eyes lifted.
"Do you?" she asked.
Lila nodded.
"He believed love outweighed mathematics," she said.
The sentence hung between them.
"And you?" Nadia asked.
Lila looked back out at the street.
"I believe mathematics outlives love," she said.

The café door opened and closed. A draft of cold air moved across the floor and vanished.

Nadia felt something inside her shift—not break, not collapse.

Reposition.

"You don't see it as theft," Nadia said.

"I see it as trade," Lila replied. "For something I didn't ask for," she added.

Nadia absorbed that.

"Voluntary enrollment," Lila continued, "created involuntary outcomes."

"Yes."

"But the alternative," she said, "would have created involuntary collapse."

Nadia closed her eyes briefly.

When she opened them, Lila was still watching her.

Across the café, a digital wall display cycled public metrics without commentary:

Urban biodiversity index: sustained.

Atmospheric particulate levels: reduced.

Population curve: declining within projected range.

No slogans.

No moral framing.

Just numbers.

Lila followed Nadia's gaze to the display.

After a moment, Lila reached into her bag and removed a thin folder.

She slid it across the table.

Nadia didn't touch it immediately.

"What is it?" she asked.

"My thesis," Lila said.

Nadia's eyebrows lifted slightly.

"On?" she asked.

"Civilizational triage," Lila replied.

The words were calm.

"Case study: ARC Phase II demographic stabilization."

Nadia's fingers moved toward the folder, then stopped.

"You're defending it?" she asked.

"I'm analyzing it," Lila said.

Nadia looked at her daughter's face.

There was Adrian in the set of her jaw.

There was herself in the stillness behind her eyes.

"You don't resent me?" Nadia asked.

Lila's answer was immediate.

"No."

"Why?"

"Because you fought," she said.

Nadia swallowed.

"And you lost," Lila added gently.

Not cruelly.

Just accurately.

The café noise rose slightly as more people entered. Chairs shifted. Cups clinked.

Lila leaned forward.

"I don't need a personal stake in continuity to feel complete," she said.

Nadia felt her chest tighten.

"But you did," Lila continued.

The air shifted.

"And they took that from you," Lila said.

Nadia's composure thinned at the edges.

"Yes," she said quietly.

Lila reached across the table and rested her hand on Nadia's.

It was the first physical contact since sitting down.

"I'm not the loss," Lila said.

Nadia inhaled sharply.

"You're not a sacrifice," Lila added.

Silence pressed in.

Outside, the light had shifted toward late afternoon. Long shadows stretched across the sidewalk.

Lila withdrew her hand.

"I'll meet him tomorrow," she said.

Nadia nodded once.

"He's afraid," she said.

"I know," Lila replied.

They both stood at the same time.

No dramatic hug.

No collapse.

Just two women adjusting coats.

At the door, Lila paused.

"Mom," she said.

Nadia turned.

Through the window behind Lila, the city moved in steady lines.

No sirens.

No panic.

Just a population that had thinned and held.

Lila studied her for a long second.

Then she opened the door and stepped into the cold.

Nadia remained inside the café for several seconds after Lila left.

She looked at the folder on the table.

Civilizational triage.

She picked it up.

Outside, Toronto continued—cleaner air, quieter streets, balanced systems.

Inside her chest, grief still lived.

It had never been dosed.

It had never been flattened.

It had simply endured.

Nadia stepped out into the street.

The wind off the lake was steady.

And the new world that had been engineered was thriving.

Made in the USA
Las Vegas, NV
06 March 2026

Made in the USA
San Bernardino, CA
13 May 2019